Advance Praise for *Words to Die For*

"Lynn Kostoff is noir to the bone: dark, twisty, baroque and thrilling. And, like all the best writers in the genre, he's never afraid to burst into new corridors of the American underbelly, offering stories that are rich in character, desperate in tone and bold in consequence. His books are not to be missed."
- Megan Abbott, Edgar Award-winning author of *The Fever* and *Dare Me*

"Lynn Kostoff is one of the very best writers out there today. His latest, *Words To Die For*, deals with spin doctors and damage control artists, what they do, how they do it, and why they do it. ... There are very few writers out there today with Kostoff's mastery of craft. I've been a fan since his first novel and I haven't stop reading him since."
- Charlie Stella, author of *Shakedown*, *Johnny Porno* and *Rough Riders*

Praise for Kostoff's Prior Crime Novels

"Kostoff proves that southern Florida is the ideal location these dope-dealing days for the noir thriller ... [*A Choice of Nightmares* is] a noir thriller that delivers with vivid writing, smart plotting, and a deeper-than-usual insight into its flawed central character." - Kirkus Reviews

"[The hero of *A Choice of Nightmares*] starts off in a Carl Hiassen novel and ends up in a Jim Thompson story in this dazzling, unputdownable South Florida thriller." - Sara Gran, author of *Dope* and *Claire DeWitt and the City of the Dead*

WORDS TO
DIE FOR

WORDS TO
DIE FOR

Lynn Kostoff

NEW PULP PRESS

Published by New Pulp Press, LLC, 926 Truman Avenue, Key West, Florida 33040, USA.

For information contact:
editor@newpulppress.com
ISBN-13: 978-0989932394 (New Pulp Press)
ISBN-10: 0989932397

This one is for Melanie Kostoff and Marian Young

An organ for real shape-feeling exists probably only in the human hand, and there is more than mere coincidence in the fact that in his hand man possesses a tactile organ which can take over some of the distinctive achievements of his eye ... Blind men can "see" by means of their hands, not only because they are devoid of eyes but because they are beings endowed with the general faculty of "vision" and only happen to be deprived of the primary organ of sight.

— Hans Jonas, The Phenomenon of Life

Anger is the tongue of Pain. Pain is the eyes of Fear. Fear is the fingers of Humiliation. Humiliation is the skin of Time. And Time is the breath of God.

— Dr. Tolson Whormer, The Guide, Book Two

PART ONE

THE WORK OF HANDS

ONE

Fall was the only season that didn't lie. The sky above Alamonte Avenue was a soft uniform gray, the surrounding light clear as a handshake, a tacit agreement to accept what was there and not without necessarily settling for either.

Through the coffee shop window, Raymond Locke watched Larry Hahn hesitate in the middle of the crosswalk when he tried to beat the light, then break into a long-legged run, like a scarecrow suddenly flushed from its post, the tails of his black trench coat flapping and whipping around him and his briefcase awkwardly cradled against his chest as he dodged horns and fenders.

A few seconds later, Hahn tried to fit his six-nine frame into the booth across from Raymond. Outside the 4,700 square feet of the basketball court at the University of Illinois and the moves he'd made on it a decade ago, the world had not been kind to Larry Hahn, forever throwing up obstacles that prevented him from negotiating them with anything approaching grace. Every doorway and each piece of furniture was a potential insult.

Hahn dropped his briefcase beneath the booth and held up both hands. "Ten minutes, Raymond."

Raymond signaled for coffee. "Sounds about right. This won't take long."

Hahn looked briefly away and leaned back in the

booth. "I wish you wouldn't call at home."

"You're a hard man to reach sometimes."

The waitress appeared, pouring coffee, smiling, and exiting in an unbroken series of gestures, a minimum wage dance step.

Across the shop, a television was mounted on the wall behind the cash register, the sound too low to carry to their booth, and Raymond watched a dumb-show replay of the lead story he'd watched earlier at home, Reagan at this desk in the Oval Office categorically denying any involvement in or knowledge of the sale of arms for hostages with Iran or any illegal diverting of funds to the Contra cause in Nicaragua.

Reagan had the look down. Raymond would give him that. He knew how to appear Presidential when the cameras were rolling. When necessary, he could deliver his lines. Someone, though, should have keyed in on the hands.

You needed to keep your hands still when you lied.

Larry Hahn gingerly picked up his cup. "In fact," he said between sips, "I wish you'd stop calling me altogether."

"People helping each other. Without that, where would we be?" Raymond paused and rested his hands on the table, palms down. "I think I can confidently say that one place you would not be, Larry, is currently dwelling in a handsomely restored brownstone near Liberty Park in Birchfield Heights with your lovely wife Susan and two charming and well-heeled daughters. Not on an Assistant District

Attorney salary."

Hahn began tapping his spoon on the rim of his coffee cup. "I've talked to Susan about budgeting. We'll be okay."

Raymond shook his head. "Property taxes, upkeep, insurance, the payments on the new Volvo, the Montessori tuition, the orthodontist bills, the cottage on the Lake, the boat, vacations. All that adds up, Larry."

Hahn looked out at the traffic stalled on Alamonte. Raymond waited, studying his profile, its long and bony lines and the small cluster of razor cuts cross-hatching the knob of a chin.

Hahn bit his lip, let out a slow breath, and faced Raymond again. "I'd just as soon let it rest. Right here, okay? We drop it." He shook his head. "Nothing personal, Raymond. I have to get back to the office. Thanks for the coffee."

Raymond grabbed Hahn's forearm and squeezed. "The *personal*, my friend? It disappeared while we were changing channels. So how about growing up, Larry, ok?

Raymond let go, and Hahn remained slumped in the booth, shoulders hunched, his gaze centered on the white-segmented bowl of artificial sweetener and sugar packets setting between them.

"You know what bothers me most?" Hahn asked. "I sleep fine. Deep. Straight through the night. It doesn't seem right."

Raymond notched down his impatience and softened his voice. "The Bushel of Love thing was rough on everyone involved. Nothing like that's ever easy, but it's bound to be harder on people like us with kids. It's over though. Yesterday's mail."

Hahn lifted his head. "I didn't know you had kids."

Raymond nodded. "A boy. Eight. Same age as your Maria. His name's Andrew." Without thinking, Raymond added, "He's autistic," and then immediately shrugged it off, surprised and embarrassed by what he heard bubbling around the edges of the words.

He picked up his coffee. It was Hahn's turn to study him. Raymond felt like a car salesman who had inadvertently distracted a customer just as he was reaching for his wallet.

"Crosses to bear and all that," Raymond said and shrugged again. "You deal with it."

"I didn't know," Hahn repeated, and Raymond relaxed. Hahn wasn't going anywhere. He was a human-interest junkie, his compulsion a bottomless idealism that left him craving for a connection that he still hadn't figured out was nothing more than an excuse for him to parade his guilt. He was perfect fodder for the District Attorney's office, each case a potential crusade to set things right once and for all, Hahn chasing justice like his own shadow.

Fortunately, for Raymond, he had met Hahn's wife at a New Year's Eve party two years ago and discovered through the course of their conversation that Susan Hahn's interest in the law did not extend much beyond that which applied to real estate, particularly if the real estate in question was located in one of the fashionable Birchfield Heights neighborhoods.

Raymond had nodded and smiled and filed the information away. It had come in handy a year later when the Bushel of Love scandal broke.

The Bushel of Love chain was a longstanding account at Public Domain, the public relations firm Raymond worked for, and Raymond had been brought in for damage control. The son of the owner of the daycare franchise had managed to run afoul of a number of man's and God's laws, and the District Attorney, Arthur Cavanaugh, had assigned Larry Hahn to the case. Raymond bypassed Larry entirely and went straight to Susan Hahn and offered to escrow her upwardly-mobile desires if she convinced her husband to temporarily sublet his moral and social convictions.

Predictably, Larry Hahn refused. Predictably, Susan Hahn squeezed. In the end, Larry came around and doctored, misplaced, or misrepresented just enough of the evidence to create some healthy doubts in the mind of a grand jury, and the case against the owner's son was thrown out.

The waitress reappeared and filled their cups. Hahn poured two packets of sugar into his coffee. Raymond waited a moment before moving in.

"Look, this one's simple. An ear to the ground, Larry. A couple calls. Nothing more. You hear something, you let me know, and I take it from there. Minimal involvement on your part."

Hahn stirred his coffee.

"What's the point of pulling me into this?" he asked finally. "From what you just said, you're talking about a food poisoning outbreak, not criminal activity. Lamar Ditell ought to be worried about the USDA and the Health Department. They're the ones who'll try to hang Happy Farms."

Raymond less than patiently reminded Larry that District Attorney Cavanaugh and Lamar Ditell, owner and CEO of Happy Farms Inc. hated each other with an intensity usually reserved for showdowns in spaghetti westerns.

Lamar Ditell had pumped thousands of dollars into the campaign coffers of Cavanaugh's opponents each time Cavanaugh came up for re-election, and though Cavanaugh had persevered and held on to the office, his margin of victory at the last election had been so narrow that it resulted in two re-counts, each accompanied by ugly and sordid side-orders of political maneuvering where innuendo inevitably held hands with the libelous.

"I'm not asking for anything more than some inspired eavesdropping," Raymond said.

"I still don't like it."

"Your sensitivities, as heartfelt as I'm sure they are, Larry, are not my top priority at the moment." Raymond picked up his spoon and balanced it on the knuckles of his index and middle fingers, then let it drop back to the table. "Happy Farms is one of the agency's biggest accounts, and I need to know we're keeping our energies focused in the right places."

Hahn looked away.

He closed his eyes and then nodded. "It stops there, right?"

"Strictly a need to know basis," Raymond said.

"You call me if you hear anything suggesting that Arthur Cavanaugh is about to do more than simply gloat over Lamar Ditell's troubles. Nothing more, nothing less than that. Conveying information, that's all, Larry."

"You always make it sound so simple."

Raymond glanced at his watch. "That's because, at bottom, most things are."

He needed to get back to the office, but Raymond thought he heard a small tremor in Hahn's voice, one off-key note in the well-practiced scales comprising Larry's usual repertoire of self-flagellation and self-pity. Raymond sipped his coffee and waited him out.

Hahn lifted his briefcase from beneath the booth and set it next to him and glanced at the check. He began fumbling for his wallet.

As with their other meetings, Raymond indulged him the gesture, Hahn picking up the tab for drinks or a meal, a flickering shadow play of conscience that enabled Hahn to temporarily forget the weight of the sealed envelope wedged between the folds of the newspaper he would pick up from their table on his way out.

There were safer and more practical ways to exchange the cash, but Hahn needed the drama. It made everything more real and added some texture and luster to the hair shirt Larry enjoyed wearing.

"Nothing beyond a couple phone calls, right?" he asked.

Raymond threw out a dismissive wave. "Nothing more, Larry."

Hahn unfolded himself from the booth, shifting

from foot to foot, conscious of the momentary attention he drew whenever he stood up.

"I'd like to believe that," he said. "Except I've seen how quickly that can change whenever we do business. So I'm telling you now I can't - and won't - go through another Bushel of Love scenario. I'll go to Cavanaugh first. There are limits, Raymond."

Hahn turned and quickly left, tucking the newspaper under his arm on the way.

Raymond let him have the last word. There might be limits to everything, but they didn't matter much in the long run. Raymond's work at Public Domain had taught him that. Limits, like the Law, were a human invention. The world wasn't interested in them, and Raymond figured, as long as Susan Hahn had anything to say about it, Larry Hahn had a long way to go before he discovered where his limits truly lay.

Raymond checked his watch and finished his coffee. He couldn't afford to let down, not now, and the caffeine was a small stay against exhaustion. He'd gotten what he'd come for. Larry Hahn would cooperate.

It was Raymond's policy when troubleshooting an account to isolate the worst-case scenario at the first tick of the clock and cap it. Then he could work on fixing things so that worse case never materialized, setting up an embargo against unruly surprises.

He watched Hahn disappear around the corner. The crowd of passersby on the sidewalk in front of the coffee shop window eddied and stalled.

A man glanced inside.

In a trick of the light, the man's features were

superimposed on Raymond's reflection, the man's face momentarily overlapping and replacing his.

Raymond involuntarily raised his hand as if to wave the face way and then stood up and put on his coat. He kept his back to the window. He glanced down at Hahn's neat stack of ones resting on the check.

Raymond looked around, then added another bill to the tip and left.

TWO

If you took Cleveland on a good day and Chicago on a bad, then split the difference, you'd find yourself in St. Carlton, Indiana, a steel and port city of 125,000-plus notched in the southeast corner of Lake Michigan.

The conference room on the ninth floor of the building housing Public Domain was an elegant box, a long rectangle with dark, heavy furniture and minimal lighting, and across from where Raymond Locke sat, stretching the entire length of the east wall was a mural holding a wide-angle enlargement of an aerial photograph of the city taken from out over Lake Michigan in the early 1940's during St. Carlton's boom. The photograph's perspective was dramatically foreshortened so that the cityscape simultaneously loomed and retreated, seeming to bend under the pressure of the camera's lens, leaving the viewer feeling as if he were plummeting through space, caught in a careening headlong free-fall toward the sepia-toned skyscrapers, factory smokestacks, and docked grain barges below.

Raymond glanced at his watch and went back to reviewing the contents of the file in front of him.

Things were not happy at Happy Farms.

Under the decidedly singular leadership of Lamar Ditell, Happy Farms had grown from a moderately successful poultry processing business with only regional recognition into one of the richest and largest poultry concerns in the country. Lamar Ditell's break came when Happy Farms cornered a number of very lucrative and long-term contracts on the local, state, and federal level and ended up supplying the food service operations for a cross-section of government agencies and school systems, eventually icing the whole enterprise by landing a contract with the Defense Department. Those contracts, coupled with the sales in the private sector, left Lamar Ditell a very rich man.

They also fed Lamar Ditell's ambition to be the emperor of the poultry world. Ditell was determined to supplant the image and pull of Colonel Sanders on the hearts, minds, and wallets of America and hired Public Domain to spearhead the campaign, giving a green light to an unprecedented public relations and marketing budget in the process.

Public Domain, for its part, got results, perhaps not as fast as Ditell would have liked, but the inroads in national recognition were solid and steady enough for Ditell to find himself in the company of some very eager and enthusiastic investors when he decided to expand and diversify his base of operations and open fast-food restaurants that would aggressively go beak to beak with the Colonel and any other competitors.

Happy Farms was planning to go nationwide with the restaurants within six months, and Ditell had decided to pilot-test two franchises on home ground. One was mall-based and the other set up as a prototype for individually housed restaurants.

The grand-openings had been staged the Saturday

and Sunday after Thanksgiving with all the expected attendant hoopla. Balloons. Prizes. Live music. Free samples. Guest appearances by local celebrities and dignitaries and sports figures and Lamar Ditell himself.

There had been enough advertising coin spent on radio, newspaper, and television commercials to grease some gratis on-site coverage. The whole show had been orchestrated smoothly and on schedule.

No hitches. Smiles all around.

Until a very definite pattern of symptoms - fever, body aches, swollen glands, dizziness, bouts of double vision, vomiting, and diarrhea - had begun to emerge among those who had feasted upon Happy Farms' bounty, and the after-effects from the grand-openings of Lamar Ditell's restaurants turned out to be as savory as the contents of Pandora's Box.

Lamar Ditell expected Public Domain to put the lid back on.

Raymond looked up from the file when Daniel Pierce, CEO of Public Domain, came through the door and moved to the head of the conference table.

Under the recessed lighting, his suit took on the color and sheen of metal shavings. His silver hair was clipped close to his skull, his posture as if at perpetual present arms.

Pierce had the reputation of giving little or nothing away. The half-joke circulated by his rivals was that Daniel Pierce didn't bother trying to recreate the world in his image; instead, he re-priced it, knowing in the long run it would turn out to be the same thing.

Pierce looked around the room, then said, "Atwell?"

"Frank will be here shortly, I'm sure," Raymond said. He landed on a coda, trying to cover for Atwell by creating a makeshift excuse about some misplaced files and Xeroxing machine problems.

Pierce let that go by. He brought up Atwell's wife instead.

"Is Atwell divorced or widowed?" he said.

"Judy's been dead going on a year and a half now," Raymond said. "Breast cancer."

"I've learned," Pierce said, "that grief has a way of bringing out what's always been there but nobody noticed."

"Frank's a good man," Raymond said. "I still go to him for advice. With Judy gone, it's been a difficult stretch for him, but Frank's weathering it. They were married close to thirty-five years."

Raymond could feel Pierce studying him.

"Loyalty, Raymond, is a fine thing, commendable even, but only if it is judiciously and strategically applied. You need to keep in mind where to place it and for how long. Otherwise, it becomes a quicksand pit."

Pierce remained standing at the head of the conference table. Raymond waited for him to go on, but Pierce looked over at the mural and didn't say anything more.

Ten minutes later, Frank Atwell broke into the room, a comet-tail of rushed apologies following him. He dropped into a chair across from Raymond. The smell of cigarettes and last-call scotch leaked around the edges of his aftershave.

Pierce asked Frank for an update.

Atwell touched the knot in his tie and cleared his throat one more time than necessary. "A Luis Murano from the *St. Carlton Courier* dug up an unidentified source at the Health Department. Right now we're looking at an unofficial confirmation."

Meaning, Raymond thought, by tomorrow morning, noon at the latest, it would be official.

"This Murano," Pierce said, "how did he get through the door in the first place?"

"I assumed he'd go through Hendricks at the Health Department," Atwell said. "I had things covered with Hendricks. But Murano didn't go through Hendricks. That's how he landed the source and statement."

Now that the *Courier*'s in, the *Herald* won't be far behind. Talk to Hendricks," Pierce said. "Keep the leaks contained and the statements to a minimum."

"We should make sure Hendricks is the one who talks to any TV news people too," Raymond said. Hendricks was perfect for sound-bytes and interviews. He was bland and bureaucratic. His presence softened the edges of anything potentially controversial.

"Official or unofficial, the numbers are not reassuring," Pierce said. "I've already been on the phone with Lamar Ditell three times this morning. He's more than upset."

"The numbers are muddy," Atwell said.

"What exactly does that mean?"

"It means," Atwell said, "once the story broke, the numbers jump dramatically. They always do. A food poisoning scare is an opportunity to call in sick to work. It's a free pass. A lot of people are taking the day off at Happy Farm's expense. Can't be helped. The numbers will plateau and drop off in the next couple of days. Things aren't as bad as they appear."

"I still want you and Raymond on-site at Ditell's place by or before noon tomorrow."

"Whoa," Atwell said. "What's going on here?" He looked at Pierce, then Raymond, then back to Pierce. "I can handle Lamar Ditell."

"Can you clear your docket by tomorrow?" Pierce asked Raymond.

"I don't get it," Atwell interrupted. "Ditell is *upset*? He wouldn't be Ditell if he wasn't. For him, everything's D-Day. He's not exactly a big fan of subtlety. The point here, Daniel, is that I know Ditell and how he operates. It's my account. I don't need help."

"I believe focus has become something of an issue here." Pierce kept his voice quiet and even. "I don't want Lamar Ditell's hand held. I want *both* of Lamar Ditell's hands held."

Atwell shook his head, then pushed himself out of his chair.

Pierce waited until he'd left, then turned to Raymond and asked if he could have his work docket cleared by tomorrow.

Raymond nodded yes.

THREE

They were curious.
They were desperate.
They were afraid.
They were arrogant.
They were lost.
They were strong.
They were affluent.
They were self-absorbed.
They were empty.
They were weak.
They were full.
They were charming.
They were quiet.
They were deluded.
They were brilliant.
They were vulnerable.
They were ruthless.
They were confused.
They were cruel.
They were loud.
They were powerful.
They were careful.
They were oblivious.
They were devious.
They were naïve.

They were grasping.
They were proud.
They were furtive.
They were showy.
They were obtuse.
And finally, they were lonely.

And because they were, they went out and jammed up their lives and the lives of others and then came to Raymond Locke and Public Domain to fix or clean up what they'd done.

Raymond had developed some basic moves for the work that came his way.

The first was the simplest: whenever possible, buy your way out. It became a matter of finding the right palm or pocket, gauging the level of greed, and matching it to amount, the trick being not to over-or-under-pay and thus add to the original or create a new problem. You worked the person, waiting until he revealed his selling price, and then met it to the penny.

Or you covered up, Raymond breathing life into a lie that became a truth the client and public could live with, the Word not so much made flesh as prosthesis.

Then there were those clients whose messes, mistakes, sins, or crimes had left them in deep trouble, very deep trouble, and they were unable to buy or lie their way out. Raymond stepped in and helped them package their guilt, leaving the sins in place but emptying them of content and bite. He crafted elegant excuses. He booked the clients on talk shows, set up press conferences, arranged television, newspaper, and magazine interviews. In each, the client tearfully or stoically admitted to his guilt and replayed all the damning details, making them palatable and letting the public glut itself on the scandal until its familiarity did not breed contempt but rather a subtle complicity and shadowy identification.

At that stage, the trick was then to coax the identification along but not let it become too overt or uncomfortable. Then you turned everything in the campaign on its head. The client tearfully or stoically admitted not guilt but rather that he had a problem, one that was out of control, running and ruining his life. He then immediately went on to announce that he was now making progress coping with it.

That was the nice thing about problems. They implied solutions and closure. Evil didn't.

At that stage, the public was privy to the details of the treatment, the one-day-at-a-time, one-foot-in-front-of-the-other drama of hope and recovery, the client recounting his struggles to come to terms with what he'd done and who he was. Raymond orchestrated a large supporting cast of specialists and experts who testified and documented the source of the client's inner turmoil and who after praising his honesty and determination, went on to give roseate predictions for the client's eventual recovery under their care and guidance, pitching the tenets of whatever movement, camp, twelve-step program, center, clinic, or support group they represented along the way.

By that point, the client and his problems had been explained away. Blame substituted for cause.

Therapy replacing effect.

The original squalid and tawdry details of the scandal lost any personal content, and the client disappeared between the lines of his life script, his former actions attributable to a comfortable and predictable array of dysfunctions: abuse, addiction, co-dependency, family dynamics, or the anomalies of his own body chemistry.

As Daniel Pierce had requested, Raymond went on and cleared his work docket before heading home, his docket currently holding two clients whose problems were most pressing. One batch belonging to Paul Crosley aka Gary Ghoulmaster, the host of *Nightshade Theatre*, who after eighteen months of sobriety jumped, rather than fell, off the wagon and ended up sounding like he was speaking in tongues during his lead-in to last Saturday night's feature, *Sea of Blood*. The other batch of personal problems belonging to Candace Wright, wife of the CEO of a national chain of video stores, Raymond working to tactfully remove the hand and replace the lid on the cookie jar after Mrs. Wright as chair of the city-wide fund drive for the American Heart Association had siphoned off substantial portions of its proceeds to pay off her credit cards and refurnish the east wing of the Georgian Revival mansion fronting Lake Michigan that the Wrights called home.

Raymond spent the afternoon on the phone. He pulled strings. He cajoled. He threatened. He wheedled. He placated. Then he started all over again.

It was already dark, deep in the evening, when he left the building.

FOUR

At the dinner table, Raymond listened to Kate try to coax grace out of their son Andrew, then finally give in and say it herself, her voice clear and strong and unwavering, the blessing backdropped by the cough and rumble of the furnace, a behemoth of an oil-burner stutter-stepping its way into what Raymond knew would surely be its last Midwestern winter.

The house, three and a half stories of Victorian excess and fussy comfort, was beached in a transitional neighborhood between the terra firma of Woodborne Circle and the shifting crosscurrents of Alton Park. At the time they bought it, Kate had still been working, and they'd fallen in love with the house and its collection of widows' walks, wide curving balconies, high ceilings, cavernous fireplaces, leaded and stained glass windows, gingerbread molding, and sweeping balustrades. But over the last couple years, the upkeep and repair on its battered charm and haughty second-hand elegance had come to feel as costly, grandiose, and doomed as the British Colonial impulse itself.

Supper was Midwestern basic: center-cut pork chops, peas, mashed potatoes, and biscuits. Kate had put Andrew's portions on separate plates, a concession to his refusal to eat if any of the different foods touched each other.

She cut Andrew's pork chop into small brown squares, then sat back for a moment before reaching for the glass of red wine next to her own plate.

"Can you tell Daddy what we did today?" she said. "I'll bet he'd like to hear."

Andrew was wearing a pair of bright red pajamas that resembled a jumpsuit. He stared at the meat on his plate, then picked up a piece from its center and replaced it with another as if he were testing puzzle pieces.

"Did you have fun today?" Raymond asked.

Andrew repeated the process of moving the meat pieces. He was humming, the sound low and atonal, like slow-moving machine parts.

"We looked at pictures," Kate said, "didn't we?"

Andrew set the plate of meat aside and pulled the ones holding the peas closer. He counted off five and nudged his spoon under them.

"What kind of pictures?" Raymond said. "The ones with airplanes in them? Or the ones with cars?"

Andrew kept his face partially averted, head canted and held at an angle as if he were expecting someone to knock on the front door at any moment.

"Today we looked at the special pictures, didn't we, Andrew, the ones of people's faces, and we worked on telling the happy faces from the sad ones and the nice ones from the mean ones."

Andrew counted out five more peas from the pile and got his spoon under them. He dropped them into his mouth and chewed until they were a fine paste.

"Can you tell me what kind of face Daddy has tonight?" Kate said. "Is it a happy face or a sad one?"

Raymond looked across the table at his son and smiled.

Andrew corralled five more peas. He worked his spoon under them.

"Okay," Kate said. "Mommy's going to eat now."

For a moment, Raymond remembered a time when signs had yet to become symptoms and symptoms had yet to harden into a condition, when Andrew had been a newborn and then an infant and love had no fine print and each day was filled with quotidian miracles, Raymond holding and feeding and changing his son, sure that having watched this life delivered into the world had forever changed him, marked him in some fundamental and indelible way. He was a *father*.

He looked across the table at Kate. The dining room light fingered its way through her hair. She caught his eye and smiled. She looked tired, and her face held a kind of bruised beauty, a combination of bloom and shadow.

She said she'd talked to her brother earlier in the day. They'd discussed the logistics of the upcoming round-robin Christmas visits.

Kate's younger sister was still single and lived in-state, near Bloomington, and her brother and his family and her parents lived in the suburbs outside Toledo.

Raymond's family consisted of an aunt in an assisted-living center in Gary and a handful of cousins, most of whom he'd lost contact with.

"Ted wanted to know if it'd be all right if they visited after the twenty-fifth this year," Kate said. "I told him that would probably work for us."

Raymond nodded. He liked Kate's brother Ted and his family. Unlike the majority of Raymond's clients at Public Domain, his brother-in-law cultivated such refreshing habits as not cheating on his income taxes, keeping his pants zipped outside marriage, and not overloading his neural circuits with a smorgasbord of illegal substances. Raymond was also guiltily looking forward to spending some time with his niece and nephew who, unlike his son, could tell the difference between a smile and a frown and who did not feel compelled to repeatedly count their vegetables at mealtimes.

The rest of the Christmas visits were complicated by the fact that Raymond and Kate's father literally could not be in the same house, let alone room, together. Leonard Simco had made it known early on that he believed Kate could have done better than Raymond, and Raymond for his part stonewalled every effort by Kate's father to run Kate and Raymond's life as if their marriage were one of the branches of the Midwestern insurance kingdom Leonard Simco oversaw.

Kate's voice touched him like a hand unexpectedly dropping on his shoulder.

He picked up his glass of wine, then set it back down. "What?"

Across the table, Andrew dropped his spoon and started rocking in his chair.

"It's okay," Kate said.

"What?" Raymond said. He wasn't sure whom Kate was talking to.

The tendons in Andrew's neck were rigid. Eyes closed, he moved back and forth in a steady and insistent rhythm. The chair legs bounced and jumped on the dining room floor.

Raymond frowned.

She held up four fingers.

"The peas," Kate said. "There aren't enough." She pointed at Andrew's plate.

"Andrew," Kate said. She leaned over and touched his arm.

Andrew abruptly stopped rocking.

Andrew turned and hit her in the face, then jumped up from his chair and ran out of the room.

Raymond moved to the other side of the table. He stood behind Kate and cupped the back of her neck.

"Did it break the skin?" he asked.

Kate shook her head no.

"I'll get some ice," Raymond said.

On the way back from the kitchen, he found Andrew in the living room standing in front of an end table and making a repeated series of minute adjustments to the angle of a soft beige lampshade.

On the end table's surface, like an abandoned poker hand, were flashcards from the pediatric therapist's office, the cards holding close-ups of people's faces, a suite of basic human expressions and the everyday emotions tied to them.

Raymond looked down at the ice cubes he'd wrapped in a white dishcloth.

The furnace kicked in again.

Andrew let go of the lampshade. He turned so that he was facing Raymond, and for a very brief moment, they made eye contact.

"Everything's ticking," Andrew said.

FIVE

The thunderstorm which had been boiling over Lake Michigan since late morning opened and spilled in an Old Testament deluge a few minutes after Raymond Locke and Frank Atwell boarded the Bell Ranger helicopter that would take them to Wilkesboro, Indiana and a meeting with Lamar Ditell, owner and CEO of Happy Farms Inc.

The copter struggled to gain altitude, jerking and wavering in its ascent, bucking the heavy winds off the Lake. Outside, the cityscape was hooded and glazed with rain. Raymond could just make out the contour of the shoreline and the wavering necklace of lights comprising the interstate beltway before the copter abruptly shifted direction and they were thrown into the roiling underbelly of clouds filling a sky that had turned the color of dirty motor oil.

The rotors pulsed and shuddered in the buffeting crosswinds. From the cockpit, the captain looked over his shoulder and winked. Raymond heard the co-pilot whistling, the melody line a little too insistent for comfort.

He crushed a tiny blossom of panic, but its roots were still intact. They ran thirty-eight years deep and ended in a July wheat field with a charred fuselage of a DC-8 and 187 dead, including his parents, Raymond one and a half years old, the lone survivor of the crash.

The newspaper headlines had christened him *A*

Child of Luck and *Fate's Favorite.*

Across the aisle, Frank Atwell unbuckled his seat belt, leaned over, and hollered in the direction of the cockpit, "Is it ok to smoke?" When the captain thumb-downed the request, Atwell nodded and began adjusting the knot in his tie.

He was a large man who had unexpectedly dropped a lot of weight but hadn't bothered to fully adjust his wardrobe. Everything bunched and sagged on him. He had a head full of televangelist hair and a pair of throwback 70's sideburns that needed trimmed. His skin tone was a half shade from healthy. Atwell looked exactly like what he was: a widower waylaid by grief. A man lost who didn't realize he was.

Outside, the wind drove the rain, and the rain sheeted the landscape.

"You know," Atwell said after a moment, "it's not like this thing is another ... " He paused, searching. "That Russian place from a few months ago." He snapped his fingers.

"Chernobyl," Raymond said.

Atwell nodded. "Yeah. It's not that I don't appreciate the help, but at bottom, we're talking chickens here, Raymond."

Raymond pointed out what he should not have had to, that Daniel Pierce was playing it conservative on this one. Pierce was flying to New York next week to meet with Public Domain stockholders. Or *stakeholders* as a very vocal and powerful bloc preferred to be called. They still wanted a fat return on their investment but at no cost to their social conscience. They were big on corporate ethics and would ask some difficult questions about the way Public Domain was handling the Happy Farms campaign. Pierce wanted to make sure all the bases were covered.

When Raymond finished, Atwell nodded twice and then ran his index finger down the inside of the window. Outside, the clouds churned, the winds turning them inside out.

"Psychics. What's your take?" Atwell said. "I mean, you ever get curious?"

Raymond shrugged. "Really haven't thought about it, Frank. Why?"

Atwell tapped the window. "The thing about our job, Raymond, you do it long enough, at some point, you either start believing or quit believing altogether that there's something out there, God or Spirit World, something, that's bigger than we are."

Raymond waited a moment before saying, "I guess."

Atwell started nodding again. "I mean, you can't sleep, so you get up, have a couple drinks, watch some television, and it's late, and you should know better, but right there in front of you, there's this woman talking about making *contact*, you know, and you get to thinking what if she can, and it's not like you forget she's just some cut-rate cable guru and it's 2:45 a.m. and a toll-free number's flashing at the bottom of the screen. No, what you start thinking about is the *idea* of it, how nice, just how goddamn nice, it would be if it was all *true* and that easy."

Atwell looked over at Raymond. "Just her voice," he said. "To hear it one more time. I mean, they cut both off, and it still got her." He paused. "My Judy. I miss her."

Raymond nodded again.

The wind thinned, and the clouds began breaking up, and twenty minutes later, Wilkesboro, Indiana appeared, its eastern limits defined by the white-capped crescents of a series of abandoned stone quarries, the Happy Farms slaughterhouse and processing plant to the north, the interstate to the south, and the walled-compound of the Ditell estate to the west. The town itself was laid out in a quadrant, each grid defined with a tic-tac-toe regularity, a no nonsense right-angled symmetry.

From the air, Lamar Ditell's home embodied Frank Lloyd Wright's prairie style writ large, the house long and low with a lean roof line and wide eaves, its lines possessing a spare and simple elegance, but as the helicopter descended, Raymond noted small anomalies, an aggressive bluntness to the design that owed less to Wright and more to Ditell's livelihood. The closer Raymond got to the ground, the more the house resembled an oversized, opulent chicken coop.

Lamar Ditell met Raymond and Frank Atwell in the living room. The furniture and furnishings were either low to the floor or scaled down to compensate for Lamar Ditell's height. He topped out at four foot ten and wore his trademark outfit, the brown suit, white shoes, yellow shirt, and yellow and white bow tie that had appeared in every major Happy Farms advertisement and publicity shot for over a decade. Without the aid of an airbrush, Ditell's face was heavily lined and creased. Raymond thought he resembled a freeze-dried fifth grader.

Ditell did not ask them to sit. He stood between Raymond and Atwell before a wide picture window overlooking the rear of the estate.

"First question," Ditell said. He held up an index finger. "How many cases?"

"At present, approximately 103," Atwell said, "and we'll probably top off just shy of 140. The figures aren't fully trustworthy though. There's always a discrepancy between reported and confirmed cases. Confirmed cases require specimens. Specimens require people taking stool samples to their doctor, and that's something most people would just rather not do." Atwell paused and touched the knot in his tie. "We'll be able to live with the final figure."

"Second question," Ditell said, another finger popping up. "How much longer before people quit shitting and puking?"

"The typical incubation period for nontyphoidal Salmonella is between eight and seventy-two hours," Atwell said, "but we're facing a few new wrinkles here, Lamar."

Atwell went on and detailed the preliminary findings of the independent pathology lab Public Domain had hired to run tests on samples taken from the two Happy Farms franchises. The Health Department and USDA were running their own tests, but Atwell predicted they'd eventually get around to confirming what the path lab had come up with. Some very sick birds had ended up in the fryers of the franchises.

The primary contaminants were mixed between Salmonella and Campylobacter, but there had been traces of Clostridium perfringens, Escherichia coli, and Staphylococcus aureus present in varying degrees also, all of which affected the interval for incubation and increased the severity of the primary symptoms. Atwell said he had asked the pathology lab for a more detailed series of follow-up tests on additional samples.

"Third question," Ditell said. "What's the source of the contaminants?"

"That might take a while to pin down." Atwell outlined the possibilities. Things could have gone awry at any stage of production. The feed shipped to the poultry growers could have been bad. The conditions at the poultry farms themselves could have produced sick birds. There could have been screw-ups when the birds were processed at the Happy Farms plants. Something might have gone wrong when the processed birds were shipped from the plants. Or the birds might have been prepared improperly at the franchises themselves. Anything was possible. In the mean time, all they could do was monitor the progress of the overlapping agency investigations and hope when one of them put its finger on the source of the outbreak that Public Domain could step in and keep that same finger from pointing too insistently at Lamar Ditell and Happy Farms.

Four fingers shot up in the air. "The media people. They're everywhere, swarming the town or trying to get inside here. I want them off my back."

Atwell cleared his throat and nodded. "I'm afraid

I'm going to have to ask you to sit tight for a while longer. The outbreak's news, and the media people are scrambling for any workable angle. We'll do our best to distract them."

Ditell held up four fingers again. "Listen to me. The media people. Luis Murano in particular. What do you intend to do about him?"

Atwell broke open a smile. It was not reassuring. "I think you're overestimating Murano, Lamar. He's just a kid. He's showboating, flexing his muscles on this one. A lot of preening while he tries to make a name for himself."

"In case it escaped your notice, Frank, young Mr. Murano is doing his preening on page one of the *Courier*. Find a way to cut him off at the knees and fast."

"Perspective," Atwell said. "You've got to hold on to your perspective, Lamar. This outbreak's hot right now. A newsmaker. But these things have their own rhythm. We can dismantle anything the media comes up with. But right now, patience. Once the regulatory agencies launch their investigations, the whole process turns snail. We'll have all the opportunities we need to bury or sidetrack anything damaging to Happy Farms and you. By the time the Health Department and the Food Safety and Inspection Service people publish their findings, even Murano will have a hard time remembering what set the whole thing off in the first place."

Despite Frank Atwell's assurances, things did not get any better as the afternoon went on. Lamar Ditell kept flipping up fingers. Atwell kept coaching patience and perspective.

Ditell then brought up Eileen Connelly, the director of And Justice For All, a consumer advocacy group that over the last three years had evolved from watchdog to pit bull status. Though the organization ran on a shoestring budget, Eileen Connelly had the knack for making her presence felt, and Ditell was worried she'd team up with Luis Murano and honeymoon their careers at Happy Farm's expense.

Ditell finally got tired of throwing up fingers. He seemed to register Raymond's presence for the first time. He cocked his head and asked, "Are you going to talk to me about perspective too?"

Raymond shook his head.

"That's good. Because I'm going to show you the only perspective that counts." Ditell crossed the room and stood before a small fireplace. Lining the mantle were six stuffed roosters of varying sizes, their wings outstretched and heads raised.

Ditell scooped something up in his palm and returned to the window. Raymond was hoping they'd sit down. Adjusting his frame to the tiny-tot dimensions of the furniture would be easier than the awkward contortions in posture he felt compelled to maintain in Ditell's presence.

Ditell opened his hand.

In its center lay a small ring, a pair of cutters resembling nail clippers, and a miniscule pair of spectacles with faint rose-colored lenses. Raymond and Atwell had no idea what they were used for.

"We need to get one thing straight," Ditell said. "The world is a chicken yard. Nothing more, nothing less. And it's to your advantage to know how it works. There's a pecking order to everything. That's the first principle of the yard.

"Chickens like to flock together," he said. "There's safety in numbers. That's the second principle of the yard.

"The problem starts when you try to reconcile the two principles. Now your poultry experts have come up with a variety of causes, everything from boredom, heat, incorrect feeding, too much light, or routine stress, but they can't say for sure what causes one chicken to begin pulling at another's feathers and to continue pulling and pecking until the skin is broken.

"But this is a fact. Once blood is drawn, the others join in. They'll pull and peck until they've cannibalized the first bird. The taste of blood leaves them hungry for more. In very short order, the flock consumes itself in a feeding frenzy."

Ditell paused and held up the palm holding the three objects. "There are some proven methods for avoiding cannibalism. One is to fasten a ring in the bird's nostrils to restrict movement. Another is to hinder their vision by outfitting the birds with rose-tinted spectacles. You can also simply go in and debeak the son of a bitches. Which leads us to the third principle of the yard."

Ditell's smile was tight and grim. "Care to hazard a guess as to what that might be, gentlemen?"

Atwell patted his jacket pocket and looked around for an ashtray. "They really put glasses on chickens, Lamar?"

"How about you?" Ditell turned to Raymond.

"You're the guy, the one Pierce told me about over the phone, that cleaned up that mess Bishop DeMarco got into, right? You haven't said anything all afternoon. What's your take on the third principle?"

Raymond looked out the window and then back at Lamar Ditell. "There are no final solutions," he said. "The glasses fall off, the rings work loose, and the beaks grow back. You can't completely avoid cannibalism."

There was a prolonged and uneasy silence while Ditell squinted and studied Raymond. It was followed by a sudden explosion of laughter and Lamar Ditell's tiny fist pummeling Raymond's lower back.

"Son of a bitch," Ditell roared. "I think I better buy this man a drink. Fellows, step up to the bar."

Frank Atwell looked happy for the first time that afternoon.

SIX

Raymond propped his head on the arm of his living room sofa and briefly closed his eyes and tried to summon up the image of what had lain on his supper plate a little over an hour ago, but he could not recall with any certainty what he'd eaten.

He concentrated harder. It seemed important to recover the details though he could not exactly say why.

That temporary jolt of dislocation became wedded to the moment earlier in the day when Raymond stood next to Frank Atwell in Lamar Ditell's living room and Ditell lifted his tiny fist of a face and challenged Raymond to verify that he was who he said he was, Raymond's name ultimately less important than the fact that Raymond had been the one to fix things for Bishop DeMarco.

Raymond had looked at Ditell and nodded. He was that Raymond Locke, yes.

The Raymond Locke who stepped in eight years ago on Christmas Eve when Bishop DeMarco's mistress committed suicide and forwarded a copy of her send-off letter to the *St. Carlton Courier*. The paper printed the letter in its entirety. It contained a none too subtle account of the Bishop's sexual predilections and his extravagant gifts and promises as well as cataloging the emotional pain and torment the woman had undergone when he finally dumped her.

The Diocese had wanted Daniel Pierce himself to handle all the attendant problems personally, but Pierce was in the Bahamas for the holidays and was afraid by the time he got back to do a full assessment of the damages it would be too late to do any real good.

Raymond, new to the Special Services Division of the agency, was the only one close by and at hand. Pierce reluctantly gave him a shot at damage control.

Raymond went one better. He erased the problem completely.

He had bracketed any individual moral qualms and treated the situation as if it were an exercise in problem solving, reducing the Bishop's dilemma to its barest elements and systematically addressing each.

The first step had been a phone call to the owner of the lounge where the Bishop's mistress worked as a waitress to get the name and address of the head bartender. Next was tracking down the bartender on Christmas day and convincing him to talk. The convincing took the form of a pair of airline tickets for a weekend in Miami Beach. The bartender had the usual knack for remembering names and faces. Raymond left with a list of the regulars.

Then, using the newspaper version as a model, he spent the rest of the day in the office working on five carefully worded variants of the original suicide letter. At nine p.m. he put in a call to the Police Commissioner and foreclosed on a couple past favors the agency had done for the department.

A day later, the *St. Carlton Herald* broke the story

that police officers had discovered a secret cache of letters at the woman's apartment, all of them suicide notes and addressed to a bank vice-president, a hometown relief pitcher for the Cubs, a city councilman, the Streets Commissioner, and an anchorman at Channel Five.

By the time each of them got done denying the allegations, claiming that they only knew the woman through her capacity as a waitress, the Bishop had been quietly included in their number, a victim of a poor deluded woman's self-destructive sexual fantasies.

Raymond had just moved into the Special Services Division of Public Domain. The Division functioned in an advisory and adjunct capacity to Daniel Pierce and was set up to handle sensitive matters that fell outside the range of standard public relations services for the agency's clients.

Raymond had originally balked at the move, despite the fact that it was common, if unspoken, knowledge around the agency that a slot in the Special Services Division was the surest and quickest way to fast-forward a career.

After acknowledging the success of his strategy, on reflection Raymond had not been so much bothered by what he had to do to get Bishop DeMarco off the hook as quietly frightened by how easily the solution had come to him.

Daniel Pierce called it a gift. Raymond was not so sure.

He remained disconcertingly good at his job.

From upstairs came the sound of running water

and then Kate's voice as she worked on getting Andrew ready for bed. Raymond had tried earlier, but Kate had had to step in and relieve him when Andrew refused to cooperate. Raymond had choked off his frustration and returned to the living room. He might be the man to see if your mistress committed suicide on Christmas eve and sent her send-off note to the media, but not if it was something as simple and uncomplicated as convincing his eight year old son to put on his pajamas. Andrew had flinched and flailed every time Raymond got near him.

He listened to Kate's voice drift down the stairs and wondered what it would be like not to love his wife, to find himself swept up in some outworn middle-aged fantasy shadowing what so many of his clients inevitably ended up chasing until the fantasy caught them and they ran to Raymond for help. Raymond almost envied them their lab-rat predictability, the all too easily negotiated maze of their desires. Even when things were strained between Kate and him, as they had been lately over finances, Raymond could not imagine a life separate from his wife. They'd been married a little over eleven years, and what started out as a private joke - Raymond's claim that he could not help but fall in love with Kate because her name, after all, rhymed with *fate* - had come to take on the tricky weight of lived truth.

Living with the truth of his son's autism proved to be a different matter.

Kate and he had spent hundred of hours in clinics and experts' offices discussing the aetiology of their son's condition and various treatment regimens, but in the end, Kate and Raymond were marooned, left with a bewildering array of competing theories on the care and education of autistic children, none of which contained much practical help or guidance in dealing with Andrew.

Kate's response was to leapfrog the distressing daily confirmation of the specialists' prognoses and embrace the long shot, hoping for a significant reversal or breakthrough promised by case studies and anecdotal evidence, but what fed her hope had seriously depleted Raymond's. He was tired of paying hundreds of dollars to specialists only to be told that he needed to love his son *because* he was autistic and not in spite of it. That, according to the counselor, was the duty of the ideal caregiver. That, as far as Raymond could see, was cheerleading masquerading as therapy.

Raymond turned his head and watched Kate and Andrew come down the stairs. Andrew was tented in a pair of red and green flannel pajamas. He was small for his age and pale, his skin too tight for his bones. His eyes were as dark as something charred and bullied the rest of his face. He ignored Raymond and moved to the opposite corner of the room where he began making a series of minute adjustments to the angle of a soft beige lampshade.

Kate glanced at Andrew and then stepped over and lightly kissed Raymond on the forehead. He caught the faint scent of soap and shampoo and started to reach for her, but she bent over and pulled a puzzle box from beneath the couch and then moved to the large oval blue and white braided rug in the middle of the living room floor.

As she upended the box, she started in coaxing Andrew to join her. Andrew continued adjusting the angle of the lampshade. A dull ache bloomed at the base of Raymond's neck, and he shifted positions on the couch.

Kate sat cross-legged in the middle of the rug and held up a blocky piece of the puzzle and said, "Look, Andrew. A red airplane. That's what I'm holding in my hand. A red airplane, and it's a very nice one."

The ache spread from Raymond's neck to his shoulders.

Andrew abruptly turned, moved to the edge of the rug, circled it twice, and then sat down.

Kate nodded and smiled. "A red airplane needs some sky. A blue piece, Andrew, can you find that, the sky, something blue like this?" Kate slipped the pieces together, repeating the sequence, her voice steady and calm and shadowing each movement. "The red airplane, Andrew, we take the red airplane and put it in the blue sky where it fits."

Andrew grimaced and swiveled his head as if he were ducking a swarm of bugs.

Kate said, "A red airplane in a blue sky is very nice, but there's no sun, and a sky has to have a sun, and what's the color of the sun, Andrew? You tell me, and we'll find it."

The ache wrapped itself around Raymond's shoulder blades. He tried, once again, to remember what he'd eaten for supper.

"Can you tell me the color of the sun, Andrew? I'll bet you can. The sun lives in the sky and makes things warm." Kate paused, then tried again. "Can you tell me the color of the sun, Andrew? I bet your father knows."

Raymond sat up and rubbed the back of his neck. The words were out before he realized he'd spoken them. "For Christ's sake, Kate, give it a rest."

She winced, then said quietly, "Stop it, Raymond."

The furnace kicked on, and the house began its cleared-throat creaking. Andrew stood with his head bowed, opening and closing his right hand.

The light in the room seemed too bright.

"Put the puzzle away, Kate, okay? I'll help you with the dishes, and then we'll get him to bed. It's been a long day, and we still have the end of the month bills to write out."

"It's been a long one for Andrew and me too. The puzzle calms him. You know that, Raymond. Or should."

Raymond headed for the kitchen, passing the dining room table and the plates and serving bowls coated in wide waxy smears and dotted with miniscule food particles that provided no more than generic clues to what they'd held at supper. To Raymond, the napkins wadded beside the plates and the empty glasses dotted with fingerprints seemed vaguely incriminating.

In the kitchen, he poured a large glass of red wine and leaned against the counter.

Kate's voice drifted from the living room, holding the same even, patient cadences as before, Kate delivering a litany of colors and shapes and fit. A red airplane, blue sky, yellow sun. Kate adding a green tree and a little boy and girl.

Raymond knew he should set down the glass of wine and join his family. He could remember all too clearly when that's exactly what he would have done.

Tonight though, he remained in the kitchen with his love and rage and the feeling that it was becoming increasingly more difficult to tell the difference between the two.

SEVEN

Raymond Locke followed the same route to work each morning, leaving the house and taking Hermitage Street east through blocks of rehabbed Victorians and Georgians that eventually bordered the campus of John Thomas, a small, private Presbyterian-based college. Then taking Hughes Avenue north where the student strip of stores and restaurants disappeared into old working-class neighborhoods once populated by Italian, Irish, and Balkan immigrants when the city's steel mills were flourishing but which now were sunk in a real estate purgatory. A few blocks later, he got on the Beltway that lifted him above fourteen square-blocks of absolute inner-city poverty and over the warehouse district that serviced. St. Carlton's still-thriving port system.

During the morning commute, Raymond thought about money.

He ran the numbers.

The tab on the house and its growing roster of renovations and repairs.

The tab on the nursing home in Gary where his Aunt Elizabeth stayed and the extra tab for the new accommodations after a recent round of falls and broken bones.

The monthly status quo tab for two cars, groceries, utilities, clothes, and entertainment.

The tab on Kate's student loans from when she went back to get her Masters in Nursing shortly after they got married.

The tab on the boom and bust cycle of his investments.

All no different from most upper-middle class Americans except for one looming and burgeoning price tag.

The one on his son Andrew.

Driving into work each morning, Raymond could get no further than the autism and the dismal odds that Andrew's condition would improve or change significantly.

Kate refused to accept the prognosis, believing that the simple fact of motherhood was powerful enough in and of itself to change things for Andrew. Raymond's faith faltered on that one. He wanted to believe in those eleventh-hour miracles, those uplifting made-for-TV-movie-moments when the negative and positive poles of fate were reversed, but that faith and belief inevitably broke down sooner or later for him, and Raymond was left with the hard-line truth that his son would more than likely never be able to support himself and would require supervised or institutional care, and that care over the course of a life required money, lots of it.

And Andrew's care would have to be bankrolled on one income because despite floating some open-ended references about returning to work, Raymond knew Kate would stay at home with Andrew as long as he was under their roof.

It added up, all that lost income. After going back

for her Masters, Kate had barely worked a year when she discovered she was pregnant.

That was eight and a half years ago.

It added up.

A couple of blunt-edged truths each morning that served as a reminder of why he was working at Public Domain.

At the 36th Street exit, the Beltway began a slow rising curve that at its apex looked as if it were emptying into the sky. On the downward slope, to Raymond's right, where the warehouse district ran into the outer blocks of downtown was a mammoth billboard mounted on pylons.

The billboard looked like a vandalized drive-in theatre screen, its face peeling in a tattered pastiche of images and broken slogans.

The billboard produced the same uneasy sense in Raymond as half-remembered dreams. In the upper left corner was what appeared to be a huge set of fingers, but what they were reaching for had disappeared. Below them was *E er   b d   r d s.* The bottom left held a large door and adjacent window, the middle portion an immense open mouth, below it *Bu l   y   r   dr a s,* the upper right holding an eye and a gold wristwatch, the lower right a smeared patch of blue that faded into a bare shoulder and then a sleek black pen and *It' a l tr* .

After a decade of commutes, Raymond could not say with any certainty what the billboard had originally advertised before it was abandoned to time and the elements and started to peel and tatter.

He thought it might have been a public service

announcement, something about the early symptoms and warning signs of heart disease.

He glanced at the dash clock, then turned on the radio to catch the news. He took Exit 27 for downtown. The sky leaked November snow.

Raymond took Williams Avenue to the parking garage two blocks north of the Public Domain building. The news held a small reprieve. Happy Farms and the food poisoning episode had been temporarily back-burnered by the ongoing Iran-Contra controversy, the questions piling up and Ronald Reagan still doing the equivocation shuffle.

Raymond pulled into his parking slot. The newscaster segued into a segment about Oliver North and someone named John Tower. Raymond shut off the car, locked it, and went to work.

EIGHT

Raymond started his morning by dealing with the very tight corner Commander Sunshine had painted himself into. The Commander along with his canine mascot, Pep, was big with the after-school and Saturday morning crowd. He hosted a children's program on Channel Five entitled *The Commander Rules!* which featured cartoons, comedy skits, sports and entertainment guest appearances, lessons in manners and grooming tips, and clumsily plagiarized *Sesame Street* educational segments that, if necessary, could be presented as parody in a court of law.

Off the set, Commander Sunshine enjoyed an active social life, part of which included hiring hookers, taking them back to his apartment, and shaving their pubic region. The Commander considered himself a Gillette Artist, and in a burst of inspiration the Tuesday before Thanksgiving, he hired two hookers, one of whom brought along a video camera.

Raymond negotiated the retrieval of the original and extra print and then put in a call to Indiana Escorts, working out a deal and escrowing it with a Channel Five slush fund so that the next time the Commander was in the mood to trim and shave someone's pudenda, he could contact Indiana Escorts rather than freelancers.

Around ten, Raymond took a call from Kate. She reminded him that he needed to be home no later than 6:30 if they were going to keep their reservation for the evening. The sitter would be there a little after six.

Raymond spent the next hour and a half reviewing the Happy Farms files, checking for new developments and flagging areas for follow-up questions. As of today, the number of confirmed food-poisoning cases had topped out at 91. They cut across all demographic lines. The Health Department, goaded by media coverage, had upgraded its inquiries to an official investigation and ordered the two franchise operations closed. The Food Safety and Inspection Service from the USDA was moving on a full-scale investigation of its own, centering on the Happy Farms plants and subsidiary companies.

Raymond swung his chair toward the north window. The skyline was streaked in a fine snow. He closed his eyes for a moment and rubbed his temples.

He looked over his shoulder at this desk calendar and the large *X* he'd inked two and a half weeks ago when Kate had started bleeding, and the pregnancy with its seemingly transparent symptoms disappeared.

A false start. The body's sleight-of-hand. A counterfeit fetus.

Pseudocyesis.

All the regular symptoms of pregnancy. Except for an actual fetus.

Kate and he had not quite talked about it.

A basic question: how do you mourn a trick of the

body?

He had no idea how to answer that one.

Raymond left the office to meet Frank Atwell for lunch. He took the Happy Farms files with him.

Very little in the décor of Bismarck's suggested a Teutonic ambiance beyond the inevitable line of festive beer steins behind the bar or the tight bodices and short accordion-pleated skirts of the waitresses. Uneasy vestiges of the restaurant's two earlier incarnations - Andre's and Antonio's - persisted, hanging around like unwelcome relatives.

Frank was at a window seat and working on his second Scotch. He saluted Raymond with an amber-colored glass.

Raymond ordered coffee and waved off a menu and without opening the file, brought up the numbers.

"They're stable," Raymond said.

Atwell swirled his glass like a doorknob. "I know."

"Not a good sign. I thought you said they'd be falling by now. Dramatically falling."

"They should be," Atwell said. "That's the standard trajectory. We're looking at a couple of anomalies here."

"Like Eileen Connelly? Is she another anomaly?"

Atwell shook his head. "Come on, Raymond. She's just one in a long line of Lamar Ditell's enemies. No news there. They have a history."

"Sandlow Feed then?" Raymond asked.

"The shredder in their main office should be working overtime. I'm going to do a follow-up after lunch." Atwell paused. "Hey, don't give me that look, Raymond."

51

Raymond tapped the file. "Luis Murano? Rumor is he's in Wilkesboro nosing around. There's talk of the *Courier* running a series of sidebars."

"What can I say? Murano got in through the back door. Nobody, not just me, saw that or him coming."

"We're looking at a lot of loose ends here, Frank. Pierce and Ditell are not going to be happy."

Atwell caught the waitress' eye and held up his Scotch glass. The ashtray at his elbow held five crushed Marlboro butts. To the left of that was a plate with a club sandwich and two irregular bites taken out of it and a pale green dill pickle pointing to a small pile of soggy potato chips.

Atwell looked back over at Raymond. "We both know that if it had been any other reporter, I could have kept things locked down. You can count on most reporters being lazy as hell and easy to steer." Atwell waited until the waitress set the Scotch in front of him before going on. "This Murano guy, though, he's on some kind of crusader kick."

Raymond glanced out the window at the snow-wet streets and noon traffic. "I'm hearing things, Frank. I'm not sure I can keep covering for you."

"Don't worry, my friend. Twenty-seven years I've been at the agency. Peaks and valleys. It all evens out."

"You're whistling," Raymond said. "The sun's down, and it's dark, and you're whistling, Frank."

Atwell burned a Marlboro.

"It's Donner, right?" he said. "The one behind this?"

Raymond slowly let out his breath.

"When Donner hired on, he was young and green, and Pierce asked me to help bring him along," Atwell said, "just like I did for you, Raymond, when you started. And this is how he repays me."

"It's not Donner," Raymond said.

"Donner and that piece on the fourth floor, what's her name, Julie something. You can't trust either. They have no idea. *Loyalty* is just three syllables to them. Noise."

Frank pointed his cigarette at Raymond. "And Donner, that little shit, is a whole new species of *ambitious.* You better watch out."

"Let's forget about Eric Donner for a minute," Raymond said. "You're getting sloppy, Frank. Careless and sloppy. That's what it comes down to."

Atwell dropped back into his chair. He shook his head twice. "Any more advice, Raymond? Something else I should know for my own good?"

"Jesus." It was Raymond's turn to sit back. "You've gotten too used to looking at the world through the bottom of a Scotch glass, Frank."

"I remember a kid knocking on my office door, and he was scared, it was all over him, but he was doing everything he could to hide it, not acting cocky, not anything like that, just the opposite, because he had a good-looking wife who he had just found out was pregnant and a job he had backed into and wasn't sure he had the stomach to do." Atwell paused and crushed out the cigarette. "The kid knocked and asked for my help."

"That was a long time ago," Raymond said.

NINE

It felt like the world could be redeemed in the time it took for a brown-haired woman in a white sweater dress to walk through a crowded room in your direction and then smile as she sat down across from you.

In a moment like that, Raymond Locke fell in love with his wife all over again.

They were in the Blue Rose, a small jazz club in the heart of St. Carlton on Evans Avenue, and they were celebrating their anniversary, not of their wedding, but rather of the night they had first met. In Raymond's mind, however, the two were inextricably joined because, despite what rationality and common sense might dictate, he had fallen in love with his future wife at first sight.

Literally. Nothing metaphorical about it. As far as Raymond was concerned, you could bypass a couple hundred thousand song-writing clichés. At first sight happens. It happened.

Tonight, over drinks, Raymond looked at the woman sitting across from him, the light brown hair just shy of her shoulders and offset by the darker walnut of her eyes, her mouth a little too wide for the contours of her face, a fullness that mocked symmetry and replaced it with ripeness, and he marveled once again at finding her in his life. He wanted another ten, twenty, thirty years with her.

"Do you think … " Kate began.

"Andrew's okay," Raymond said. "Mackenzie's watched him before. She can handle things."

Raymond drew a set of imaginary brackets in the space between them. "Remember. Tonight it's us. We set everything else aside."

Kate nodded. He took a sip of his drink, then took her hand, and they moved to the small dance floor that began where the cluster of tables ran out.

Billy Faulk, the owner of the Blue Rose, dictated the music selection. Tonight it was Sarah Vaughn and "It Could Happen To You."

Raymond pulled Kate close, and they left everything outside their movement on the floor, no extended discussions of Andrew's autism and treatment options, no talk of the emotional minefield hiding the recent false pregnancy, no arguing over money, where it went and how much, no lamenting the workload and hours Raymond put in at Public Domain, no tense silences and standoffs about Kate's family, her father in particular, overstepping and interfering in their lives, no round-robin working out of all the holiday plans and obligations, all that set aside, so that when Raymond tilted his head and leaned down and found Kate's lips, he tasted the moment and the music, its smoky melody soft and haunting, evoking the neon and nightclubs and sultry romances of the 40's, the kiss and the night full of moody saxophones and moonlight, white gardenias pinned in a dark shimmering fall of hair, of lingering perfume and lipstick traces and the sharp clean bite of gin.

They danced to and in the music. There were no false bottoms to it or their movement, no jaded nod or knowing wink, no world-weary smirks or self-congratulatory irony, nothing beyond Raymond's hand in the small of his wife's back and the rich multi-layered promise of his love for her.

Right then, it felt like the music and that love could eclipse or clean anything the world brought to them.

And yet.

There was always the *and yet*.

And the name attached to it: *Michael Cardell.*

Meeting his future wife had come down to what had also defined so much of Raymond's life. Luck and timing.

Coattailed by a little fast-thinking calculation and cunning.

A Friday evening, almost twelve years ago, Raymond stopping for a to-go coffee at the Cup and Saucer after a long day at work and while in line, seeing a striking brown-haired woman sitting at a window table by herself.

At the counter, the server, taking his order, noticing him watching the woman and then saying, *You must be Michael.*

Raymond looking at the server, then at the woman in the window seat, hesitating, timing it just right so that the server went on to fill in the blanks or enough of them for Raymond to pick up his coffee and cross the room.

It's so romantic, the server had said. *A blind date. She's pretty. You make a nice couple.*

Kate had looked up, expectant, Raymond leaning over and smiling again long enough for her to ask, *Michael?* Raymond nodding, keeping the smile in place and extending his hand, saying, *And you're?*

Kate, she automatically went on to answer.

The first fifteen minutes or so of conversation were stiff, a little awkward, but then suddenly, everything changed, and it was as if they were not so much following a script as spontaneously writing it between them, trading lines that didn't feel old or shopworn, Kate and Raymond unexpectedly caught up in the eerie and automatic collaboration of couples who had been together for a long time and completed each other's sentences and the thoughts behind them.

Outside, the rain broke into sleet, and the street began to ice up. At the time, Raymond didn't know the deteriorating weather was part of his luck.

Kate and he left the Cup and Saucer for the Blue Rose five minutes before Michael Cardell showed up.

Raymond still remembered the song that had been playing when they entered the club: Billy Holliday's "Night and Day."

They had drinks. Listened to more Holliday. Danced. Had some more drinks. He continued pretending to be a man named Michael Cardell, and he continued to fall in love with the woman sitting across from him.

Outside the Blue Rose, the world iced over.

Later, in the doorway of her apartment, a long kiss, followed by another, slower and deeper, and when they broke it off and Kate turned to open the door, after having promised a second date, Raymond finally told her, *I'm not exactly who you think I am*, and he was still able to clearly remember the abrupt shadow-play of emotions across her features, the move from confusion to shock to anger and finally to outright fear, before she slammed the apartment door on him, and the door remained closed and her phone unanswered even while he filled her answering machine over and over again with every movie line and its variation he could think of, each *I can't quit thinking about you* and *just one more chance, please, to show you who I really am and make things right* going unacknowledged until the closest thing he'd ever known to an outright act of unearned grace when Kate finally picked up the phone, heard him out, and consented to another date and chance.

They were married less than five months later.

TEN

If Tuesday were a shotgun aimed at Lamar Ditell and Happy Farms, then Luis Murano pulled the trigger for the first barrel and Eileen Connelly the trigger on the second.

Neither had any trouble hitting the target.

Things were in apocalyptic mode at Public Domain, and Raymond Locke was back in the ninth floor's windowless conference room sitting across from Frank Atwell and the wall-sized aerial photograph of St. Carlton.

They were waiting for Daniel Pierce.

"Jesus, Frank." Raymond tapped his pen on the edge of the table. "This isn't good. I'm hearing they're setting up betting pools all over the city. Three-to-one odds the numbers will top out at 110. Even for them staying under 100.

"What can I say?" Atwell slowly shook his head. "What we're looking at. Circle the wagons right now."

"I called, Frank. Gave you a heads-up."

"It's not my fault the office manager at Sandlow rushed things, " Frank said. "I explained what we needed."

He reached up and began tugging on his left earlobe. His skin tone had not improved much since Raymond had last seen him. The stripes in his tie were a shade and a half away from a match with his shirt and jacket, and the right sideburn was noticeably shorter than the left. The friend and colleague Raymond had known up to a year ago had disappeared, and the Frank Atwell sitting across from him had managed to turn himself into walking synonyms for *lost* and *unlucky*.

"His name?" Raymond asked.

"Who?"

"The office manager. What's his name?"

"Why's that matter? Pretty much after the fact at this point."

Raymond sighed. "Because we need to check him out, Frank. Make sure he's clean and we're not looking at any repeat performances."

Atwell pointed to the folder in front of Raymond. " He's okay. I've known him for a long time."

Raymond pursed his lips. Frank should know better. How many times had someone - a husband or wife, family member or friend or co-worker - said exactly the same thing only to end up looking at the fist raised, gun pointed, wallet lifted, character assassinated, pants unzipped or bra unclasped, life dismantling and mocking every one of their assumptions and certainties?

Raymond flipped open the file and flagged the name and made a note to watch the guy's bank account for any irregularities or unusual activity for the next few months.

"I'm doing what I can here, Frank," Raymond said, "but you need to step up."

"It's not as bad as it looks," Frank said. "A little elbow grease, and I'll have everything cleaned up and looking good again."

Daniel Pierce showed up five minutes later and stationed himself at the head of the conference table. Under the recessed lighting, his customary silver-gray suit was the shade of a new quarter suspended in a cloudy ice-cube.

Pierce asked for updates, starting with Sandlow Feeds.

Frank Atwell began talking about circling the wagons again.

Pierce rapped the tabletop as if it were a door. "Start over," he said. "I don't want to hear any metaphors."

Frank cleared his throat. He looked at Raymond, then at Pierce, and cleared his throat once more. Then he began again to explain how Sandlow Feeds had come to figure so prominently in the *Courier*'s investigation of the Happy Farms food poisoning episode.

"This Murano, that's the same kid that was down in Wilkesboro harassing everyone in the main office of Happy Farms?"

Frank nodded yes.

Raymond had taken the temperature on Murano's ambition and figured he was going to push things with Happy Farms, and he'd guessed Murano's move and had given Frank a heads-up on containment.

Since the source for the contaminant of the tainted chicken had not yet been determined, Luis Murano went alpha on them, starting at the first stage of the production process. Sandlow Feeds was the primary distributor of the feed for the network of growout farms that produced the birds for the Happy

Farms line. It wouldn't be the first time that bad feed got shipped out.

As it turned out, Luis Murano caught a break. A couple of them. He'd been crossing the lot on his way to interview the distribution managers at Sandlow when he noticed some high-energy activity around the dumpsters at the rear of the main office.

Murano snagged two bags of trash, secreting them in the trunk of his car, before he was caught and escorted off the premises.

The two bags of trash were part of the five bags of documents that had been shredded and tossed in anticipation of Luis Murano's visit.

Hastily shredded and tossed.

Which constituted Murano's second big break because the office manager at Sandlow had emphasized speed over efficiency and three of the five bags contained only partially shredded material.

The details from which fell short of anything approaching an indictment but were still incriminating enough, coupled with Sandlow's previous history of violations and fines, to raise Lamar Ditell's blood pressure to Wrath-of-God levels.

Because, with a little research, Luis Murano had also been able to report that Sandlow Feeds was in fact one of a number of shell companies that resided like Russian nesting dolls within the Happy Farms corporate structure, Lamar Ditell holding a controlling interest in each.

The feed, the trucks that transported it to the grow-out farms, the chickens the farms raised and shipped to the processing plants, and the birds that landed in the kitchens of restaurants and homes and eventually people's stomachs, Luis Murano made sure the *Courier* readers understood Lamar Ditell was tied, directly or indirectly, to each phase.

No Place To Hide.

That had been the title of the sidebar article that Murano had written about the shell companies.

"So where are we on this Murano?" Pierce asked when Frank Atwell finished.

"The thing with a food poisoning episode like this, Daniel, is there's never one, but a lot of fires to put out."

"There you go again with the goddamn metaphors," Pierce said. "I don't trust them. The world doesn't run on or need them."

The tenor of the meeting did not improve when Daniel Pierce abruptly shifted the discussion to Eileen Connelly.

Raymond helped out the best he could, throwing out the rhetorical equivalent of life preservers to Frank when the opportunity presented itself.

In the meantime, the longstanding and deeply acrimonious history between Eileen Connelly and Lamar Ditell unfolded.

Eileen Connelly was in her mid-thirties and the head of a consumer-watchdog and advocate organization named And Justice For All.

She had also come to enjoy quasi-celebrity status in the media with a potent combination of striking good looks and fiercely articulated idealism. That idealism had always buffered most of the fallout from the gossip and tabloid mills about her sex life, and she countered whatever remained by refusing to apologize for being a woman with a healthy sex drive and went on to feed her mystique by refusing to either confirm or deny involvement with whomever the media had currently linked her.

With donations and support from other animal-rights groups, Eileen Connelly went after Lamar Ditell, and their first skirmish took place four years ago when she began hammering away at the image of the parent company, her wrath directed at the line operations of Happy Farm's plants, particularly the methods used to prepare the chickens for processing. Invoking the organization's name, Eileen Connelly had maintained justice applied to all sentient beings, even those of the beaked and feathered variety, and called for ethical treatment of the birds that ended up on the dinner plates of Americans, and she had gone on to graphically detail their fates at the hands of Happy Farms, a Dantesque nightmare of overcrowded and contaminated holding houses, debeaking procedures gone awry, stun gun malfunctions that left the birds conscious even after the throat-slitting phase, and the eventual immersion in scalding feces-choked water to facilitate the removal of feathers.

Ditell and Connelly had again clashed when the United Food and Commercial Workers Union at Happy Farms went on strike after contract negotiations stalled. Ditell refused to concede or compromise on a single demand from the union's rank and file concerning safety, working conditions, cost of living adjustments, health benefits, or pay raises.

A month and a half into the highly publicized strike, Lamar Ditell held a press conference and pulled the rug out from under the whole show by threatening to shut down the plants and move the base of operations to South Carolina.

The union caved in and went back to work. The move generated a maelstrom of negative publicity that Eileen Connelly kept seeded by helping to underwrite a documentary by a young film-school auteur who put a human face on the strike and Lamar Ditell's retaliation by tracking the effects on the workers and their families as they struggled to cope with the original punishing work conditions and the disappearance of what they had once called their dignity.

The film's title, *Only the Rooster,* was an allusion to the now infamous slogan that Lamar Ditell had coined when he launched Happy Farms Inc. two decades ago: *Only the Rooster Gets A Better Piece of Chicken.*

Now Eileen Connelly was on the attack again.

Under the aegis of And Justice For All, a series of billboards were popping up across the country depicting a cartoon-version of a blood-covered Lamar Ditell smiling and waving a large cleaver while surrounded by towering piles of chicken carcasses. Running underneath and highlighted in red was: *Who's Next?*

Frank Atwell sputtered to a stop. He cleared his throat. He looked at Raymond. He rifled through the file in front of him. He looked at Raymond. He went back to the file. "This looks thin," he said. "I was sure."

He looked around the room. "I was sure," he said again.

What had become painfully apparent, even to Frank himself, was his proposed PR response to the problems facing Happy Farms had been built between hangovers on a handful of ad hoc hunches, blind luck, and a threadbare optimism that had run long past its expiration date.

Daniel Pierce stood up and said, "To point out the obvious, I think it's time to make some changes while we still can because what I've heard today, I don't like, and I particularly don't like what I'm not hearing."

ELEVEN

Murray's Steaks was a St. Carlton institution founded by its namesake in the late 40's on the cusp of the city's boom years. An army vet who had a short run as a pro boxer before turning restaurateur after having fattened the wallets of some mobbed-up friends who appreciated the strategic dives he'd taken during that short-lived career, Murray Sinclair opened his steak house on D-Day plus one. In the course of turning Murray's Steaks into an icon, Murray ran through four wives over the years, only one of whom delivered heirs. Heir number one, a daughter Julie, ran off in 1969 to Haight-Ashbury and became an earnest groupie for any number of reverbed three-chord psychedelic bands before turning Born Again and moving to Waco, Texas where she met and married a Christian hairstylist, the two of them operating a boutique unironically and earnestly named Sampson and Delilah's. Murray's second heir, a son predictably named Murray Junior, possessed no more ambition beyond patiently waiting for Murray Senior to die, then taking over the restaurant where either through lack of imagination or laziness or both, he kept his father's original blunt-itemed menu - drinks from a well-stocked bar, three inch steaks, potatoes as large as a size nine shoe, homemade cherry cobbler, complimentary cigars to accompany cups of strong black coffee - all of which more than amply justified the nickname given to the place by the locals: the Coronary Cathedral.

Frank Atwell was a regular.

Raymond found him in a dark corner booth. He had two scotches on the way before Raymond sat down. Setting in front of Frank were a large sirloin with its pink heart exposed and a half-finished baked potato. A salad in a small white bowl with a side of house dressing remained untouched.

The waitress brought the drinks. Frank lifted his glass and saluted her, then the Christmas lights and poinsettias flanking the bar.

"You doing okay?" Raymond waited a moment before adding, "I'm sorry for the way things turned out this afternoon with Pierce."

"A little time off, that's all it is," Frank said. He nodded twice. "And a big weight off."

He drained half his scotch. "I appreciate what you tried to do."

"It wasn't enough."

Frank lifted his scotch and leaned toward Raymond. "It's that I lost something," he said. "Not just Judy. My story too."

"I'm not sure I follow."

Frank nodded. "You don't know how important your story is until you lose it." He paused and shook his head again. "I've been thinking a lot about this lately."

He explained his idea behind stories over the next forty-five minutes and a slow parade of scotch and waters. "At bottom," he said, "humans make stories, and stories make us human. They are who we are.

What we are. Without them, we're not much more than high-end amoebas."

Frank went on to maintain that all these stories were "out there," part of the world and in their own way as real as trees or stones. The trick was finding and recognizing the one story that truly fit you and then fully inhabiting it.

"It's simple," Frank said, "but it's not." He shook his head. "I mean the story is but not what it does. That's the thing."

Raymond tried to keep his expression neutral. He reminded himself he'd known Frank a long time.

"You can lose your story or have it taken away," Frank said. "It happens, believe me. Then you know."

He went into a long cough, then leaned back in his chair and closed his eyes. "I've been thinking about this," he said. "Stories and what they do and finally mean. It's more complicated than it sounds."

"And these stories," Raymond said, "they're just 'out there?'"

Frank nodded.

Raymond looked down at this drink. "I don't know, Frank. You're going a little too mystical on me here."

"Don't humor me, Raymond. It's not a joke, and neither am I." Frank leaned over and rapped the tabletop with his knuckles. "This is not the booze talking. This is not my wife dying. This is not some goddamn agency account. This is my life."

"It's just that you don't sound like yourself, Frank."

"That's the point I've been trying to make. What

can happen."

"Okay," Raymond said. "Okay."

"You quit believing in stories, Raymond, and it can happen to anyone, even countries, and you end up more than lost." Frank looked at Raymond and continued to look at him a few beats longer than was comfortable.

"What?" Raymond asked.

Frank lit a cigar, got it going, then balanced it on the lip of the ashtray. He finished his drink, set down the glass, picked up his knife and fork, and started in again on the steak, cutting crosswise to the grain of the meat.

"We're *amigos*, Raymond," he said. "Still are. What happened this afternoon ... " He waved the rest of the sentence and sentiment away.

"Kate and Andrew are probably expecting you by now," he said. "You should go. You have a family to think about. I'm fine. We'll talk again. I'm a little tired is all. Some time off is not so bad."

Despite himself, on the drive home, Raymond started doing the math. He couldn't ignore what the extra money from taking over the lead on the Happy Farms account would mean.

Since 1982, each month had turned into a photo finish between what he made and what he owed.

He'd panicked when Andrew was diagnosed and Kate quit working, so when Phillip Branch, an old college buddy and a then very successful broker, offered some ground-floor investment opportunities with the potential for quick and large returns, Raymond took him up on them, and he made some money.

No. He made *a lot* of money.

In a very short period of time.

Phillip Branch had what amounted to a head start on news about certain deregulations coming out of Washington.

Telasco became the proverbial sure bet, a large trucking empire that through a choreographed series of mergers seemed destined to become a world-beater shipping conglomerate, branching into rail, ship, and air venues.

In the end, Raymond had diverted Kate's and his savings, as well as a second mortgage on the house into Telasco.

The move had almost worked.

Telasco, though, overreached.

So did Raymond and a lot of friends of Phillip Branch. By the time Raymond understood that and tried to dump the stocks, it was too late.

So he stayed at Public Domain and worked on, learning not to flinch at what his clients dragged into his office, and he started and ended each day at the agency by courting the equivalent of temporary moral amnesia.

By the time he got home, the streets and sidewalks were starting to ice up. Before going in, Raymond salted down the front walk and driveway. He stood in the street and looked through the front windows at the top half of the artificial Christmas tree he'd promised Kate he'd bring down from the attic but then had forgotten about.

He was working on another link to what was

becoming a very long chain of apologies as he followed the sound of Kate's voice into the living room where he found her hovering over Andrew with a pair of scissors. Andrew seated on a stool in the middle of the floor patterned in overlapping layers of newspapers.

Andrew's hair was a mess, hacked-up, full of jagged lines with pasty patches of scalp showing through.

"What happened?" Raymond asked.

"Andrew and I were working on Christmas decorations. I stepped out of the room for a moment. That's all it was. A moment." Kate stopped to wipe her eyes. "I left the scissors on the table. Andrew found them. And then he did this." She pointed at what remained of his hair.

Raymond moved to the sideboard and made two drinks. Behind him, Kate still upset and breaking one of her own cardinal principles, one for which she'd reprimanded Raymond many times over, was bluntly talking about Andrew as if he weren't there before them. It was an easy habit to fall into with autistic children. After a while, any attempts at conversation felt like dropping pebbles down a well, the answering echo so faint or delayed that you eventually quit hearing it. Kate had always refused to give into the habit and had been furiously adamant about never forgetting to speak to Andrew as they would any other child.

Raymond held out one of the drinks. Kate waved it off. She said there were some leftovers in the refrigerator, and then she went back to trying to corral the damage from Andrew taking the scissors to his hair.

Andrew sat calmly, his head impossibly small above the folds of white sheet. To Raymond, his son's profile resembled something stamped on a foreign coin, a portrait of an obscure banana-republic despot whose whim and ironclad will underwrote every law.

Raymond finished off his drink and watched Kate edge a long jagged line above Andrew's left ear, the skin around her eyes tight with concentration.

He went into the kitchen and made a sandwich and ate it standing at the sink. Then he did the dishes and finished the second drink.

Back in the living room, he found Kate on the couch. She was crying. Andrew was still sitting on the stool in the middle of the room, the newspapers around him strewn with clumps and scattered fans of brown hair.

"Just hold me," Kate said. "No talk."

Raymond joined her on the couch. She tucked her head against his chest. He could feel the exhaustion cording her neck and shoulders. He also saw that her attempts to repair Andrew's self-inflicted haircut had backfired.

The only way she'd been able to fix the damage was by cutting off most of Andrew's hair, and the child that emerged looked hopelessly alien and unattractive. The bristly pelt covering the bony contours of the pale skull was the color of dry dirt and threw the features beneath it into grotesque relief. The eyes were empty and protuberant, the cheeks stark and hollowed. It was a face that had been robbed of its humanity, shadowed by something feral and forlorn, a face that could have been staring through the barbed wire at an Auschwitz or Belsen.

Raymond knew Kate saw that too. It was impossible not to. Tonight there was no place she or Raymond could hide. The haircut had stripped away what their hope had window-dressed.

The truth was that Andrew was not a loveable or winsome little boy. The odds were he never would be. He was not *special* either, no savant in terms of music or numbers or drawing. Despite early intervention and the work with specialists, Andrew eclipsed the second-cousin symptoms of Asperger's and showed no signs that might indicate the capacity for anything approaching high-end functioning.

In the face of that, all the easy pieties of parenthood collapsed. There was no implicit profile-in-courage warranty to Andrew's condition, no uplifting subtext to their days.

Andrew was his own tautology.

Raymond held Kate until she cried herself out. Right then, he didn't know what else to do. He sat across from his son. He held his wife. And he remained marooned in his love.

TWELVE

On the drive into work the next morning, Raymond Locke tried to remember what it had been like to still feel superior to his ambition.

A moment of panic then, because he suddenly couldn't remember the last time that had been the case or the barest outline of what it had felt like.

His job conferred its own blunt grace on everyone but himself. His clients brought him a mix of the Seven Deadly Sins, and he turned them into a half dozen and one minor inconveniences. He silk-pursed the sow's ear, fixing it so that Public Domain's clients were granted absolution without the bother of having to do anything to earn or deserve it beyond cutting and endorsing a check.

Raymond had been up late the night before taking notes for strategies to repair the missteps and messes Frank Atwell had made with the Happy Farms account.

First off, he needed to do some CPR work on Lamar Ditell's public persona. He had to find a way to ensure that a grandfatherly, salt-of-the-earth, generous, God-fearing, socially-concerned, and charmingly eccentric Lamar Ditell took up lodging in the hearts and minds of consumers, so that privately Lamar Ditell could continue being the megalomaniacal, pompous, tight-fisted, opinionated, selfish little prick that he was.

Raymond started off with a basic bread-and-circus move: a love interest.

He put together a heartstrung scenario. Carly Waite, a beauty proportioned along Amazonian lines, had briefly and self-servingly married Lamar Ditell in the very early stages of her modeling career, concurrently with she changing and shortening her name simply to *Ursula*. Later she truncated it even further so that she became known simply as *U*.

Raymond had checked around and found that *U* had ended up in Robert Palmer's music video for "Addicted to Love." *U* was the second one on the left in the string of women behind Palmer, but Raymond was not sure if that was the viewer's or Palmer's left, and even after repeated viewings, Raymond could still not say for sure which one was *U* because all the women were made-up and dressed exactly alike - black mini-skirts, black hose, black heels, shiny black lipstick, and black slicked-back hair - all of them blurring into the equivalent of a ground-fog of viewer lust.

Raymond made some late-night calls to the west coast and discovered that *U* at present was between jobs and agreeable to the deal Raymond worked up. She'd pocket a quick paycheck and garner some easy center-stage and spotlight action.

Raymond had scripted a tearful reunion scenario between Lamar Ditell and *U*, she returning to him in his hour of need, but what would start out as simple support and concern would flare into rekindled passion. Lamar and *U* once again becoming an item, every facet of the relationship on display for the public.

Then a little good-sport fun at Lamar Ditell's expense, Raymond bringing in a high-end photographer for a series shoot centered on Lamar Ditell in his trademark outfit and *U* echoing her "Addicted to Love" look, Lamar at four foot ten standing on a wooden stepladder in order to kiss his former bride and soul mate.

Lamar and *U* would then put in customary appearances at a benign series of charities, clubs, and sporting events, their renewed courtship culminating in a well-publicized repast at each of the new Happy Farms franchise restaurants that had been the original sites of the food poisoning incidents.

It was edging noon by the time Raymond finalized the majority of the details for the campaign. He took the elevator down one floor to the fourth. Each floor of Public Domain's offices had a similar layout, the décor consisting of the same patterned fleur-de-lis wallpaper bisected by cherry wainscoting, tapestry rugs rather than carpeting, and dark heavy furniture. Mirrors, rather than paintings, dominated the wall space. The mirrors were in a variety of sizes, all with elaborate frames, and hung in a number of strategically different heights so that no matter where they stood or looked, clients at Public Domain never had to doubt their existence or their importance in the scheme of things.

The Research Division occupied half the fourth floor, and once he walked through its doors, Raymond became self-conscious about his age. He was thirty-eight and found himself wanting to or starting to append *only* to that number. He figured he was twelve years the senior of the average age of the men and women working in the Research Division, a mini-nation of Wunderkind that Daniel Pierce had established to colonize the late twentieth century.

Pierce was slowly building a network of connections that would eventually enable Public Domain to systematically jacklight anyone's personal, professional, or public life.

After becoming CEO of Public Domain, Pierce had used his background in Army Intelligence to structure the Research Division. Pierce maintained close connections with a number of former colleagues who on occasion provided selective access to information not normally available through other avenues.

Daniel Pierce buttressed that move by scouting out hotshot college students majoring in banking, law, business, and computer science information systems and providing some of them under the table financial support and favors so that after graduating, they were ready to return those favors by a variety of helpful, if clandestine, means.

Others, like Julianne James, came to work directly for Daniel Pierce and Public Domain.

Julianne was one of the Division's stars, impossibly young - a blink from twenty-three - and impossibly brilliant, and someone who as far as Raymond could tell from their previous dealings existed wholly without a shred of self-doubt or conscience when it came to her job description. Julianne methodically set about locating the rocks and turned them over and didn't flinch at what she found underneath them.

In her office, Raymond asked for the file on Eileen Connelly, but it didn't take long to realize it didn't contain anything that he hadn't already seen. He asked Julianne for the follow-up material.

"That's it. What's in your hands."

"Frank Atwell said there was more. This looks too thin."

"Mr. Atwell never requested anything further. He said he didn't think Eileen Connelly would do much beyond those billboards she commissioned attacking Lamar Ditell."

Raymond slowly let out his breath. "Okay. I need you to make Connelly a priority. She's poised to do more than billboards at Ditell's expense." Raymond tapped the file and explained that Connelly liked to hit hard, then wait until your guard was down, and come back even harder. "She's not going to go away," Raymond said. "Get me something that will do more than slow her down."

Julianne nodded.

And frowned a moment later after Raymond asked her for the updated material on the reporter for the *Courier*, Luis Murano.

"You should already have it," she said.

"*Should* does not translate as *does*."

Julianne opened and checked her log. She hesitated.

Raymond leaned over the desk and checked the sign-out time. Eric Donner had signed off on the Murano file.

"That one was a little thin too," Julianne said.

"In the future," Raymond said, "any material pertaining to Lamar Ditell and Happy Farms is to be routed solely to me. No intermediaries. Not Frank Atwell. Not Eric Donner."

Julianne James hesitated again, then finally nodded.

When he reached the door, Raymond stopped and looked back across the office.

Ms. James already had the phone cradled between her neck and shoulder and was punching in numbers.

THIRTEEN

Raymond turned up the volume on the portable television setting on the kitchen counter below the spice rack. His son Andrew took a bottle of ketchup and a jar of mustard from the refrigerator and moved to the counter, walking on tiptoes and taking small steps, reminding Raymond of the exaggerated movements meant to convey stealth in cartoon villains.

He slid a rack of hot dogs under the broiler and called Andrew over to stir the chili. On the evening news, Dan Rather tried to process for viewers the burgeoning mass of details connected to the Iran-Contra Affair, a welter of competing narratives full of gaps, coincidences, mistakes, misjudgments and cover-ups, a left-hand-not-knowing-what-the-right-hand-was-doing scenario writ bewilderingly large.

The Boland Amendment. Iran. Seven hostages. National Security Advisor Robert McFarlane. Lebanon. Israel. Nicaragua. Defense Secretary Caspar Weinberger. Ayatollah Khomeini. Arms dealer Manucher Ghorbanifar. Swiss banks accounts. Panama. Manuel Noriega. TOW anti-tank missiles. Ground advisors. Cocaine. William Casey, CIA Director. Oliver North. Reverend Benjamin Weir. Sandinista Junta of National Reconstruction. Hezbollah and the Army of the Guardian of the Islamic Revolution. Ronald Reagan. Hawk anti-aircraft missiles. Spare parts. Air space violations. U.S. Attorney General Edwin Meese. Secret London meetings. Admiral John Poindexter. Human rights watchers. Secretary of State George Shultz. Fawn Hall.

Listening to Dan Rather, Raymond envied Reagan, North, Weinberger, Casey, and company. They were going to get away with it.

Maybe not all of it and maybe not for the short-term, but in the ways that really mattered, they were going to get away with it. Nothing finally would stick because the details never quite cohered. Dan Rather was doing his damnedest to lay it out for the American people, but the sheer weight and number of details defeated him. Again and again, the storyline broke down, and in the end, Rather became nothing more than a tour-guide in a hall of mirrors.

Raymond was worried that Lamar Ditell and Happy Farms wouldn't be so lucky. Eileen Connelly and Luis Murano were working hard to make sure cause was distressingly close to effect in the public's mind when it came to the food poisoning incident or *epidemic* as Murano, in particular, was trying to paint it.

"Okay on the chili stirring, buddy," Raymond said. "What's next?"

"Chips, dip, soda," Andrew said. "Soda, dip, chips."

"How about coleslaw? Some pickles?"

"No coleslaw. No pickles," Andrew said. "Hot dogs, chips, dip, soda, then chili."

"I hear you," Raymond said. He handed Andrew two plates. "We're all systems go here."

Andrew carried the plates to the counter. He opened the bag of buns and set one on each plate. He looked up at the television.

"*Fresh from the grave,*" Andrew said, perfectly mimicking the rhythm of the lead-in to *Nightshade Theatre*. "*Don't touch that dial. I'm dying to show you tonight's feature. It's a Ghoulmaster favorite.* "

Raymond looked over his son's shoulder at Gary Ghoulmaster aka Paul Crosley. Tonight's feature - *Dead Time* - was a re-run, the Ghoulmaster on a short-term Channel Five leave of absence after showing up on the set drunk and brandishing a sprig of mistletoe which he proceeded to hold over his crotch at inopportune moments during the taping.

Andrew went to work preparing his meal with the focus of a surgeon. He counted out twelve chips so that they ringed his plate, then went back and coated the lower portion of each with dip. The bun was in the exact center of the plate, and he placed the hot dog inside so that it was equidistant from either end of the bun. Next he took the ketchup and lined one side of the hot dog, then set up a parallel yellow line of mustard. Andrew then put four dollops of chili along the spine of the hot dog and pronounced it ready.

Raymond and he carried their food and drinks into the dining room where they sat side by side at the table.

Raymond had forgotten to turn off the television. A string of commercials, most of them Christmas-themed, ran in the background.

"Jungle bells. Wreck the halls," Andrew said. "Everybody rides. Priced to sell."

Raymond pointed at Andrew's plate. "Well, Champ," he said, "I bet your mom wishes she was eating with us instead of with her friends. They won't get hot dogs this good at their restaurant."

In the living room, the Christmas tree remained half-decorated. Kate had stopped when Andrew had taken the scissors to his hair. She was getting ready to start in again, adding a little at a time, testing Andrew's reaction to the changes. Christmas was particularly difficult. You could never be sure if Andrew would be fascinated by or infuriated over a string of blinking lights or the gossamer angel topping the tree.

"It's Girls' Night Out for your mom," Raymond said, "so we have the place to ourselves. What do you want to do?" He started ticking off the standard possibilities: reading stories, working puzzles, drawing, painting, building Lego cities, playing Checkers or Go Fish.

He waited.

Andrew refused to respond.

Raymond ran through the options again.

"*Don't touch that dial,*" Andrew said. He walked quickly away, again on tiptoes, disappearing up the stairs. A minute later, the banging around started up in his bedroom.

Raymond followed and stood inside the door and watched Andrew take a red plastic bat to a bare section of wall. At one point, Andrew stopped and looked down at the floor and said in a rush *chipsdiphotdogsodathenchili* and turned and began rhythmically working the bat again.

Raymond went back downstairs.

He checked the answering machine in the study. There was one message from Frank Atwell inviting Raymond over to his apartment for some beer, pizza, and Chicago Bulls-Indiana Pacer action this weekend.

Nothing from Eric Donner despite the fact that Raymond had spent a good portion of the afternoon trying to get in touch with him.

If first impressions counted, Eric Donner occupied the negative side of the ledger. At twenty-seven, he was another of Daniel Pierce's Wunderkind, a spoiled boy with powerful and affluent parents and a top-end IQ and a case of arrogance that was frequently mistaken for confidence. He was not someone Raymond was looking forward to working with. On paper at least, Donner came across more like a client needing Public Domain's services than a junior account executive working to implement them.

Raymond erased Frank Atwell's message and looked up. Andrew was in the doorway and dressed in a black stocking cap, overcoat, mittens, and boots.

"The ships," he said.

"It's cold out," Raymond said.

"The ships," Andrew said. "The ships. I'm seeing them in my head."

Raymond got his coat.

Twenty-five minutes later, he pulled into the parking lot behind the lakefront warehouses for the Total Shipping Company. Andrew and he crossed to the security station.

A man in his early fifties with a graying fighter-pilot mustache and a pale blue uniformed bump of a paunch set down his coffee and opened the station's window.

"Hey Mr. Locke," he said. "Hey Mr. Andrew."

"Anything?" Raymond said.

"They're just finishing up at Slip 6. They started on Slip 4 about ten minutes ago."

"Thanks, Carl." Raymond set a folded twenty next to the coffee cup.

Carl opened the gate, and Raymond and Andrew walked down to the docks. A thin slant of wind-driven snow started up. Their breath broke white around their faces.

There was the slow throb of a ship's engine idling and the smell of diesel fuel and the cold metallic taste of the wind moving across the Lake. Andrew walked closer to the edge of the dock. To the right was a tall crane that resembled Erector-Set models Raymond had assembled as a boy.

Andrew and he stood within the shadow of the ship's hull. The ship was still sitting high in the water, and the hull rose like an iron wall, blocking out any view of the port and its waters and dwarfing Raymond and Andrew.

Andrew started up a low rush of words.

"What?" Raymond leaned as close as Andrew would permit. It took a moment to understand that Andrew was detailing the ship's specs.

"LOA 490, the LBP is 471, beam 73, depth 41, draft of 30, the numbers are feet not meters, and they are where the ship lives, draft is loaded ship keel to water, width is the beam, length overall is in the LOA, depth is keel to deck, length between

perpendiculars is LBP, all the letters, they are the words and the words are the numbers and I can see all of them because they are white in the air when I say them."

Andrew abruptly stopped and tilted his head and looked up at the side of the ship's immense hull.

The crane's arm swung out and deposited a cargo container on deck.

Andrew began keening, the sound high in his throat and his face still pointed at the sky.

The crane's arm swung out again with another container.

Raymond lost track of time. It disappeared into the smell of diesel fuel and the cold that slowly had settled in his shoulders and hands.

Over and over, the crane's arm swung out, then back. The rectangular containers were at least twenty feet high and colored red, blue, green, and yellow.

Andrew kept his head tilted and watched their movement.

Raymond watched his son.

He was struck once again by the fact that Andrew did not resemble Kate or him. From the moment Andrew entered the world through the subsequent eight years, Raymond had scrutinized his son's features, sure he'd see Kate or himself or some telling combination of them in him, but it hadn't happened. Andrew was Andrew was Andrew.

The cold settled. The snow picked up speed. Andrew counted containers. He tracked their colors. Raymond looked down at his wrist, then remembered he'd left his watch, along with his gloves, back at the house.

High above them, in a square of yellow light was the silhouetted profile of the crane operator.

The arm of the crane swung out. From where they stood, it looked as if the container had been slotted into the sky itself, as if it were filling or replacing something that was lost or missing.

The lines of snow. The dark hull of the ship. The crane. The silhouetted operator. The containers. The smell of diesel fuel. Andrew with his upturned face. Their breath in the cold air.

The arm of the crane swung out with another container, this one wider and larger than the others.

"Yes," Andrew said. "Yes. Oh yes."

Raymond rubbed his wrist, the patch of skin, which his watch usually covered, and he watched the container disappear into the sky.

FOURTEEN

Public Domain was housed on Mercer Boulevard, a half block from the corner of 12th Avenue, and overlooked a terra cotta paved plaza holding an elaborate angel-encrusted fountain commemorating the beneficent public side of various nineteenth century robber barons. The building was from the turn of the century, designed when Louis Sullivan and the Chicago School ruled the architectural streets and skyscrapers began eclipsing church spires as a reference point on a city's skyline. The building and its banks of casement windows, scalloped cornices, and tiered façade had been scheduled for a mid-twentieth century tryst with a wrecking ball when Nathaniel Greene, the founder of the agency, picked up the building on the cheap from a state landmark commission back-door deal and went on to restore and renovate it. Public Domain occupied half its floors and leased the others to a hive of lawyers, accountants, psychiatrists, and financial advisors.

The lobby was dominated by an immense skylight and a couple tons of well-polished Italian marble.

Raymond Locke was waiting for one of the south bank of elevators when Eric Donner stepped next to him, glanced over, and said, "Morning, Boss."

Donner was holding two take-out cups of coffee. His eyes were red and bruised-looking.

"I was looking for you," Raymond said, "all

afternoon yesterday."

"I was setting some things up." Donner took a large gulp of coffee and grimaced.

"Without my authorization."

"Believe me, you'll like this angle."

"That's not the point."

"Oh, man," Donner said. "Please don't start going all hierarchical and patriarchal on me."

The elevator arrived, and the doors slowly opened. They stepped inside. Raymond pressed the sixth floor. "We finish this in my office."

Once there, Raymond sat behind his desk. Donner kept moving around. He went at his coffee again, finishing off one of the two cups in an abrupt series of swallows. He made a show of incredulously shaking his head. "I wasn't expecting something like this," he said. "Not from you."

"I want daily updates," Raymond said. "Three of them. *Full* updates."

"You know," Donner said, "when I moved to our Division, I asked Pierce if I could work with you. *Begged* Pierce. I'd heard about you. Knew your reputation. Bishop DeMarco. The Bushel of Love thing. All of it. But Pierce paired me up with Pops Atwell instead." He made a show of shaking his head. "Jesus."

"Frank Atwell was a good man, one of the best." Raymond inwardly flinched at the verb tense.

"Maybe so," Donner said, still moving. "But I came here to rock and roll, not square dance."

"You told Ms. James in Research that you were going to pass on the Murano file to me."

"Ms. James?" Donner paused for a moment. "Oh, you mean Julianne." He smiled. "She's something, isn't she? You ever tap any of that?"

Raymond sat back in his chair and let his silence answer.

Donner tilted his head, noting the photo on the corner of the desk. He nodded twice. "No need, right? That's the wife. Hey, stone cold."

"The file on Luis Murano," Raymond said.

Donner set the remaining cup of coffee on the desk and rummaged through the leather pouch he carried in lieu of a briefcase. He eventually found and held it up.

Raymond began flipping through the material. He didn't look up when Donner said that he had everything covered.

"What's that mean exactly?" Raymond said.

"Hey, what I said." Donner picked up his coffee cup. "Luis Murano. I set some things up. They're unfolding as we speak."

Raymond closed the file, sat back and looked at Donner. Late-twenties. Tall and thin. Pale-skinned with high cheekbones and no trace of facial hair, not even the shadow of sideburns. A crushed posture from the attitudinal slouch. Baby-fine hair pulled back into a pale blonde apostrophe of a ponytail.

Everyone in the agency knew Donner owed his job to his parents' influence. They ran a joint venture north of Chicago along the Lake, a private and exclusive clinic for the Rich and Famous and the Rich and Powerful. Donner's father practiced cosmetic surgery, and Donner's mother was a psychiatrist who oversaw a rehab and mental health spa. A significant portion of Public Domain's clients used the clinic's services, and a significant portion of their patients were referred to Public Domain. It was a cozy arrangement made even cozier by the fact that Eric Donner also had access to the files of his parents' patients and no reservations about playing fast and free with the dictates of doctor-patient confidentiality.

Raymond begrudgingly, very begrudgingly, admitted to himself, if not Donner, that Donner's response to the problems Murano presented was workable, particularly given Frank Atwell's late start at capping them off.

"Okay," Raymond said finally. "We'll run with that for now. But I expect you to keep me in the loop."

"Hey," Donner said. "A regular Marconi. That's me. Count on it."

Raymond spent the rest of the day going through the Happy Farms files, checking and double-checking problems and responses and trying to tease out future complications.

The numbers from the poisonings were not reassuring. They remained distressingly stable when they should have been on a downward trajectory.

He put in a call to Larry Hahn at the District Attorney's office, reminding Larry that he was expecting any word concerning the DA, Arthur Cavanaugh, who resided near the top of the list of people who hated Lamar Ditell. It was a foregone conclusion that Cavanaugh would give his support, tacit or otherwise, to any smear campaign directed at Ditell.

Raymond then called the lawyers representing Sandlow Feeds, making sure they were throwing as many roadblocks as possible in the way of the USDA investigation of tainted feed shipments.

He rescheduled appearances of Lamar Ditell and his Amazonian squeeze, Ursula aka *U*, at two charity benefits.

Julianne James in the Research Division called with an update on Eileen Connelly. Julianne said she was pursuing a couple promising leads, very promising leads, but ones that were requiring quite a bit of overtime on her part. Raymond gave the package a green light and promised a bonus if things panned out.

His wife Kate called and asked if he'd heard the weather report. A large low-pressure system was bullying its way down from central Canada and was about to drop the first major snowstorm of the season.

"It might be a good idea to postpone the drive to Gary and come straight home this evening," she said.

"My aunt's expecting me," Raymond said.

"She'll understand. The weather's supposed to turn bad, and we still haven't gotten snow tires put on the car yet."

Kate paused. "Speaking of your aunt, we got a past-due notice for this month's Meadows bill."

"I covered it," Raymond said. "It was only a little late."

"The thing is," Kate said, "it wasn't the only over-due notice we got in today's mail."

She paused again. "Have you talked to Sean about helping out with the Meadows bill? It's his mom, after all."

"Not going to happen, Kate. We both know that."

Another measured pause. "I talked to my father earlier today. The offer's still there."

"Please, we've discussed this."

"He just wants to help. We're family."

No, Raymond thought. There was no *just* with Kate's father. Leonard Simco, insurance magnate, dealt in absolutes. He established any and all terms in family or business matters.

No way Raymond was opening the door to that.

He got off the phone after promising that he would call the Meadows Assisted Living Center and talk to his aunt rather than make the drive after work to Gary.

The weather was an unexpected break though.

Like the standard-issue sentiments tied to the Christmas season, a patch of bad weather re-routed public attention. It gave people something to talk about for a while besides the havoc wreaked on intestinal tracts by tainted Happy Farms chickens.

Raymond's aunt had moved into the Meadows Assisted Living Center three years ago after her husband died and two years after her son Sean wiped out her savings and the insurance settlement with his accumulated gambling losses, dropping the money on one sure booze-soaked bet after another.

Raymond had picked up the tab on the Meadows. He owed his aunt and the memory of his uncle that much. The two of them had taken him in and raised him after his parents died in the DC-8 crash when Raymond was eighteen months old.

His aunt and uncle never complained, and Raymond had grown up keenly aware of the sacrifices they were making on his behalf. Raymond was literally a second family. His uncle was forty-five, his aunt forty-one, when they took him in. His cousin Sean had already joined the army and moved out by then.

Raymond's aunt and uncle did not openly or easily show affection, but they were good people, reliable and solidly blue collar. The defining ethos of the household was duty, and duty became the standard by which everything was measured. They took Raymond in out of duty. They fed, clothed, and sheltered him out of duty. They were there for him, year after year, out of duty.

They were who they were, no more and no less, and Raymond could count on them, and that was something in itself, particularly when he saw the careless train wrecks most of his friends' parents made of their marriages.

For his part, Raymond was grateful and tried not to disappoint them. He did well in his studies. At fifteen, he started working after school. He stayed out of trouble. He finished his four years at Indiana University on a combination of part-time jobs, scholarships, and student loans. After college, he stayed in touch and visited his aunt and uncle regularly. He delivered the eulogy at his uncle's funeral.

And whenever necessary, he lied to keep his aunt's illusions alive.

She needed to believe Sean was a successful,

happy, and devoted son.

Raymond made sure that belief was kept intact even while his cousin's life followed a cycle that unfolded as regularly as the seasons: Crash. Burn. Rehab. Relapse. What the booze didn't undermine, the gambling did. His cousin had managed to pass into his mid-fifties bankrupt in every possible sense of the word and world.

So he let his aunt believe that Sean was paying for the Meadows. He let her believe that birthday, Christmas, and Easter presents that Kate and he bought for her came from Sean. He let her believe that all the times Sean did not show up for visits or call were the result, not of indifference or neglect, but of a busy work schedule and family demands.

He willingly conspired with his aunt and turned every one of her son's excuses and shortcomings into a virtue.

He did it because she needed the lies.

He did it out of love or out of duty or out of some shadowy combination of the two that he did not have a name for.

FIFTEEN

As predicted, the first major snowstorm of the season hit, and in the midst of it, at 11:38 p.m., Tina Brackett happened.

SIXTEEN

In the meeting with Daniel Pierce, Raymond Locke explained that they were looking at the tail end of the incubation period, so it should have been the beginning of the end of Lamar Ditell's and Happy Farms' problems.

Should have.

Nobody, however, had seen Tina Brackett coming. She was the blur on the periphery of your vision that suddenly loomed and became the car that ran the light as you were crossing the intersection.

What remained from the wreckage was a handful of facts.

Tina Brackett was a week and a half shy of her tenth birthday. She lived in Wilkesboro, Indiana. She was in the fourth grade. She weighed sixty-one pounds. She had black hair. Her father's name was Ken. At the time, there was no word or sign of the mother.

Everything started at 10:55 the night before, when Ken Brackett took his daughter to the emergency room at Wilkesboro General.

He told the attending physician his daughter Tina had the flu.

It had looked that way at first. Tina's body had cooked up a 102-degree fever that left her semi-delirious and severely dehydrated from several days of nausea and vomiting. She'd lost nine pounds.

Brackett had brought her in when there'd been signs of her bringing up blood when she vomited. The ER doctor barely had a chance to get beyond the initial examination when Tina's stomach ruptured. Complication followed complication. Anemia. Wildly fluctuating blood pressure. Shock. Heart murmurs and a brush with cardiac arrest from a childhood bout of rheumatic fever. And finally acute toxemia. The ER doctor got her on glucose and IV antibiotics and called for an airlift. The weather caused extra delays, and by the time Tina Brackett was installed at the ICU in Mercy Medical in St. Carlton, she had gone into a coma.

The toxemia was eventually tied to the Happy Farms franchises when the lab work showed a virtually identical mix and strength of Salmonella and Campylobacter and E-Coli and Clostridium perfringens and Staph as other profiled samples.

Raymond might have had a little more time and room to work the fallout if Luis Murano had not also been part of the equation. As it was, Murano was able to verify early on that Ken Brackett and his daughter had been at the Happy Farms franchises' grand-openings in St. Carlton.

Murano had been nosing around Wilkesboro where he'd added a couple more journalistic notches to his notoriety by trying to bully his way into the main Happy Farms plant and ending up with a bloody nose after getting in a fistfight with one of the security guards. Murano was then taken to the hospital, but not before heroically posing in his blood-splattered shirt for the local television mini-cam crew.

An hour later, Murano was on his way out of the emergency room just as Ken Brackett brought his daughter through its doors.

Murano had ended up riding shotgun with Ken and Tina Brackett and the paramedics on the airlift to St. Carlton. The trip gave him the opportunity to ask more questions.

Murano made sure there was a camera crew waiting when they landed. The snowstorm provided a nice dramatic backdrop to their arrival.

Raymond paused.

The Office Manager knocked and poked her head into the conference room. She told Raymond and Pierce that Lamar Ditell was scheduled to show within the hour.

Pierce turned back to Raymond. "Please tell me there's something else."

Raymond looked down at his almost non-existent notes. Pierce's *please* had not been rhetorical; there'd been an undercurrent of genuine anxiety in it. Pierce was looking at a difficult stockholders meeting at the beginning of the new year. Despite his penchant for turning profits, there was a very vocal bloc of stockholders who detested Pierce and his methods, most of which were grounded in and translated from military maneuvers.

"I have Ms. James and a Research Division team working overtime," Raymond said, "and I sent Eric Donner to Wilkesboro to see what he could dig up first-hand about Brackett and his daughter as well as who Luis Murano has been talking to."

Anything else, Raymond explained, had been

hastily gleaned from employee records at Happy Farms.

"You mean Brackett worked for Happy Farms?" Pierce said. "Jesus."

"Works," Raymond said. He went on to lay out what he had. "It's not fully complete, and some of it needs updating," he said, "but it's what we have for now."

Kenneth Brackett. No middle name. Thirty-seven years old. High School education. Military service, army. Married. One child. Employment history, twenty-one years at the Wilkesboro Division of Happy Farms. Current position, part of the in-house line inspection team. Raymond added Brackett's salary, social security number, phone, and home address.

"And?" Pierce said.

"At present, Brackett's bedside, and he won't leave the ICU. He's also refusing to talk to anyone but the doctors."

Pierce waited.

"That's it," Raymond said.

SEVENTEEN

That evening, Raymond parked in his driveway and sat behind the wheel for a few moments before going inside. The meeting with Lamar Ditell had run late. Outside the car, the sky was layered in white - a skein of wind-driven snow, a soft patina from the streetlights, and a luminescent slice of swollen quarter moon.

Next to him on the passenger seat was a ten by twelve black and white photo of George Pullman.

It was a little object lesson from Lamar Ditell.

Something to buttress the very real and adamant threat to pull the Happy Farms account if Pierce - and now, Raymond - couldn't neutralize all the attendant problems tied to the food poisoning incident.

Lamar Ditell making sure everyone got his point.

Pullman, one of the richest and most powerful men of his time. Inventor and manufacturer of the Pullman Coach and Sleeping Car. By 1880, his influence running so wide and deep that he had his own city - named after himself, of course - built south of Chicago. Four thousand acres. Pullman leaving his fingerprints on every phase of the city's life and literally owning all the houses, parks, utilities, shopping centers, hotels, libraries and allowing no outside newspapers, churches or town-meetings.

Then the labor strike in 1894, violent and acrimonious and eventually infamous enough to attract the notice and intervention of the Governor and President. Four years later, in an Ozymandias moment, the town was divested and annexed to Chicago.

Pullman dying in 1897, so absolutely hated and vilified that he had to be buried at night in secret in a specially designed vault buttressed with reinforced steel and tons of concrete, the coffin itself lead-lined and bound in tarpaper and then coated in asphalt, and the whole thing topped off by cross-hatched steel I-beams and another layer of concrete, the grave so large and obsessive in its design that it took two days work to fill it, all to prevent Pullman from being exhumed and desecrated by mobs of his former workers.

The workers and their families he had at one time called *My Children.*

The weight and teeth of History. That's what Lamar Ditell had said as he dropped the black and white images of Pullman in front of Pierce and Raymond. *I will not be crushed or eaten. That's why I hired you bastards.*

Raymond set the photo back on the front seat. The windshield had blurred white with wet snow.

Once inside the house, before he'd even taken off his coat, he kissed his wife. The kiss had become part of an eleven-year ritual, the first thing he did when he got home.

Kate leaned in and lightly pressed two fingers on the side of his neck. She broke the kiss, smiled, and said, "Hello there."

Raymond looked over her shoulder into the living

room. "Andrew?" he said.

"An early bedtime." She glanced up, reading Raymond's expression. "No, nothing like that. It was a good day. I was able to finish putting up most of the Christmas decorations, and Andrew was all right with that."

Raymond hung up his coat and went into the kitchen, pouring two glasses of wine and putting a plate of leftovers from dinner to reheat in the oven. Then he joined Kate in the living room. She was on the couch, and the television was on low.

"Oh, before I forget," she said, taking the glass of wine, "Frank Atwell called for you. I told him you'd get back."

"He say what he wanted?"

"I think it was just to talk. He sounded lonely." Kate took a sip of wine. "We should have him over for dinner sometime soon."

"Okay," Raymond said, "but let me get on the other side of this Happy Farms mess first. I'm more than likely looking at a string of late nights for a while."

"The girl?" Kate said. "I remember something on the news about an airlift."

"Among other things," Raymond said. He got up and headed back to the kitchen. He brought the leftovers and the rest of the bottle of wine into the living room and sat down next to Kate again.

"I like this red." She poured them each another glass.

"Which one is this?" Raymond pointed at the screen. *Gimme A Break! Silver Spoons. Punky*

Brewster. Family Ties. Different Strokes. He could never remember which was which. They all blurred into the same laugh track.

"*The Facts of Life*," Kate said.

Then, shoulders touching, she leaned closer, lifting her hand and turning Raymond's face toward her. "You look tired, friend."

"I always look tired," he said. "That's nothing new. So do you."

Kate stopped the glass halfway to her lips. "Ouch."

"Come on," Raymond said, "you know what I mean. My job. You working with and taking care of Andrew. Running the house. The money worries. It adds up. No surprise we're tired." Raymond omitted mentioning, *the false pregnancy*.

"Okay," Kate said. "This, then. Friend, you look *more* than tired."

"I'm fine, and it'll pass."

"When was the last time you slept through the night?"

Raymond looked at Kate through the side of his wineglass. "Why do I get the feeling you're going to tell me?"

Kate shook her head. "Go on, finish your meal." She leaned over and gave him a quick kiss. "I'm going to take a hot bath. A long one."

Raymond watched her walk toward the stairs. She paused along the way to shake out her hair. It spilled over the shoulders of her old around-the-house sweater, bulky and banded in wide alternating swaths of green and blue. Her jeans were faded almost white. Kate stopped at the bottom of the stairs, looked over her shoulder, wiggled her ass at him, then laughed and continued upstairs.

Raymond poured another glass of wine. He stayed where he was, watching television while he ate. Along the way, the phone rang, and he let the machine take it.

Frank Atwell again.

"Hey Raymond, I just heard about the Brackett girl. A tough break, that. We need to powwow. Give me a call. I'll do what I can."

Raymond finished his wine, turned the television off, and took his dishes into the kitchen. He left them in the drying rack after he got done washing them.

Upstairs, he checked in on Andrew. The room had the close smell of children at rest, which had always reminded Raymond of the smell of ripe vegetables under a hot sun.

There were three nightlights along the baseboards. The only other light in the room came from the aquarium tank against the wall directly across from the foot of the bed. The tank was filled with Neon Tetras, silver-stomached with an iridescent stripe and a bright red one that started mid-section. The fish were barely an inch long and moved en-mass in shimmering waves.

Andrew owned the room. That's how Kate and he had come to see it. On the advice of a pediatric specialist, Kate and he gave the bedroom over to Andrew's tastes and whims. It was his world.

The walls were a deep olive green. The west wall was completely bare and pocked by dark spots. That was the space that Andrew periodically and rhythmically hit with an oversized plastic baseball bat when he needed to work things out of his system. Raymond had hung shelves of varying lengths and heights on the rest of the walls and mounted brackets so that he could easily move or adjust them. There were close to thirty-five shelves total, some as low as eighteen inches from the floorboards or as high as six feet, which was as far as Andrew could reach for now. Some of the shelves were as short as six or eight inches, the longest five feet. The arrangement, with the minimal lighting, gave Raymond the uncomfortable dream-like feeling of everything being unmoored and suspended in space.

Raymond could never be sure what would end up on those shelves or for how long. Andrew was constantly adding, replacing, and switching position and location of the objects occupying them. Andrew's choices managed to feel both inexorable and arbitrary, growing out of some shadowy intersection of his personality and his autism.

One of the shelves above the bed held a miniature toy car, a nickel, a spoon, a #2 pencil, and a blue sock.

The shelf to its left contained an old watch of Raymond's, a piece of gravel, a pink rubber eraser, a large marble with green, blue, and red swirls covering it, a shoelace, a Band-Aid, a pack of saltine crackers, and an acorn.

The rest of the shelves held the same dizzying array of objects, and at best, Raymond could only guess at the logic behind their number, sequence, and placement.

The room had its own taxonomy, and Andrew was

its official curator. Once in a while, Kate or he could coax an explanation out of Andrew. Sometimes, but not often, Andrew would tell them on his own. Most of the time, though, Kate and he were left to puzzle it out.

Initially, the objects on the shelves had been organized by something as simple as color or weight or size, but as Andrew had grown older and more inward, the organizing principles became more esoteric. The objects on a shelf might be there because the words for each were exactly one syllable and they ended with the same consonant. The objects on another might be grouped because they were associationally tied to Andrew's favorite television shows on a particular day of the week. Or they were things soft to the touch and that fit in a hand. Or were in the opening chapters of books that Kate or Raymond read to him. Or an object from each room in the house.

Raymond looked down at his son. Andrew lay on his back, his head in the center of the pillow, the blanket pulled up and folded so that it stopped at and crossed the middle of his chest. His arms were outside the covers and lay straight at his sides. His face was coated in the underwater light from the aquarium.

Raymond slowly, very slowly, lowered his hand and rested it on his son's head, grateful for any touch, however fleeting, because Andrew had never liked or tolerated much physical contact from Raymond. At a touch or hug, Andrew either stiffened, statue-like, or flailed wildly.

Raymond decided to risk one kiss before he left

the room.

He was within a couple inches of Andrew's brow when Andrew's eyes snapped open.

"Double prints at one low price," Andrew said, the words coming out slow and flat. "A complete line of home accessories. No credit check. Action News Live at Five."

"It's okay. Go back to sleep, Andrew."

"The two-ply tissue that doesn't act like a two-ply tissue. Bigger and better burgers, all meat. Power away mold and mildew. Turn the page. We're here to help."

"It's okay," Raymond said. "I'm going."

"Color-fast. Tumble dry. Remember, you count. Crunchy and delicious. Results, not promises."

Raymond made the doorway. "It's okay now. Sleep, Andrew."

Andrew kept his face aimed at the ceiling. "Don't be the last to know. If you have to ask. We can, and we will."

Raymond started to close the door. "Good night."

"One size fits all," Andrew said.

Raymond stood outside the door, waiting and listening until Andrew had talked himself out. Then he walked down the hall.

There was a bathroom right off the master bedroom, and Raymond had just set his wallet and keys on the dresser and unbuttoned his shirt when he looked up and across the room and saw Kate step from the bath. She was framed in the light by the doorway.

He watched her begin to towel off.

She didn't realize he'd been watching until he softly called her name just as she was about to slip on her nightgown. She hesitated, then crossed the room with the gown bunched in her hand. She paused at the foot of the bed.

Raymond waited.

He felt he'd been doing that a lot lately. The false pregnancy had temporarily rerouted the paths of attraction between them. The attraction was still there. That wasn't the issue. The problem was Kate and he barely had time to adjust to the idea of another child when the pregnancy had simply disappeared. They hadn't found a way to talk about it. At least not in the way Kate and he were used to.

So that left them right where they were, Kate at the foot of the bed, her nightgown bunched in her left hand, Raymond four feet away and feeling the same way he had at the end of their first date when, headlong in love, he finally admitted he was not Michael Cardell, the man she had been expecting on the blind date.

Raymond said his wife's name.

She tilted her head, expectant, as if he were going to continue.

Raymond said her name again.

Kate dropped the nightgown on the floor, then slipped off her panties.

Then, in bed, touch became the sign language for what they could not give words to, and that's where they lived, in those touches, Raymond's fingers tracing the inside of Kate's thighs, Kate moving closer, resting her cheek on his shoulder, her breath warm, its rhythm shortening when he slipped two fingers inside her and lightly pressed her clitoris with the pad of his thumb, Raymond continuing to cup and press and circle, Kate curling around his touch, her toes braced against his calves, then a slowly gathering heat, slickness, and a long shudder as Kate pushed hard against him and tightened around his fingers.

Then she shifted and leaned over Raymond for another kiss, her breasts grazing his chest. She straddled and slipped him inside.

And they began moving.

The sex was wet, messy, and lovely.

Everything went away, except Kate and him, the fit of flesh to flesh, and Raymond found the grace of and the grace in lips and hands and hips, and he wanted to hold onto that grace, to lose himself in its rhythms, and push everything else out of the bedroom so that it held nothing but Kate and him, no Lamar Ditell, no tainted chickens, no Sandlow Feeds, no Luis Murano or Eileen Connelly, no Daniel Pierce or Frank Atwell or Eric Donner, no Gary Ghoulmaster or Commander Sunshine, no pediatric therapists and specialists, nothing but the practiced ease of long-time lovers and the refuge they created for each other.

Raymond closed his eyes.

His orgasm, when it arrived, left him feeling as if he'd been split in two.

EIGHTEEN

"It's a Wonder Bread and wiener kind of place," Eric Donner said. "Honest to God, I'm in a diner, and it's right there on the menu: *Wieners Any Way You Want 'Em. Try Ours Fully Loaded.*" Donner shook his head. "I'm telling you, Wilkesboro, Indiana, it's an outpost in the Land That Time Forgot."

Raymond watched Donner move around his office. He suspected that Donner's energy after a very early morning return drive to St. Carlton resulted from the by-product of the coco leaf rather than coffee bean. A thin rim of red outlined each nostril.

"About Tina Brackett," Raymond said.

"I checked," Donner said. "No surprises. She's almost ten, and guess what, her favorite bands are The Bangles, Pet Shop Boys, Wham! and Huey Lewis and the News. She also loves Amy Grant and Madonna and Michael Jackson. Her favorite movies are *Karate Kid II, Star Trek IV, Great Mouse Detective,* and *Top Gun.* She watches *Highway to Heaven* and *Magnum PI* and was crushed when *Knight Rider* got cancelled this fall. She likes to wear jeans or leggings and headbands and *Flashdance* sweatshirts. She can't bring herself to give up her *My Little Pony, Strawberry Shortcake,* or *Glo-Worm* collections."

Donner paused, bouncing on the balls of his feet. "She has three best friends - Casey, Toni, and Dory - and guess what, they all like exactly the same things.

Toni, though, isn't quite sure how she feels about Huey Lewis."

Donner closed his eyes for a moment. "Let's see. Tina's a B average student. Her favorite subjects are Language Arts and Biology. She came in third in last year's Spelling Bee. She's quiet and polite, so no problems with teachers. Not a lot of extra-curricular activities though, but she's just popular enough with her peers to be indistinguishable from the bulk of them."

"Family life?"

"She's a Daddy's Girl," Donner said. "The mother's dead. Accidental."

"I like the sound of *no surprises*," Raymond said. "We have some room to work here. When it comes to the Brackett girl, I want you to set up a response in case we have an opening to make Happy Farms and Lamar Ditell look beneficent and concerned, but not responsible."

Donner cracked his knuckles twice and started moving around the office again. The blonde sprig of a ponytail bobbed with his movement. "I hear you. I'll get something worked out for either scenario, coma or post-coma."

"Julianne's digging up more on the dad," Raymond said, "and should have that later this morning. That'll help gauge how we approach the girl and this whole thing."

Raymond then asked Donner what headway he'd made reining in Luis Murano.

Eric quit moving, turned toward Raymond, and held out two empty hands. "I ran Marie and Duncan right at Murano. I scouted the places Murano likes to eat and hang out after work and did a tag-team number. They're both lookers. It should have worked."

"You think Murano suspected?"

"No way." Donner went into an elaborate head-shaking routine. "Duncan and Marie, they're good, very good, and practiced. They come on to someone, it's an art form." More head shaking. "Gay, Straight, or Bi, Murano had his chance. From what I can see, if he's got a hard-on, it's for his job."

"Okay," Raymond said. "We're going to have to come up with another angle then. Murano has turned himself into a problem that's not going away."

Raymond spent the bulk of the morning brainstorming on that angle. A little before noon, Julianne James sent up the report on Ken Brackett from Research. Raymond read it standing at his office window. The sky was cloud-heavy and leaking flat light. Below him was the eastern portion of downtown in the midst of a sandblasted and rehabbed metamorphosis. The middle distance was dominated by the steel roofs of warehouses. Beyond them, the silhouettes of the cranes and loading platforms at the port district and Lake Michigan disappearing into the horizon.

The view from the office window was a lot more palatable than the one that Raymond was left with after reading Ken Brackett's file.

They guy was a lightning rod for bad luck. In less than a year, he'd lost his wife, house, and all his savings.

Now his only child was in a coma.

The rest of the file detailed a life that was utterly forgettable. Ken Brackett was born and raised in Wilkesboro, Indiana. He graduated near the bottom of his high school class. He'd been at Happy Farms for over twenty-one years and had worked most of the line positions at one time or another. He eventually married a girl he knew from high school, and they eventually had Tina.

A small-scale life full of small-scale dreams propped up by small-scale beliefs played out in an endless sequence of small-scale days.

Julianne also corrected some small inaccuracies and omissions in the earlier report gleaned from Happy Farms employment records. Brackett was now living at 1313 Sandstone Lane, not 832 Perry Street. He had eight months of military service before an unspecified medical discharge. He was thirty-eight, not thirty-seven years old. Brackett had changed his religious affiliation from Methodist to NA at the last Human Resource update.

Raymond worked through lunch and went through the material on Ken and Tina Brackett three more times, making notes on points of emphasis and looking for anything he might have missed, but Ken Brackett and his daughter appeared to be exactly what they were. The question that remained was how Ken Brackett would handle the stress of his daughter's illness and the inevitable onslaught of media attention.

And the biggest concern was whom he'd end up retaining as legal counsel for the equally inevitable lawsuit against Happy Farms. A lot of the PR response would be contingent upon who Ken Brackett was lawyered-up with. Raymond worked up a list of probable and possible candidates and started cross-referencing personalities, settlement packages, and trial outcomes.

Late that afternoon, Eric Donner called in with the next round of distressing news. He'd just found out that tomorrow's edition of the *St. Carlton Courier* was running three lengthy related articles by Luis Murano on the food poisoning outbreak.

"Any chance at all of killing the coverage?" Raymond asked. "Or maybe delaying it?"

"Not according to my source," Donner said. "He told me the top brass at the *Courier* is behind Murano on this one, and they're going to push it and hard."

The editor was behind Murano, Raymond thought, and the *Courier* brass was behind the editor, and Arthur Cavanaugh, prosecuting attorney, mayoral aspirant, and Lamar Ditell's life-long enemy was behind the brass at the *Courier* on this one. A lot of markers were being called in.

It didn't take a psychic to predict things were about to get a whole lot uglier.

NINETEEN

The ambulances at the emergency room bay were decorated for Christmas: reindeer antlers on the hoods, wreathes on the grills, Santas impaled on antennae, bright tinsel and garlands around the doorframes. The drivers and paramedics stood outside the bay doors in small groups, smoking and sipping coffee.

Raymond was parked in the third row in Lot C directly facing the new wing of Mercy General. The wing, like the rest of the hospital, was all anemically tan bricks and narrow mirrored windows that resembled slots in electrical outlets.

He was waiting for Gerald White to take his morning break. On the passenger seat, next to Raymond, was the day's *Courier* and a plain white envelope holding a thousand dollars.

The three-part series in the *Courier* had given Luis Murano the opportunity to develop an unfortunately convincing subtext for the sequence of events leading up to Tina Brackett's hospitalization.

There'd been enough paper shredding at Sandlow Feeds to keep the fed and state regulatory agencies backpedalling on conclusive findings, but Murano was still able to make a persuasive and damning case with what remained. He cited a half dozen incidences where the agencies were lax in inspecting the Sandlow facility and in testing feed for contaminants, making sure that there were some strong precedents in place for the present problems. Murano then resurrected the controversy over the sub-therapeutic use of antibiotics and chemicals in feed as a growth stimulant and prophylactic against disease in chickens and then pointed the finger at Sandlow for exceeding the agency guidelines established for acceptable antibiotic levels in processed poultry feed.

Then, according to Murano, the adulterated feed from Sandlow was supposedly shipped to Midwest Poultry Growers Inc. who subcontracted growout houses with a network of farmers to produce birds for Happy Farms. A typical house raised 26,000 chickens in forty-two days. The antibiotics kept a lot of sick birds alive which would not have otherwise survived, and the sick birds mingled indiscriminately with the healthy, all of them eventually crated together on flatbed trucks and shipped to the plant. Murano pointed out that once again there were agency guidelines for the minimum time interval between the use of feeds containing antibiotics and processing, but that it was a common practice among growers who were under pressure to produce and keep down costs to ship the birds early. The chickens then entering the slaughterhouse carried an unacceptably high residue of antibiotics.

Luis Murano was able to create a damning picture of contamination levels at the slaughter and processing plants. The crated birds, deprived of food during transport, usually compensated by eating each others' feces or each other. At the plant they were quickly hung by the feet and sent down the line where they were stunned by electric shock and their throats cut, the birds then dipped in a scalding tank to loosen feathers. The temperature of the tank also unfortunately opened the birds' pores, allowing them to sponge up bacteria, and things did not get much prettier at the eviscerating stage where automated machines gutted the birds at high speed, usually spilling and coating them with the contents of their own intestines, before they were dumped in a chlorinated chilling tank whose waters became increasingly dirty and bloody during each shift, the equivalent, Murano maintained, of washing your hands in the toilet after using it.

He then cataloged the conditions on the line during the final stages of production, creating tightly packed vignettes of horrific details for his readers. Equipment covered with rotting meat and left uncleaned at the close of each shift. Chickens dropped on a floor covered with maggots and put back on the line. Oil, rust, paint chips, and metal shavings falling on the meat. Roach and rat infestations. Poor plant ventilation that filled the air with a miasmal bacterial mist from the washing vats. Harried inspectors using mirrors to check the condition of ninety carcasses a minute passing before them. A Grand Guignol system of evaluating sick birds: one cancer tumor or two sores or two abscesses allowed, three of any one not and blue tagged, the numbers inevitably juggled in the end and the bulk of the lot passing if the tumors, sores, or abscesses were trimmed off.

Finally, there were the bureaucratic delays in USDA recalls so that contaminated meat might enter the market for months before anything was done or even publically acknowledged if the numbers of sick consumers were low enough.

Tina Brackett provided a dramatic coda to Murano's findings, putting an all too human face on the facts and statistics and thus letting Murano cast her as the penultimate victim, an innocent beautiful ten year old who had had to weather the grief of losing her mother and who now found herself, through no fault of her own, in Mercy General, her young life tragically hanging in the balance. It was the stuff television movies were made of.

And Pulitzer Prizes.

The emergency room doors slid open and Gerald White, Head of Hospital Security, stepped out, looked around, then headed in Raymond's direction, nothing extra or wasted in any of his movements, a focused economy of muscle and purpose that he'd carried over from his years as an MP. Despite the cold, he hadn't bothered with a coat or hat.

Gerald White took immense pleasure in the double takes his last name produced in people meeting him for the first time. He was quite possibly the darkest-skinned person Raymond had ever run into. Gerald's skin carried the same purple-black color, sheen, and texture of an eggplant.

Raymond reached over and unlocked the door, and Gerald slipped into the passenger seat. They shook hands. Raymond handed Gerald the envelope, and Gerald handed him one in return. They asked about each other's families. They watched an ambulance tear out of the parking lot.

Gerald folded the envelope with the thousand dollars and tucked it in his front shirt pocket and buttoned it. Raymond shook open the list of people who'd visited Ken Brackett since his daughter had been put in the ICU and scanned it.

"Carlon Leaf?" he said. The name sounded vaguely familiar.

"He's the preacher-man," Gerald said, "the one from The Church of the Eternal Truth that wants to lay the healing hands on that girl."

"He's persistent," Raymond said, running down the list.

"Man's got the spirit," Gerald said. "Had to shut him down two times yesterday and already once today."

Raymond went back to the list. "Still no media, I see."

"The girl's daddy, he's refusing to speak or let them in the room."

That one didn't fit expectations. "Any idea why, Gerald?"

"Don't know I can say." He waited a moment. "The man, he's wound pretty tight. Of course, a sick child can do that to you." He paused again. "Still, there's tight and then tight. With Brackett, there's something in his eyes or not there in the eyes that reminds me of someone who's about to go AWOL."

Another ambulance, sirens going, tore into the lot and ate what White said next.

He started over. "Sometimes he talks to himself. Not all the time, but he does," Gerald said. "You can't help but notice. That and the book he carries with him everywhere. He's always underlining and marking it up."

Raymond nodded, then pointed to the middle of the list. "They come in separately or together?"

"Together in the morning," Gerald said. "Separately in the afternoon."

Brewer and Nelson. They were two high-profile lawyers from one of the most powerful and influential law firms in the Midwest, and they were the first two Raymond had predicted would approach Ken Brackett. Luckily, another of their number, Walker Anderson, was out of the country.

"How'd they leave each time?"

"Put it this way," Gerald said. "Straight-out not happy."

"Any idea why?"

Gerald shook his head no. "Brackett's supposed to meet with a couple more this afternoon though."

"I appreciate everything here, Gerald. Keep me up to date, okay?"

Gerald patted the front pocket of his uniform shirt, nodded, and got out of the car.

He was almost a third of the way back to the emergency room bay when Raymond called him back.

"I just thought of something," Raymond said. "There'll be a little extra in the next envelope if you can get me the title and author of the book Brackett's been carrying around with him."

TWENTY

Raymond dropped onto the couch next to Kate. "The mall thing's supposed to be on next," she said.

They watched a string of commercials, and that was followed by the theme music for *Nightshade Theatre* and a close-up of Gary Ghoulmaster in his coffin, eyes snapping open as he slowly lifted himself halfway up and announced through a shroud of dry-iced fog that later this evening he would be premiering *Demon Diner*.

Andrew carried his wooden desk chair and set it in front of the north window overlooking the yard and street. The window, along with the others flanking it, was outlined in blinking red and white lights.

He sat down in the chair and began rocking, neatly bisecting his torso with each dip and rise. He timed his movements so that his reflection appeared red, disappeared, appeared white, and disappeared over and over again.

Kate touched Raymond's wrist, and he turned back to the television screen.

The anchor for Channel Five did the lead-in: the scene, Loganview Mall, the food court and the Happy Farms franchise in particular, noon, hundreds of hungry holiday shoppers.

Then a close-up of Eileen Connelly, all black Irish beauty, in a tight-fitting And Justice For All T-shirt as she stood among a dozen protesters holding signs and placards at the entrance to the Happy Farms restaurant.

The camera panning, then lingering on the messages: the signs evoking the traditional image of the skull and crossbones but replacing each with a headshot of a leering Lamar Ditell over two oversized crossed drumsticks. The placards holding a school picture of Tina Brackett in their center with photos of heaping platters of Happy Farms chicken nesting in each corner and arching rainbow-like over Tina's head, *It's Enough To Make You Sick!*

Then a cut back to Eileen Connelly and a couple of leading questions from the reporter that let Connelly showcase some righteous indignation as she hammered away at Happy Farms' treatment of the birds from the grow-out farms to the menu items and plates, Connelly then segueing to Tina Brackett and highlighting the connection between ethical treatment of the birds and consumer safety.

"They can't be separated," she said, "and Happy Farms has woefully fallen short on both ends." She then mentioned the need for vigilance by groups like And Justice For All, particularly given industry developments like the new Streamlined Inspection System.

Eileen Connelly efficiently laid out the system's parameters. "It's part of quality control or what passes for it," she said. "The SIS is a joint venture between the USDA and the poultry industry. The plant provides in-house inspectors to assist the regular federal inspectors with their duties." Connelly went on to explain that the in-house crew could vouch for the quality of the products, but they didn't have access to the USDA stamp.

Cut to a close-up of Connelly ruefully shaking her head. "The SIS is one sweet deal for someone as unscrupulous and unethical as Lamar Ditell and Happy Farms."

Kate looked over at Raymond. "There's really an in-house program like that?"

Raymond nodded yes and kept to himself the standard canned response he'd drafted for press releases: *The system, like any other, has, by necessity, its drawbacks, but it's important to remember deregulation isn't synonymous with irresponsibility.*

Across the room, Andrew continued rocking. Raymond watched his son's reflection pop up, loom, recede, and disappear in the center of the window.

Eileen Connelly's diatribe on the ramifications of the Streamlined Inspection System should have ended the segment, but she understood something else: when in front of a television camera, too much talk and information blunted and buried the message.

So she introduced a little theatre.

Just as the reporter was about to tie things up, a six-foot chicken carrying a large basket stormed the entrance to the restaurant and began pelting everyone and everything in sight with rotten eggs.

Two mall security people eventually subdued the chicken while a third called the police.

The first problem occurred when one of the security guards reached up and pulled the head off the chicken outfit. The three special effects blood packs secreted along the inside of the neckline erupted and geysered, soaking the front of the guard's uniform shirt and the top half of the chicken outfit a wet bright red.

The second problem occurred when the police arrested and read the oversized chicken his rights, and it turned out that the person wearing the outfit was Jason Hatt, a current Hollywood heartthrob and leading man in *Apprentice Lovers* and *Hope Chest II*.

Jason Hatt who at one time or another had been romantically linked in the gossip rags with Eileen Connelly and who had a little time off for some guerilla theatre before he began working on his next blockbuster, *The Weekend Husband.*

Raymond had to give Connelly credit. She had perfectly choreographed and packaged the protest. First, the visual shorthand of the placard slogans. Then her verbal elaborations with the reporter. Topped off with some high profile Jason Hatt brand name protesting.

The rest of the evening news unfolded.

There was a segment on the Tower Commission pushing Oliver North for a full disclosure about White House and Congressional involvement in the Iran-Contra Affair.

One updating the coverage of a recent earthquake in the Balkans that destroyed the town of Strajica, Bulgaria.

One on the neurochemistry of dreams in sociopaths.

One on do's and don'ts in holiday decorating.

Then closing out on the early rounds of the national Air Guitar competition, highlighting two college students fighting it out as they ripped through and laid down imaginary tracks to Cream's and Clapton's "Crossroads."

Kate leaned in and touched his arm. "Raymond," she said, inflecting his name as if it were a question or the beginning of one.

The phone rang.

When Raymond picked up, Gerald White passed on that Ken Brackett had met with two more lawyers late that afternoon, but he didn't seem that taken with either.

"At the least, Brackett wasn't promising anything," he said.

Gerald waited a moment before asking, "That offer still good? You know, the little extra coming this way if I got you who wrote that book and the title?"

Raymond hunted a pen, then copied down the particulars. "You sure that's what he's reading all the time?"

"My own eyes," Gerald said.

Raymond glanced over his shoulder. Kate was watching him. He mouthed *what?*

Kate tucked a rogue swath of hair behind her ear, got up from the couch, and moved to the window with Andrew. She dropped her hands to his shoulders to slow his rocking.

The phone call should have made Raymond feel better than he did. Brackett, though, didn't make any sense. His daughter was in a coma. He was looking at a gold-strike of a lawsuit and settlement. Why, then, wasn't he pressing and pursuing both?

There had to be a reason.

Raymond wasn't sure he had enough time to find it.

He looked down at what he'd written and shook his head. He then called Eric Donner and told him to hunt down a copy of the book ASAP.

"Kemosabe," Donner said. "This isn't some kind of joke?"

Raymond looked over at the window. Kate and Andrew had left the room.

"I wish," he said.

PART TWO

LIVE FROM THE GRAVE, IT'S...

TWENTY-ONE

Subtract exhaustion, desperation, and a half-dozen deep-seated moral qualms, and what was left was an undeniable adrenalized buzz, one that Raymond Locke did not so much feel as live inside for a while.

Raymond Locke was *there*. He burned and threw no shadows. He made things happen. It was as if the world came with a set of instructions that nobody but he had taken the time to read.

He'd found a way to significantly slow, if not fully stop, the problems accumulating around Ken and Tina Brackett for Lamar Ditell and Happy Farms.

The details.

The details and an imperfectly remembered quote: God was supposed to be in the details. Or perhaps it was the Devil. Or maybe it was both, but whatever the case, that's where he'd started, with the details, returning over and over to the files, reading through them until his eyes blurred and ached, and then he started again, looking, just looking, waiting to discover what he only dimly sensed in all that paper and all those words and numbers, waiting for the moment to break open and reveal what had previously been hidden, camouflaged, or nested in all those details, a small thing that was easily overlooked and became the small thing that turned out not to be small at all, Raymond teasing it out and holding it up to the light and then seeing exactly what he needed to do.

Convincing Lamar Ditell of that was a different matter.

Raymond laid out his case. Ditell balked.

Too risky was the consensus of Happy Farms' chief counsel.

Raymond didn't deny the assessment. What he'd come up with was risky, perhaps too risky for the straightjacket of logic or rationality, but it would work, Raymond was sure of that, the certainty underwritten by everything he'd seen and fixed in the past for Public Domain clients.

Raymond pointed out that when you had a ten-year-old girl in a coma and your product put her there, you couldn't afford to play it safe. With Luis Murano and Eileen Connelly gunning for you, there was no *safe*.

That risk had cut both ways. Raymond was all too aware of what would happen to his career if his take on the problem collapsed.

He pushed it anyway.

Raymond had been there before. He'd cleaned up the Bushel of Love account and the suicide of Bishop DeMarco's mistress and had mopped up all manner of clients' mistakes, mishaps, and messes. He'd discovered the trick of fixing the seemingly unfixable was not a trick at all, but rather the willingness to set up a base of operations in the equivalent of a lunar no-man's-land where all moral convictions and judgments were irrelevant and then have the courage or the stomach to go on and explore and map it.

Raymond had started with the central discrepancy presently at the heart of the Happy Farms mess: the fact that Ken Brackett kept meeting with lawyers but not hiring any of them.

Then he worked back through the files. Raymond collected details and constructed makeshift hunches. He tested them. Threw them out. And then tested them again.

Small details. He collected them. Bounced them off each other.

Like the fact that Ken Brackett had been born and raised in Wilkesboro and, with the exception of a truncated stint in the army, had worked virtually his entire adult life at the Happy Farms plant.

Then Raymond had put that up against Lamar Ditell's object lesson when he'd set up the George Pullman parallel, both men leaving their fingerprints all over the lives of their workers and home places.

Raymond had then jumped to the labor strikes that had threatened the images as much as the livelihood of Pullman and Ditell and how each responded to that threat.

The labor strikes had lead him to And Justice For All and Eileen Connelly and her long-running fight with Ditell and that brought to mind the slogan with which Lamar Ditell had introduced the Happy Farms line: *Only the Rooster Gets a Better Piece of Chicken*.

The slogan which when shortened to *Only the Rooster* then became the title of the documentary film Eileen Connelly had underwritten, the film detailing the strike at the Wilkesboro plant and its aftermath.

Raymond had watched the film three times before spotting him in footage of a knot of strikebreakers trying to cross the picket line. The attempt had broken down into a melee of curses, shoves, and punches. There was enough blood and broken bones to justify the police stepping in.

Raymond had paused the tape and found Ken Brackett in the midst of that melee, a younger version of the man who sat bedside in Mercy General, but Ken Brackett nevertheless, Brackett's face torn open in a rictus of rage as he swung his left fist into someone's chin.

Raymond almost missing it then, the small detail that wasn't. He backed up the VHS tape and advanced it incrementally, hitting pause again when he'd seen enough to be sure.

Raymond had found what he needed.

Ken Brackett was a scab. Brackett had turned out to be one of a very few locals who joined the crew of strikebreakers that Lamar Ditell had brought in from outside Wilkesboro.

Ken Brackett had sided with management and turned his back and then later his fists on his neighbors and co-workers.

Raymond could not say for sure how far that company loyalty might still extend with Brackett's daughter in a coma, but there was at least the real anomaly of his not immediately setting loose a team of lawyers on Lamar Ditell.

It was simultaneously a small opening and a big risk, but Raymond had recommended that Ditell reach out to Ken Brackett *mano a mano*.

Ditell ended up overriding the objections of Happy Farms' lawyers and agreed to what Raymond had outlined.

Raymond and Eric Donner had then gone about coaching Lamar Ditell on the known facts of Brackett and his life, pushing Ditell until those facts were second nature and he could reference them without hesitation.

During that time, Raymond had been drafting the letter that Lamar Ditell would supposedly write to Ken Brackett, a letter which sidestepped any references that a lawyer might be able to cast as culpability or admission of guilt, a letter which simply expressed his concern for Tina and let the offer of help reside between the lines. It would be signed *Your friend, Lamar D.*

Raymond then had Gerald White, head of hospital security, deliver the letter to Ken Brackett.

Against odds and standard-issue luck, it worked. Brackett agreed to a meet. No media. Twenty-five minutes bedside at Mercy General. Outside regular visiting hours.

Lamar Ditell showed up on time. He brought two cups of black coffee and two workingman brown-bag lunches. Raymond had coached Ditell well enough that for close to a half hour, Lamar was able to impersonate a human being and pull it off. Ken Brackett didn't quit meeting with lawyers, but he did invite Ditell back the next night and continued to invite him.

It was the door Raymond had been looking for. It opened a little more with each passing day.

Raymond went back to work again.

Raymond booked Lamar Ditell on the *Commander Sunshine Show*. After snacking on some

Happy Farms Chicken Bittles, the Commander, accompanied by his canine sidekick Pep, Lamar, and the studio audience, most of whom were as tall as Ditell himself, hunkered down on-stage and Crayolaed a large scroll-like get-well banner for Tina Bracket, the segment ending with Lamar leading the audience in a rousing sign-off: *Tina and the Commander Rule!!*

Next, Raymond arranged it so that Ditell and *U*, his former bride now on retainer and reunited, made a surprise appearance at a World Wrestling Conference match, Lamar leaping into the ring during the third round of the second match and mugging his way through a David and Goliath routine.

In the meantime, Raymond made sure the public got its share of gizmos and trinkets. He choreographed a constant barrage of advertising and promotional gimmicks. Jingles and radio contests. Reams of discount coupons for the Happy Farms franchises. Giveaways - coffee mugs and glasses, earmuffs, T-shirts, windshield scrapers, potholders, bird-feeders, pen sets, Xmas decorations - all emblazoned with the Happy Farms logo.

Lamar Ditell escorted passels of underprivileged kids to afternoon performances of *The Nutcracker* at the Royal Memorial Theatre Center in downtown St. Carlton.

He delivered take-out boxes of Happy Farms meals to the Mayor and his staff at a working lunch session.

Lamar and *U* Santa-and-Elfed it in the Pediatric Wing of Mercy General.

Raymond nudged things further along, and Ken

Brackett eventually consented to stepping into the spotlight with Ditell and others. Brackett, though, did not give up the practice of meeting with lawyers.

Gary Samuels, MVP and Goalie for the St. Carlton Cobras stopped by Tina's room and left an autographed puck.

Raymond plucked, then pulled, some ecclesiastical strings, and Bishop DeMarco made a personal visit to the hospital to bless Tina and the staff.

Frankie Wayne, a crooner from the early 60's whose career and reputation as a high-rolling ladies man had been kept on life-support by the Las Vegas lounge circuit, dropped in to the hospital and delivered his rendition of "It's Beginning to Look a Lot Like Christmas" and "Silent Night" to a mini-cam crew, Ken Brackett, Lamar Ditell, and a still comatose Tina.

Sharon Palm and Luke Calvin detoured over from Chicago and the Midwest premiere of their new romantic comedy, *Two Hearts, One Beat,* and brought Tina a dozen white roses and then mugged for a shot with Lamar Ditell, sandwiching him between them while they simultaneously planted kisses.

Lamar periodically complained to Raymond that Ken Brackett was a "strange bastard." Raymond counseled patience and emphatically reminded him that they had so far avoided a lawsuit.

Eileen Connelly and Luis Murano continued to hammer away at Lamar Ditell and Happy Farms. They were rapidly becoming the darlings of the wire services. Connelly, for her part, attacked Public Domain, condemning it for exploiting Tina Brackett in its PR campaign and equating it with child abuse. She buttressed her attacks by making sure the And Justice For All coalition circulated petitions, picketed stores selling Happy Farms products, and bombarded congressmen with letters and calls. She also managed to stage a number of highly publicized meetings with Arthur Cavanaugh, the St. Carlton District Attorney, who lent his support and political clout to anything that potentially hurt Lamar Ditell.

Luis Murano kept pushing the expose-angle, emphasizing Happy Farms' shaky and shadowy history when it came to USDA inspections and investigations and the resultant paperwork and cross-purposed bureaucratic recommendations.

Raymond counter-attacked, preparing answering statements from Lamar Ditell to deliver, charging that Luis Murano and Eileen Connelly were hypocritically doing what they attacked Public Domain and Happy Farms for - exploiting Tina Brackett for their own ends, in this case, to further their causes and careers. Raymond also attacked Murano's speculation that Tina Brackett's deteriorating condition was due to the fact that she had been eating antibiotic-laced Happy Farms chicken all her life and that her inability to beat the toxemia came as a result of contracting strains of Salmonella and Campylobacter Jejuni that had become resistant to standard antibiotic treatment regimens. Raymond brought in panels of experts who cited dozens of studies commissioned by the federal government and poultry industry, none of which established conclusive proof linking health risks to humans from agricultural antibiotic use.

Raymond answered Murano's portrayal of Happy Farms' plant conditions by creating a series of public service announcements on the proper care and preparation of poultry in the home, making sure each announcement also emphasized the fact that the vast majority of cases of Salmonella and other foodborne diseases originated in the consumer's own kitchen from improper handling or undercooking.

When it came to Arthur Cavanaugh, Raymond planted some barbed letters to the editor highlighting some of the *St. Carlton Herald's* previous disastrous rushes to judgment that resulted from Arthur Cavanaugh's temper and ambition and going on to suggest that Cavanaugh should concentrate on responsibly meeting the duties of his office and refrain from practicing wanton character assassination on Lamar Ditell.

At that point, Raymond took Ken Brackett and Lamar Ditell and orchestrated a meeting of the myths.

He pitched Brackett as the Little-man-writ-large, the homegrown-and-spun small town American hero, unapologetically blue collar in appearance and belief, a decent, simple, hardworking, practical, freedom-loving family man who'd weathered hard times, a new version of an old breed of American hero, a man of quiet strengths and character who refused to cloak himself in victimhood and exploit his misfortune, someone who instead chose to squarely face what life had served up without complaint or excuse, his rough-hewn individualism the antidote to a decade of self-indulgent finger-pointing and outrageous and irresponsible litigation practices.

With Brackett the Little-man-writ-large, Raymond then cast Lamar Ditell as the Large-man-writ-small, an all-American entrepreneur whose immense success, power, and wealth were not the spoils from the bloody tooth and claw Darwinism of the capitalistic marketplace but rather the beneficent reward for his fidelity to the basic virtues and tenets of the Puritan Work Ethic, Ditell as the Midwestern magnate with the Midas Touch who still had barnyard dirt under his nails, the self-made scion who had not forgotten his humble roots, God, family, or country.

Pairing up Ken Brackett and Ditell in the public eye became the opportunity to put the American character on display, a broad brush-stroked rendition of democratic wish fulfillment, and if things went as planned, Ditell and Brackett would be inseparable in the hearts and minds of a public already receptive to ignoring or overlooking basic contradictions.

The holiday season itself provided cover. Raymond dropped Brackett and Ditell into the unruly mix of spiritual and material demands Christmas traditionally exacted on the American psyche, and he hoped any nagging doubts or questions on the public's part would be diluted, swallowed, or lost completely in the brimming reservoir of seasonal goodwill and sentiment.

Raymond put in the hours on the campaign, hours long and arduous and caffeine-laden, and he was looking forward to having more time with Kate and Andrew and something approximating a good night's sleep.

Then Lamar Ditell called.

"He wants to see you," Ditell said.

Raymond thought Ditell was referring to his ex, the *U*, from the lineup in the Robert Palmer "Addicted To Love" video.

"Talk to her, Lamar, and I'll work something out to everyone's satisfaction."

"No. Not *U. You.*" Ditell spelled it out.

Raymond worked best behind the scenes. He wanted to stay there and told Ditell that.

"It's that goddamn book," Lamar said.

Raymond told him he wasn't following.

"The book that Brackett's always carrying around," Ditell said. "He started asking me about it, and I had no fucking idea what the strange bastard was talking about, so I bailed and said I borrowed it from you, Locke. Now he wants to meet you."

Raymond pointed out that Eric Donner had summarized and coached Ditell on the book's contents.

"Hey," Ditell said, "the son of a bitch started asking me about something called Modal Replications. No more. I will not go there. You handle it."

TWENTY-TWO

Ken Brackett was sitting at a corner table with his back to the wall, gunfighter style, in the north wing of the Mercy General cafeteria. He had enough food for two people in front of him and was in the process of systematically working his way through a cheeseburger when Raymond stepped up, introduced himself, and waited for Brackett to ask him to sit. He noticed Brackett held the burger so tightly that his fingertips had disappeared in the bun.

"The point is," Brackett said, "you *take* a seat. That's the point. Taking it."

Raymond sat down. Brackett gave what Raymond thought was a smile, but Brackett's teeth were so clotted with meat and bread that Raymond could not say for sure.

Brackett finished the cheeseburger and unwrapped another. His fingertips were shiny with grease. He had not bothered to shave that morning.

"Your assistant?" Brackett said. "You just missed him."

"Eric Donner? He was here?"

"He was wearing mascara," Brackett said. "Not a lot but it was there. He didn't think I noticed."

"Did he say what he wanted?" Raymond thought Donner was supposed to be back in the office.

"I asked him about you. He said you were an orphan." Brackett took another bite of the burger. "Is that true?"

Raymond nodded but wouldn't elaborate on the circumstances. The details of the DC-8 crash over three and a half decades ago weren't any of Brackett's business.

"That might explain a couple things," Brackett said.

Before Raymond could ask exactly what, Ken Brackett held up a plastic fork, then spoon, and finally knife. "See who we are," he said. "A civilization that's now afraid to spear, spoon, or cut. A country that likes *pretend*. We don't live. We *approximate*."

"Interesting point," Raymond said to say something.

Brackett finished off his burger and bypassed the third on his tray for a large order of fries, tearing open the bag and letting them spill across his plate, then covering them in thick runnels of ketchup.

"Actually, what's interesting," Brackett said, "is the how and why of my daughter ending up in a coma." He inserted a fry in his mouth. "She's not getting any better, you know."

"Dr. Schonenfeld knows what he's doing," Raymond said. "Lamar wanted the best in the field for Tina. That's why he brought him in."

"You think that's why?"

Raymond's gut told him not to answer that one.

"There was an editorial cartoon in today's *Courier*," Brackett said. "I was in it. So was Lamar Ditell. No caption. Just a drawing of him hovering over me and me with all these strings attached like a puppet."

Brackett reached across the table and grabbed Raymond's forearm, lifting and then letting it drop. "You feel them, Raymond Locke? The strings? You can't cut them with a plastic knife. You should know that."

Raymond had no clear idea how to steer the conversation or of the direction to take it that would placate Ken Brackett. He tried going back to Eric Donner.

"You never mentioned why he was here," Raymond said.

Brackett pointed over Raymond's shoulder. "Over there, I just noticed. It's called Wave Pattern. It also comes in Early Frost, but the Wave is what we had in the bathroom in the house on Perry Street. That's the one that burned down."

Raymond turned in his seat and looked toward the east wall of the cafeteria. The lower portion was painted the same anemic tan that dominated the hospital's décor, but its upper half was gridded in thick opaque glass blocks.

Raymond waited for Brackett to bring up his wife. She had died in that house fire, but like Raymond's survival as an infant from the DC-8 crash, she resided in the ellipses of their conversation.

Ken Brackett pushed his fries aside and pulled over two dessert fruit cups. He opened each and set them side-by-side and then took turns eating from both.

Raymond watched him finish each fruit cup in the same number of bites. He was uncomfortably reminded of his son Andrew.

Brackett wiped off the plastic spoon with a wadded napkin, then snapped the spoon in two and dropped the pieces on his plate. He did the same to the fork and knife.

He then sat back in his chair. "'The man that excuses himself ... '"

Raymond frowned. "I'm not following."

"He said it was yours."

"It? Who?"

"Lamar Ditell. He said it was your copy, not his." Brackett paused and tilted his head. "Anyone familiar with Dr. Tolson Whormer's work should be able to finish that quote."

A prop. That's all the book was supposed to be. Something to establish a working bond with Brackett. The book had been notoriously difficult to find and it took longer to get a copy than expected. Raymond had Eric Donner do a hasty overview and summary for the coaching sessions with Lamar Ditell.

A Guide To Unleashing. By Dr. Tolson Whormer. Published eight years ago in 1978 by an obscure Canadian press. 181 pages. From what Raymond had managed to gather, Dr. Whormer came across as the love child of Ayn Rand and B.F. Skinner, his *Guide* a misguided self-help book that encouraged readers to ignore the social contract and then went on to reinforce bad manners and rudeness in the guise of personal growth.

Based on what Raymond had seen today, Ken Brackett appeared to be a true disciple.

Raymond set his briefcase on his lap, hit the clasps, and rummaged until he found his copy. "I told you I had it," he said, holding it up with both hands.

"Baby steps," Brackett said. "Necessary, but still baby steps."

Raymond frowned, puzzled.

"That's Book One," Brackett said. He brushed aside a pile of napkins and picked up a paperback. It had the same title but was twice the thickness of Raymond's and had a black cover with red lettering rather than a green cover with yellow lettering.

"Book Two," Brackett said. "It's Dr. Whormer's Magnum Opus and the fulfillment of his genius."

Of course, Raymond thought.

"I didn't know there was a Two," Raymond said. "Where can I buy a copy?"

"It's not that simple," Brackett said. "There's a very big difference between *A* and *THE*." He pointed to the titles of each paperback.

Brackett went on to explain that Dr. Whormer had self-published *Book Two, The Guide*, by choice and necessity to avoid any semblance of editorial interference or fingerprints. The only way to get a copy was to literally petition Dr. Whormer personally by writing to a Post Office Box in Vancouver. There was no set price on the book. The petitioner sent whatever he could or thought fitting. Dr. Whormer was under no obligation to honor every request. He might or might not send a copy of *Book Two*, and if he decided to honor the request, the book might be shipped at any time. It might be overnight-expressed or appear six months or a year later.

"It took me four tries before I got my copy," Ken said.

Raymond waited a moment, then said, "If it's that difficult, maybe I can just borrow yours."

Ken Brackett's expression was a photo finish between a grimace and smile.

"You can't borrow the truth, Raymond," he said. He slid back his chair and stood up.

Raymond did the same. As they started out of the cafeteria, a nurse in pale green surgical scrubs stopped them. "You're supposed to bus your own tables."

Raymond said he was sorry and started to turn around, but Brackett reached over and snagged the sleeve of his sports jacket.

He then tapped the cover of *The Guide*.

"'The man who excuses himself accuses himself,'" he said.

TWENTY-THREE

Eric Donner tapped the tabletop in the Executive Conference Room and said, "I'm afraid, Raymond, you're coming down with a case of the *Frank Atwells*. Symptoms include cloudy thinking and retracted testicles." Donner launched a facsimile of a smile. "The only symptom you don't appear to be exhibiting is arriving at the office with a Mac-truck-sized hangover and then spending the rest of the day pretending to do your job, so I guess there's still some hope for you. You haven't hit *terminal* yet."

"I appreciate the concern, Eric," Raymond said, "and I hope you know it's reciprocated. Everybody on the sixth floor has chipped in to help fund your visit to an ear-nose-throat specialist and gastroenterologist. That chronic runny nose of yours and the frequency of your trips to the men's room have been duly noted by all."

Donner made no effort to hide his bemusement. He slid over a thick file and flipped it open in front of him. He was wearing a green silk shirt buttoned to the neck but no tie and a black sports jacket with its sleeves rolled three-quarters of the way up his forearms. When he turned his gaze from Raymond to Daniel Pierce, Donner's pale-blonde ponytail curled over the collar of his sports coat like a crooked pinkie finger.

"You two done yet? I'm still waiting on any new

updates about Ken Brackett," Daniel Pierce said. He sat at the head of the conference table in a light gray suit and West Palm tan.

Raymond was irritated with himself for letting Eric Donner get to him. It was the exhaustion speaking. The last few days in particular had come to feel as if they were buckling under the weight of the demands of the Happy Farms account, and any sanctuary sleep might have provided had been denied by his son Andrew for two nights running when he inexplicably got up at three a.m. and began hitting the west wall of his bedroom with his red plastic bat. Each night, it had taken Raymond and Kate over an hour to get him to stop and calmed down enough to go back to bed.

"We need to take this to the next level." Donner tapped the file before him. "I think Brackett's ripe for an out-of-court."

"I don't," Raymond said.

"The agreement's drawn up," Donner said. "All we have to do is get it and a pen in Brackett's hands."

"And I'm telling you, Brackett's not ready yet." Raymond had read various drafts of the agreement, and they all were designed toward one end: making sure Ken Brackett was bought off and in Lamar Ditell's pocket while preserving the illusion that Happy Farms was in no way responsible for what happened to Ken's daughter. The latest draft attempted to bypass any and all attendant negative publicity and costs tied to a court case. It was an out-of-court settlement without having to call it one. Ken Brackett ended up with a nice pile of cash, and all his daughter's medical expenses were picked up in a show of corporate altruism.

"Brackett's too much of a wild card right now," Raymond said.

Donner went into an exaggerated head shaking that pantomimed disbelief. "I'm majorly disappointed in you, Raymond. You've lost or you're losing your nerve. I don't know which, but it's creating problems."

Donner added a coda to the routine by throwing up his hands. "Credit where it's due," he said. "You lived up to your reputation, Raymond, more than lived up to it, by discovering Ken Brackett had been a scab during the strike in Wilkesboro and then parlaying that angle with Brackett and Ditell. That was brilliant. Honestly brilliant."

Donner then paused for effect and frowned. "But you create an in like that, and then you start equivocating. I don't get it. Brackett's our buddy. He's ripe. We need to stick it to him now."

"Brackett's daughter is the key," Raymond said. "We shouldn't go any further until we know for sure she's going to recover. And right now, she's not getting better, so that's still an open question." Raymond looked over at Daniel Pierce. "I've been over the prognosis again and again with the doctors, and I say we should wait."

"Oh man," Donner said. "The fact that nobody can say for sure she'll recover is exactly the reason why we need to push Brackett. Once he signs, he's ours."

"Not necessarily," Raymond said. "I talked to Brackett at lunch, and he's not particularly coherent or stable right now. He's totally focused on his daughter. We can't confidently predict what he'll do or not do, and that's asking for trouble. We push things, and down the road, any half-assed lawyer can claim we took advantage of Brackett's mental and emotional state and pressured him into signing, and that will come back on us in very unpleasant ways."

"Hey, I talked to him in the cafeteria too," Donner said. "They guy's a couple quarts low on charm, but we're not looking at Mensa material here. Basically, Brackett's pissed off at the world. All you have to do is let him vent." Donner paused and shrugged. "We stay on Brackett's good side, and he's ours."

"I still don't think it's that simple," Raymond said.

"It is," Eric Donner said. "Believe me."

"Why?"

"Toby Wenzler,"

"I don't know who or what you're talking about," Raymond said.

"Wenzler's the lawyer who represented Brackett after his house burned down."

"There's no Toby Wenzler mentioned anywhere in the files on Brackett or his daughter," Raymond said. "Why haven't I heard of him before now? What are you pulling here?"

Raymond kept expecting Daniel Pierce to break in, but he just continued sitting at the head of the conference table, every so often taking a sip from his glass of water and jotting something down in a small black notebook, his expression and posture at true-north neutral.

"I was going to tell you about Wenzler," Donner said. "That's why I went to the hospital cafeteria. I was trying to catch you before you met with Brackett, but we missed each other."

"Who exactly is Toby Wenzler?"

"Not *who*," Donner said. "*What*. Wenzler's our ace-in-the-hole." He paused. "We've all been trying to figure out why Brackett hasn't already gotten lawyered-up on us, and Wenzler is the reason."

It didn't take long to see why Brackett had no reason to love lawyers. Eric Donner went on to explain how Brackett had been cheated grandly by Wenzler who represented him and took on the Mayflower Development Company after the death of Brackett's wife. Mayflower specialized in throwing up subdivisions of over-priced starter homes. Ken and his family had lived in one of them, Windplover Estates, on the south side of Wilkesboro.

Ken had taken Tina roller-skating the evening the house burned down. His wife, Leah, had left work early with a bad cold and gone straight home to bed. By the end of the evening, she had turned the phrase *sleep like the dead* into a literal truth. The Fire Marshall's subsequent investigation pointed to faulty wiring, the ruling on the source becoming official when the wiring in five other homes in a two-block radius proved to be as potentially lethal.

Enter Toby Wenzler, Attorney at Law, promising justice and compensation. Toby explained that he believed the victims of tragedies such as Ken's deserved the full settlement in liability cases, and that was why he preferred to work for a flat fee - reasonable and up-front - instead of following the traditional practice of taking a percentage of the final settlement. Toby couldn't justify working that way, not with a case as cut and dried as the one against Mayflower. The Fire Marshall's ruling made it a virtual cakewalk. Toby Wenzler just wanted a fair price for his services and the satisfaction that he'd helped Ken and Tina get what they were entitled to under the law. He knew in the end there was no price tag on grief. Ken agreed to let Wenzler represent him, signing over the insurance policy he'd carried on Leah.

Wenzler then went to the other five families whose homes contained substandard wiring and made his pitch for representation, using Ken Brockett as bait, citing precedents for extravagant settlements, and offering to kite-tail the other cases to Ken's. Leah's untimely and tragic death would work to their benefit, virtually guaranteeing the success of their suits and bumping up the amount of the settlements all around. Each of the five families jumped on Wenzler's proposal, all paying ten thousand up front by taking out second mortgages on the deathtraps they'd been calling home.

Wenzler appeared to play it by the book. He filed motions and set up hearings and conferred with Ken and the other families, laying out trial strategies he knew he'd never have to institute because Wenzler had expediently left out one very pertinent detail when he'd signed Ken and the others on as clients. It was a bit of information he'd picked up in passing a month before the fire from a colleague in Chicago who specialized in tax law: the Mayflower Development Company was in serious financial trouble and about to go belly-up and file bankruptcy. Wenzler was counting, correctly as it turned out, that Ken's and the other five families' cases would never make it to trial. He pocketed all the front money and commiserated with his clients about the vagaries of the law and the imperfections of justice. In the end, Ken and Tina had to move back into his childhood home with his mother.

"Why hadn't any of us heard this before?" Raymond asked again.

"Breaking news," Donner said, and when Raymond asked his source, Donner smiled.

"Pillow talk," he said, and then recounted how he'd met one Ivan Timmons, Attorney at Law, at one of his favorite clubs and then with one thing and drink proverbially leading to another, they ended up spending the night at Timmons' apartment. It turned out that Ivan and Toby Wenzler had worked at the same law firm.

"Ivan was part of the burial detail," Donner said, "after the senior partners at the firm found out what Wenzler was up to. Ivan and the others made sure there was no residual damage because Wenzler had been passing off his freelance scams as pro bono work."

"I can see how Wenzler can be used as a wedge against lawyers trying to talk Brackett into a suit," Raymond said, "but it still doesn't change my original point. Right now, Brackett's stressed and on edge. It's not the time to push for an out-of-court settlement."

Daniel Pierce got out of his chair and stood before the enlarged aerial photograph that doubled as a mural of St. Carlton.

He reached out and touched the Metropolitan Bank Building in the center of the city, then dropped his hand, and began speaking while still keeping his back to Donner and Raymond.

"The reality of our present situation is this," Pierce said. "We cannot afford to lose the Happy Farms account. We also cannot afford the appearance of doing anything underhanded or illegal. There is a very determined and powerful bloc of stockholders that at the next meeting in New York hopes to force me to step down. These stockholders - or *stakeholders* as they like to refer to themselves - have heard rumors about some of our methods and working relationships with our clients, and to put it mildly, they do not approve."

Pierce paused and slowly tilted his head at the cityscape as if he were taking in the view for the first time. "This crowd wants their end of quarter statements served up with a fashionable show of corporate ethics. Ken Brackett is that kind of show. The two of you need to make sure you keep Brackett happy."

Pierce abruptly turned and walked out of the conference room without looking at Donner or Raymond.

"What ... the ... fuck?" Donner said. "That's it? We just let Ken Brackett hold us hostage?"

"Yes," Pierce said, turning to look at Raymond and then Donner. "Your job for now is to make sure Brackett believes that's exactly what he's doing."

TWENTY-FOUR

Raymond only dreamed of his mother during the month of December.

The dreams were variations on a single unwavering image, one of a beautiful young girl who was fifteen or sixteen years old with long, straight blonde hair, a flawless milk-white complexion, and pale blue eyes, a genetic trifecta common to Andersonville, the tightly packed Scandinavian community wedged between the 5200 and 5400 blocks of North Clark in Chicago where Raymond's mother had grown up surrounded by three generations of the Pederson clan.

It was Elena Pederson, Raymond's mother, that he dreamed of each December, the young girl who had yet to meet Billy Locke, an architectural student, some six years later at the University of Illinois during her senior year as an elementary education major or the young woman who had yet to become the young mother some three years after that who, with her husband, Bill Locke, and infant son, boarded a DC-8 that twenty-five minutes later crashed and burned, killing her and her husband and 185 others, Raymond the sole survivor.

The image that persisted in Raymond's dreams was embedded in the ritual honoring St. Lucia and Andersonville's Festival of Light. Raymond could never remember the exact date of the Festival, only that it occurred early to mid-December.

The image from the Festival: a young girl in an ankle-length white choir robe, a crimson sash belted at her waist, and wearing a crown of burning candles, the girl cupped in light by a semi-circle of girls in white robes, each holding a candle.

The image reoccurred in his dreams in different settings and forms. Sometimes Raymond was standing in the middle of a busy sidewalk full of strangers wearing T-shirts with the image silk-screened on their fronts and backs. At other times, the image occupied parts of the peeling billboard he passed each morning on the way to work. Or the image appeared on every channel on his television set. Or it appeared on the covers of magazines, the walls of art galleries, on license plates, and canned goods lining a shelf.

In one version of the dream, Raymond stood directly in front of the young girl and the others and the wall of white and flickering lights they made, and a man standing behind him explained in a voice with the carefully modulated tone of an Educational Television narrator that Lucy was the patron saint of blindness and that the candle-lit festival in her name celebrated the power of light triumphing over the darkest time of the year. Each time when Raymond turned around to thank the man for the explanation, there was no one there.

The dreams had originally started shortly after the birth of his son, Andrew, and Raymond traced their origin to a photograph he remembered of his mother as the Festival's Queen of Light that had resided along with others on his aunt and uncle's fireplace mantle, but his aunt had resolutely denied the existence of the photograph, and Raymond had never been able to find it when he'd helped box up his aunt's possessions after she had to move into an assisted living center.

With the residue of last night's dream crowded out by Raymond's end of the day exhaustion, he pulled behind Kate's car parked curb-side at the south entrance of Coleman Park.

He'd driven straight from work. He could see the silhouettes of Kate and Andrew etched along the edges of a flat snow-covered field that in the spring was used for soccer matches. Raymond got out of the car and waved, but they didn't see him.

He crossed the playground, empty now except for the tracks of children who'd been running through it earlier. A patchwork of heavy clouds bullied what remained of the light, and in a gap between masses, Raymond caught a glimpse of a silver half-moon.

Raymond wished he'd worn heavier clothes. His feet were already cold and damp by the time he reached Kate and Andrew, and he had somehow once again misplaced his gloves. The bones in his hands were beginning to feel brittle.

The wind shifted and the snowfall started to gain both weight and speed.

"Say hello to your father, Andrew." Kate pointed at Raymond.

Andrew held out a tangled mass of plastic punctuated by splintered wood pieces. He was wearing a dark ribbed stocking cap pulled low on his forehead. It left the rest of his face looking crowded, its features pulled together like a loose fist.

"It was a trial run," Kate said. "Obviously one that was unsuccessful. I brought an extra. You can use the picnic table."

She walked over and brushed off its surface, and Raymond, with increasingly stiffening fingers, went about assembling the kite. Andrew stood on the opposite side of the table and watched intently and softly repeated *It's time* over and over again.

Raymond handed the kite over, and Andrew walked out toward the middle of the field. Andrew lifted his arm, and the wind caught the kite, lifting it through the lines of snow in a series of stutter-steps.

"Thank you," Kate said. "Andrew's been waiting all day for this."

Raymond slipped his hands in his overcoat pockets.

"Any change in Tina Brackett?" Kate asked.

Raymond shook his head no and said, "Red Zone," after Kate asked about Ken Brackett. "Warp-speed stress," he added a moment later.

An abrupt updraft momentarily turned the kite's face in Raymond's and Kate's direction. The kite had been part of a campaign for one of Public Domain's accounts, and Raymond had come home with a half-dozen or so when the promotion ended. Andrew had discovered the cache of kites when Kate had been unpacking Christmas decorations. The client had been North Country Car Rentals, and the face of the kite featured a knight on a charging steed, but in place of the lance, he held an oversized set of keys out before him.

Kate took a step closer to Raymond. She was wearing a pair of bright red earmuffs, and the snow had already dampened and darkened her hair. "Someone from the Research Division called just as we were leaving. Julianne something. She said to tell you she's following up on something that's very promising and hopes to have news soon."

Raymond nodded and then nodded again when Kate told him that Frank Atwell had also called and wanted him to stop by his apartment after work one day this week.

They watched Andrew follow the kite deeper into the field. For a moment, the kite disappeared in the thickening lines of snow, leaving Andrew silhouetted with empty upraised hands.

"I can't do it all myself," Kate said.

Raymond waited for her to continue. He wasn't sure if he'd missed something or if Kate had started in the middle of what she wanted to say. Things felt a little off-key between them over the last month. It wasn't as if they were completing each other's sentences anymore, but rather as if they were getting momentarily lost in the spaces between the words.

"Have you even bought a single present yet?"

"I'm not sure what you mean."

"It's not a trick question, Raymond." Kate dropped her head back, lifting her face to a gray sky and the snow breaking from it.

"We haven't solidified any of our holiday plans," Kate said. "We've barely discussed them. In case you haven't noticed, it's coming up on Christmas."

Raymond dropped his hands deeper into his overcoat. "A little patience here, okay, Kate?"

Before he could continue, Kate started walking toward the center of the field and Andrew.

The snow, heavy and wet, continued to fall harder and harder, thickening in the last of the evening light, so that by the time Kate reached Andrew, they resembled figures wavering on a television screen that couldn't hold its picture.

TWENTY-FIVE

Ken Brackett's face had the unsettling angularity of a cubist portrait, its features seeming to come at Raymond all at once and from all directions. His eyes were dark brown blurring to black, small and widely spaced, his left a half-thumbnail-width lower than the right, and his ears were large-lobed and flared. Reversing the poles of the eyes, the right ear was slightly lower than the left. Brackett's teeth were small given the size of his mouth, and most of them held the blue-gray ghosts of fillings. His face ran itself out in a bony knob of a chin with a left of center cleft and capped itself with a thick carpet of lacquered black hair and a part so straight and sharp it appeared grouted.

Raymond had agreed to meet Brackett on the eleventh floor waiting room outside the ICU. The room was wedge-shaped with tall curving banks of windows looking out on a morning sky that was clear and full of winter sunlight.

Along one wall of the waiting room was a television with the sound low, and below it, a man of indeterminate age asleep in a chair.

"Sigourney Weaver in her underwear," Ken said.

Raymond and he were standing at the east bank of windows. Ken kept reaching up and tapping the glass. On the far edge of the morning was the tattered billboard Raymond passed each day on his way to work. The wind had been working on the upper left corner, turning _t_s A_l T_u_ to I _s a_l_ m_n_ and exposing a deep red gash below the lettering.

"Tom Skerritt with floppy black hair," Ken said.

The man across the room made small noises in his sleep.

"Harry Dean Stanton in a baseball cap."

Ken fumbled with the button on his front left shirt pocket and pulled out a Mars bar. He tore it open with his teeth. "John Hurt at a table in the ship's dining hall."

He finished off the bar in two bites.

"Can you imagine something like that?" he asked. "You got a thing living in your chest and you don't know what, and it's there all the time you go to work and come home. It's in there all the time you're going about your life, and then you sit down to eat, and right in the middle of the meal, it suddenly comes bursting out of the center of your chest." Ken shook his head. "No idea it was there. That thing inside you."

Raymond figured the best strategy right now was to let Ken talk himself out. At the moment, he wasn't sure he liked what he saw in Ken's eyes.

Ken went back to his shirt pocket. He took out a Milky Way this time.

"I refuse to see the new one," Ken said. "James Cameron should have left things alone. There's no room for a sequel in this case. Some things are perfect the first time."

He pointed the Milky Way at Raymond. "You watch *Alien*, then tell me Ridley Scott doesn't understand the workings of a Eupatrid Convection. The man is locked in. Absolutely locked in."

Raymond looked out the window and, using the billboard as a reference point, tried to locate his neighborhood and home.

The man in the chair below the television continued to make noises in his sleep. They sounded like a cross between a sob and low curse.

"James Cameron put the marines and a little girl in the new one," Ken said. "I saw the previews. I will not go beyond that."

"I don't blame you," Raymond said, searching for anything approximating common ground.

" 'Blame is a blind hyena.' Page 147, *The Guide*," Ken said. "Dr. Whormer says it's what's left after an unsuccessful or partial Croustadian Transfer."

Raymond gave a short nod.

Ken finished off the Milky Way. There were pockets of chocolate in each corner of his mouth.

"Speaking of Dr. Whormer," Raymond said, "I sent off my petition for *Book Two* of *The Guide*." Raymond had gone to Daniel Pierce, and for anything that might help Raymond stay on Brackett's good side, Pierce had authorized the funding for the order and had a cashier's check cut for two thousand dollars. They agreed that the amount ought to catch Whormer's notice. Raymond included the check with his petition that simply read: *I'm Ready.* He express-mailed both to the P.O. box in Vancouver.

Ken tapped the window and pointed at the pale reflection of the television screen.

It was a commercial for *Nightshade Theatre*.

"They've only been showing *The Best Of Nightshade Theatre* lately," Ken said. "They're all repeats. I read rumors that Gary Ghoulmaster is all the way dead for real now."

Raymond shook his head. "Gary Ghoulmaster is one of my clients. I know for a fact he's alive." Raymond decided to leave off the *and well* since at last check, the Ghoulmaster was still detoxing.

"Then you must know his real name."

Raymond nodded and smiled. "Trade secret." Keeping Gary Ghoulmaster's real identity secret had been part of the packaging of the show and persona since their inception.

"Tina and I never missed *Nightshade Theatre*," Ken said.

Raymond tried not to imagine family night at the Brackett household.

Raymond then missed something or Ken arbitrarily jumped conversational tracks. Raymond wasn't sure which.

"Okay," Ken said. "Here it is. Pretend you life depended on getting the right answer. Which would you do? A. Break a church window with your fist. B. Set fire to a beehive."

Raymond closed his eyes for a moment. "That's a hard one, Ken."

Brackett turned so he was directly facing the window. Sunlight splashed across his face and turned his profile into a dark silhouette.

"Dr. Schoenfeld told me it might be permanent." Ken kept his gaze pointed north. "The damage to Tina's heart."

"I'm genuinely sorry, Ken. You know that also goes for Lamar."

"Chapter Three, page 41, *Book Two*. 'An apology is always a gun without bullets.'" Ken turned his hand into a pistol. He pointed it out the window at the sun.

Raymond started to explain that his *sorry* was not intended as an apology but rather empathy. He decided, though, that Ken probably wasn't interested in fine-tuning linguistic distinctions.

"Walker Anderson," Ken said quietly.

Shit. It was one name Raymond had hoped not to hear. Anderson had been a hard-line hotshot at the Prosecuting Attorney's office before moving into the private sector. He'd been a protégé of Arthur Cavanaugh and shared his grudges and ambition. Walker Anderson would love nothing more than to be able to deliver up Lamar Ditell and Happy Farms. During the initial stages of the food poisoning outbreak, Anderson had been out of the country. Raymond had hoped the stay would extend through the new year.

Ken fumbled in his shirt pocket. He pulled out another candy bar. This one was a Payday.

He took a bite and said, "Anderson wants to talk to me about Tina."

Ken tilted his head, making a show of studying Raymond. "Something you want to ask me? A point you'd like to make?" He continued to watch Raymond. "I'm thinking Toby Wenzler here."

The playbook was gone. Raymond had no clear idea how he was to call this one. He settled on a temporary ignorance.

"No idea?" Ken said. "Come on."

"Can't place the name."

"Toby Wenzler," Ken said, "Attorney at Law? The guy who stepped in after the house fire that killed my wife and then cheated and robbed me and most of my neighbors by promising a suit against the construction company who put up all the deathtraps in my subdivision in the first place?"

Raymond lied again and told Brackett he couldn't place the name.

"Hard to believe," Ken said, " at least according to Walker Anderson. He told me you're very thorough." He paused and slowly scratched his cheek. "In fact, when your name came up, Walker Anderson said if you wanted to, you could probably tell me Toby Wenzler's shoe size."

TWENTY-SIX

Raymond Locke was on his way to shut Eileen Connelly down. He'd met with Julianne James from the Research Division earlier in the morning, and she explained what she'd found and how carefully and completely it had previously been hidden, and then Julianne had passed over a padded envelope with the same measured moves of a clerk handling change from a large bill.

Raymond glanced in his rear-view mirror and kept the car right at the in-town speed limit. He didn't want to think about where he was going or what he was about to do, but he recognized the signs. A thin coppery taste in his mouth. Dry lips. Nerve-ends trampolining. A persistent itch under his shirt collar.

Given Eileen Connelly's quasi-celebrity status, Raymond had assumed she'd be living in the Stohl District, a trendy rehabbed enclave that had once housed St. Carlton's earliest factories because of its proximity to the railroad yards and warehouses.

Eileen Connelly, though, lived in northwest St. Carlton near the baseball stadium the minor league St. Carlton Wildcats shared with two large local high school teams. It was a neighborhood that behaved itself. Streets with parallel lines of now bare-limbed sycamores. Sidewalks shoveled and salted. A tasteful restraint in outdoor Christmas decorations. Middle class ranches and townhouses that sat next to each other and held hands.

Not exactly where you'd expect to find the domicile of a sexy firebrand and social activist.

Raymond drove slowly down the block of 800's and pulled to the curb. He checked the house number and shut off the car. The front lawn was dominated by a single large oak, its limbs inked and stark against a sky that resembled a partially erased blackboard. Curbside, a handful of desultory sparrows hopped among dirty mounds of snow.

Eileen Connelly answered on the third knock. She held a coffee mug in her left hand and drew the top of her robe closed with her right. Raymond started to introduce himself.

"I know who you are," she said.

For a moment, Raymond thought she was going to slam the door in his face, but then she stepped away, and he followed her inside.

They sat across from each other in the living room, a coffee table between them, the surface nearest Raymond holding fanned sections of a poker hand of regional and national newspapers. Facing Raymond were sidebar photos of Oliver North and Fawn Hall and a lead-story on the Tower Commission hearings.

Eileen Connelly caught him taking in the furnishings. The house had the feel of a motel. That was something else he hadn't expected.

"A place to stay," she said, answering what Raymond had not asked. "That's what this is and the way I want it. With my work, it's all I need for now." She pulled an ashtray over and lit a cigarette. When she leaned back, the top of her robe parted. She didn't bother to close it. She watched Raymond and waited.

"I thought it would be better if we talked in private, rather than at And Justice For All's headquarters," Raymond said.

"For whom?"

"For all concerned."

"Does that include Lamar Ditell's new lapdog, Ken Brackett? You trained him well, Mr. Locke. He heels, sits, and rolls over on command. How much does a dog like that cost?"

"You're wrong about Brackett. The decision not to file suit was wholly his own."

Eileen Connelly laughed and picked up her mug, the fingers on the handle long and elegantly tapered, a description that also fit the rest of Eileen Connelly. She had the type of beauty that left both men and women uncomfortable. There was something both languid and charged in each of her movements. The face beneath the wild Medusa-mane of black hair was small and delicately sculpted, but the pale skin covering it was stretched tightly, barely fitting her bones. Her cleavage left a dark comma between the halves of her robe.

She pointed the cigarette at Raymond. "You know, you're not going to get away with covering up the outbreak. I don't care how much icing you spread on the truth or how much you paid for Ken Brackett's soul. A little girl may lose her life because of Happy Farms' irresponsibility and greed. And there are over a hundred others who are lucky they aren't in the hospital with her."

Eileen Connelly leaned over and ground out her

cigarette, then looked up at Raymond.

"Isn't this the point where you bring out the airline tickets to the Bahamas or the keys to a new car? Or smilingly offer a discrete little bankbook? Or is Lamar Ditell and Happy Farms prepared to make a generous donation to the coffers of And Justice For All if we turn our attention elsewhere?" Connelly leaned back. She slowly stroked her neck. "You'd be wasting your time though. I won't be bought."

Raymond held up two empty hands. "I'm offering nothing more than a suggestion. It's the holidays. Why don't you take some time off, maybe visit your parents? San Diego, right?"

Eileen Connelly shifted on the couch and smiled. "My parents are flying into town. They want to be part of the candlelight vigil And Justice For All is holding for Tina Brackett on Christmas Eve."

Raymond steepled his index fingers and rested them for a moment against his chin. "We can stop right here, Ms. Connelly. I'll ask one more time. Why don't you take a little vacation? Relax and enjoy yourself, put a little distance on recent events?"

"How do you sleep at night?"

"The same as everyone else," Raymond said. "I lay my head on the pillow and close my eyes."

The phone rang. As Eileen Connelly got up to answer, the short blue robe parted again, exposing a long flash of thigh and a shutter-speed glimpse of pale blue panties.

Raymond might have lost the taste for the work at Public Domain but never his nerve, but the longer he sat in Eileen Connelly's living room, the more stubbornly human she became, the mundane particulars of her life insinuating their way into his resolve. He needed to see her for what she was: an obstacle to the Happy Farms campaign, a problem. He did not need to notice the frayed hem on the blue robe or the slight crook in the otherwise delicate lines of her nose, the Spartan apartment furnishings, the careful erasures on the half-completed crossword puzzle on the table or the small red half-moons on the edges of the coffee mug used one time too many.

Connelly came back into the living room and stood across from Raymond, her hand on her left hip. "It's time for you to go, Mr. Locke. I'm not going to back down or out. Lamar Ditell is going to pay. Tina Brackett doesn't deserve what happened to her."

"Who does? I could say the same thing about the wives and families who've suffered from your practice of sleeping with married men, Ms. Connelly." Raymond took a folded sheet of paper from the breast pocket of his jacket and handed it to her. "Take a moment and look that over. There are innocent victims there too. Think of the children left behind when their fathers were foolish enough to fall in love and chase after you, all the lives you've wrecked, the trust you've destroyed."

Eileen Connelly glanced at the list, then crumbled it in a tight ball. "Leave. Get out of my house. Make all the allegations you want. I'll deny every one. I can guarantee if you push this, all you're going to end up with, Mr. Locke, is a docket full of libel cases against Public Domain."

Raymond waited a moment, then said, "You and I

both know the list isn't complete. I was hoping we could reach an agreement without having to bring her into the discussion."

Eileen Connelly bit the corner of her lip.

Raymond thought about kissing his wife before leaving this morning, her skin warm and holding the smell of sleep. Andrew's small face in the living room window impassively watching him back down the drive. In the lawn, the north side of the trees skinned in snow. It felt like he had pulled away not so much from a home but from a safe house, his marriage the equivalent of a portable witness protection program that provided him immunity from what his job made necessary.

Raymond opened the padded envelope, took out the videocassette cartridge, and held it out to Eileen Connelly.

He listened to the whir of the VCR as it started up. The television set was at his back and out of his line of vision, but Eileen Connelly wasn't, and Raymond watched her watch the screen.

He had viewed the tape twice earlier at the office. It held a series of short takes, separated by abrupt jump-cut transitions, the whole thing lasting less than three minutes.

Halfway through, Eileen Connelly dropped back on the couch. "No, No, No, No." She wrapped her arms around her waist. "Where did this come from? It shouldn't be. Nobody knew. She was safe."

An infant wrapped in a pink blanket. Attacking a bottle. Taking first wobbly steps. Bent over a coloring book. Riding a bike. Smiling with her left front tooth missing. Standing in a Brownie uniform. Holding up a gymnastics trophy. Modeling a swimsuit and new breasts. Standing in a semi-circle of girls with their arms thrown over each other's shoulders. Holding up a learner's permit and a set of car keys.

The tape ran out. Eileen Connelly slowly rocked on the couch.

"I don't understand," she said. "It isn't possible. No one should have been able. Where did you get that?"

"Two copies," Raymond said. "You keep this one. The other is locked away." Raymond let the *as long as* float unspoken. "Amy Peyton goes on to get her license next year. She keeps her life. She doesn't need to know. Nobody does."

Eileen Connelly got up from the couch and rewound the tape. She watched it again, hitting pause this time around, intently studying each interlude, watching the daughter she'd given up at birth hopscotch her way through the first fifteen years of her life.

Raymond let the tape speak for itself. He watched the backstory play across Eileen Connelly's features: Eileen Connelly three months shy of her own fifteenth birthday, the heart of a sultry summer, the lakeside summer home of her parents' friend, Senator Ted Colby, and his family, Eileen in a red bikini and a body that had already outrun adolescence, Senator Colby with a campaign-poster smile and gentle hands.

Eileen Connelly refusing to name the father, keeping it her secret from everyone, even her parents who eventually turned to their friend Senator Colby for help, Colby quietly and discreetly making all the necessary arrangements.

The tape ended. Raymond waited for Eileen Connelly to make her decision.

She nodded.

He left.

It took him two tries to unlock his car. His hands continued to shake even after he'd wrapped them around the steering wheel.

As long as he continued to feel appalled, Raymond told himself, he'd be all right. *Appalled* kept him from getting lost. *Appalled* was good. *Appalled* was the line of breadcrumbs he dropped in order to find his way back home.

TWENTY-SEVEN

Raymond met Eric Donner for drinks and an update at the Four Leaf where, if you threw in the dart boards, shamrocks, dark paneling, and a couple green-vested bartenders, then soundtracked it all with a few pennywhistles and fiddles, you might be able to convince yourself you were in something approximating a pub.

The beer, though, was dark and cold. It helped to erase the bad taste the day had left in Raymond's mouth.

Eric and he sat in a corner booth. On the wall behind them was a faux-sampler with a standard-issue Irish blessing: *May the Road Rise to Meet You Until We Meet Again. May God Hold You in the Palm of His Hand.*

"Victory, man," Eric said, lifting his glass in Raymond's direction. He dipped his head and winked. "Now dish on the spoils."

Donner stuck a finger in Raymond's face. "It's written all over you. The classic signs. Your wife takes one look, and you'll be sleeping on the couch for the next three months. No chance of exoneration or stay of execution unless you erase the evidence."

"I didn't sleep with Eileen Connelly, Eric."

Donner tapped his index finger against his thumb. "Not bad. You injected some conviction with the voice there, but the eyes and body language, they need some work." He paused. "You still look guilty as hell."

"Didn't you hear what I said?"

"No one's going to say anything, Raymond. Believe me in spades, I would have done the same thing. Eileen Connelly's a piece and a half. You don't leave something like that on your plate. You fucked her, a perk is all it is." Donner tipped his beer at Raymond again. "Anyway, who's she going to complain to? You're covered."

"How many times do I have to tell you? I didn't sleep with her."

Donner smiled. "Hey, you want to take that line, the dutiful husband and family man, fine. But you're not going to convince me, there's no way, you go in and bring the one and only Eileen Connelly to her knees on this Happy Farms thing and you didn't get in a little zipper action while she's down there on them. No way on that one."

In the center of Raymond's drink napkin was a smiling snowman in a derby, its outline smudged and melting from the condensation of his beer. He asked Donner if there was anything new on Ken Brackett. Raymond could remember all too clearly Ken's take on the *Alien* franchise, and he continued to be concerned that Brackett was going to snap.

"He's sticking close to the girl, and no change with her, by the way. Brackett was out of the ICU," Donner said, "only a couple times in the last two days. I checked with that hospital security guy."

"Any idea where he went?"

Walker Anderson stepped up to the booth and leaned over and smiled. "I can enlighten you on one count, friend."

Raymond had not seen him coming, and that bothered him given how Walker Anderson liked to play a room. In or out of court, Anderson was not a fan of understatement. He was an amalgam of Gold's Gym and *GQ* and sported a recent haircut that probably cost more than Raymond's monthly mortgage.

"Mr. Brackett and I met for lunch," Anderson said. "A *business* lunch. Your name, among others, came up on more than one occasion, Locke. You seem to have made quite an impression on Mr. Brackett."

Anderson turned and waved in the direction of the bar. "Still, I'd have to say our meeting was fruitful. Mr. Brackett and I found some common ground, maybe not as much as I'd originally hoped for, but enough to ensure some future meetings. He's an interesting fellow, our Mr. Brackett. For example, not having gained the benefits of Dr. Tolson Whormer's tutelage in *The Guide,* I had no idea that the failure of the League of Nations could be directly attributable to, as he put it, an 'Omphalosic Shear' that Woodrow Wilson underwent at the onset of adolescence."

Raymond could see, just over Anderson's shoulder, the city's DA, Arthur Cavanaugh, making his way across the room. He was holding two bottles of beer. Cavanaugh did not so much walk as lumber, his posture suggesting that he perpetually shouldered the weight of great and grave judicial matters. There was no trace of a brogue when Cavanaugh spoke. His eyes did not twinkle. He did not tear up when *Danny Boy* was played. At bottom, Arthur Cavanaugh was as humorless as a middle-school principal.

Cavanaugh joined Anderson and handed him one of the beers. He nodded once in Donner's, then Raymond's directions. "Heard you paid Eileen Connelly a visit," he said.

"News travels," Raymond said.

"Ear to the ground," Cavanaugh said. "Friends." He glanced down. "You got your own hands dirty on that one, Locke. Lamar Ditell must be very proud of you."

"A little early for campaign mudslinging and innuendo on your part," Raymond said, "and counting votes before they're cast."

"I'm thinking more along the lines of subpoenas," Cavanaugh said. "And serving them."

"Remember where that landed you," Raymond said, "the last time you rushed and pushed things along." He watched the memory souring Cavanaugh's face. He had gone after a black councilman's son and two of his friends for a convenience store robbery turned shooting, only to have the politically charged case fall apart within minutes when he took it in front of a grand jury.

"We're going to enjoy taking down Lamar Ditell," Walker Anderson added, "and I'm seriously hoping you're standing in the way when we do."

Raymond took a swallow of beer. He shook his head. "The dialogue, Walker. Too many movies. Read some books."

"You know what your nickname is around the DA's office, Locke?" Anderson squeezed out a smile. "And not just because of your fashion sense there." He reached down and rubbed the left lapel of Raymond's black suit coat.

Cavanaugh lifted his bottle and held it against the available light. "Walker, how about getting us a couple more? Put them on my tab."

"A refill is not a bad idea, Kemosabe," Eric Donner said to Raymond and slid out of the booth. "I got this one." Raymond watch Anderson and Donner slowly make their way through the crowd to the bar. Then he watched Cavanaugh watching them.

He was tired.

More than tired. There were layers to his exhaustion.

Cavanaugh tipped back his beer and set the empty in the middle of the table. "You misunderstood what I was referring to. I don't know what you did to Eileen Connelly to change her mind, and she's not saying. So I guess that's score one for Lamar Ditell and Happy Farms."

There were layers to the layers of his exhaustion.

"Those subpoenas I was talking about?" Cavanaugh leaned closer to Raymond. "They'll be for Luis Murano and what you hired out. You overstepped this time. You and Lamar Ditell both."

"I have no idea what you're talking about," Raymond said.

Arthur Cavanaugh went on to tell him.

When he worked late at the *Courier*, Luis Murano made it a practice of stopping by his uncle's restaurant for take-out, and the previous night after he made his way across the parking lot with his meal, Murano was ambushed and mugged just as he was unlocking his car. His attacker wore a ski mask and gloves. He never said a word. He sucker-punched Murano, taking his wind, and then put Murano's hand in the car door and slammed it three times. When Murano regained consciousness, his wallet was lying on his chest, and his hand had swollen to the size of a grapefruit.

"I'm sorry to hear that," Raymond said. "I really am. But what makes you think Lamar Ditell or I had anything to do with it?"

"Murano had been spending a lot of time in Wilkesboro, talking to line workers and shift supervisors at the Happy Farms plant and home office," Cavanaugh said.

"Nothing new there," Raymond said. "He'd practically made Wilkesboro a second home since this whole thing started."

"Murano believed he was getting close to a major break."

"Again, nothing new to that claim either," Raymond said, shaking his head. "I still don't see what that has to do with Lamar Ditell or me."

"It was a message," Cavanaugh said, "the attack was."

Raymond slowly let out his breath and watched Eric Donner and Walker Anderson standing side by side at the bar waiting for their beers.

"Francis de Sales," Cavanaugh said.

Raymond shook his head, exasperated.

"The Patron Saint of Journalists," Cavanaugh said. "Luis Murano carried a medal in his wallet. Whoever attacked him took it."

"The point," Raymond said.

"The attacker didn't take anything else. In fact, he left over three hundred dollars in cash and two credit cards." Cavanaugh waited a moment before adding, "He took the St. Francis de Sales medal, that's it, except for replacing it with a worthless metal slug."

Eric Donner and Walker Anderson started back toward the booth with the beers. Raymond watched Donner laugh at something Anderson said.

"*That's* your point and message, Locke," Cavanaugh said. "That metal slug and a hand slammed in a car door."

"First I've heard of either," Raymond said. "I already told you that."

"And I don't believe you."

"And I don't give a rat's ass, Arthur."

Cavanaugh held up his index finger. "Dialogue there, Locke. Anderson's not the only one prone."

Eric Donner and Anderson stepped up and passed out beers. Donner slid back into the both. Anderson remained standing with Cavanaugh.

Raymond pointed across the room. "Looks like a table just opened up." He gave a small wave. "Nice seeing you two."

"*The Mortician*," Anderson said. "That's what they call you. Not very original, but it suits you." He turned and started across the room to claim the table.

"FYI," Cavanaugh said. "Luis Murano is left-handed. The guy you hired for Lamar Ditell to hurt Murano broke the right hand." Cavanaugh smiled. "Careless, Locke. It's the little details like that that come back to bite you."

Cavanaugh nodded to Eric Donner, then walked

off to join Anderson.

Raymond was tired on more levels than he could count. The inside of his head felt like a flooded basement or sluggish blender, something invaded or barely functioning. He wanted sleep to be more than a noun with five letters.

"I'm waiting," he said.

Donner lifted, then set down his beer. He theatrically raised his eyebrows.

"I'm waiting to hear why I had to find out about Luis Murano from Cavanaugh," Raymond said.

"Hey, I was going to tell you," Donner said. "They showed up before I had the chance. It's not like I could have earlier. You weren't in the office all afternoon."

When he left Eileen Connelly's, Raymond could not quite face returning to Public Domain and the Happy Farms account, so he called in and drove straight on to Gary and the Meadow Assisted Living Center to visit his aunt. On the way, he stopped and bought flowers and candy. Raymond spent the heart of the day in his aunt's room listening to her stories and trying to quell a slowly burgeoning panic and despair when the stories she so happily and uncritically recounted all centered on the life her husband and she shared before they took Raymond in after the air crash that killed his parents. He didn't figure in any of them.

"I didn't know you, Anderson, and Cavanaugh were such pals," Raymond said.

"Whoa, there," Donner said.

"You and Anderson sharing anything more than a

laugh at the bar earlier?"

"He told a joke. The one about Jesus and the Democrats. At the end of it, you're supposed to laugh. That's how jokes work." Donner shook his head. "Speaking of Jesus, what's wrong with you tonight? I mean, come on."

"The two of them just happening to show up here," Raymond said. "I've never been a big fan of coincidence."

"How about paranoia? You a fan of that? Because, Kemosabe, you're inhabiting a whole different dimension from the rest of us right now." Donner went at his beer, then looked around the bar.

"You don't like me much, do you?" Donner said. "You're still blaming me for the inevitable. You could never see that Frank Atwell was finished. Same for his world. *Poof.* Gone. Not even a shadow."

Donner smiled, then said, "So you want to know about Cavanaugh and Anderson? Simple. They're friends of my parents. I've known them since I was a teenager. My father did a boob job on Anderson's wife, knocked her rack up to D cup, and Cavanaugh's sister is seriously depressive and did a couple stints at my mother's clinic."

Raymond rubbed his temples. There was an odd taste in his mouth, some confusing mix of the metallic and vegetative.

"You changed up the meeting," Raymond said. "We were supposed to meet at the Markson Lounge. At the last minute, a switch, here, to the Four Leaf. Then Anderson and Cavanaugh just happen to stop by." Raymond paused and studied Donner's face, zeroing in on the eyes and mouth. "Is that change-up just a coincidence too?"

"No," Donner said. "It was deliberate. And convenient because I was running late." He pointed toward the bar. "See the tender on the left, the George Michael wannabe? His name's Gordon. He's my coke connection, and he gives the best blow jobs east of Wabash Avenue. The Four Leaf's the equivalent of a two-in-one shopping experience for me."

Donner dropped both hands to the edge of the table and leaned in. "You need to get some rest and reacquainted with reality, boss."

He spread his arms, then got up and started for the door, pausing just as he reached it and returning to the bar where he ordered two beers and had them sent over to Walker Anderson and Arthur Cavanaugh.

Then Eric Donner winked at Raymond and left.

TWENTY-EIGHT

Raymond was simultaneously exhausted and wired. He told himself he should have gone straight home after leaving the Four Leaf, but as he drove Mercer Street through downtown St. Carlton and block after block of the resolutely optimistic and desperate Christmas decorations of businesses trying to gain or maintain a toehold against the shiny pull of the mega-mall and its satellites southwest of the old city limits, he missed his turn for Memorial Avenue which would have taken him to the bypass and, five exits later, home.

Instead he found himself driving toward Mercy General.

Why was not on the menu.

It was more than the weight of the day, his starting it off by turning Eileen Connelly's personal life inside out and then against her, or the numbed drive to Gary and the visit with his aunt and a long afternoon of family stories, none of which turned out to have room for him. Afterward the drinks with Eric Donner whose trust and loyalty Raymond was coming more and more to find suspect, the evening ending with the tag-team threats of Walker Anderson and Arthur Cavanaugh and a feeling that Raymond could not quite identify.

Remorse, maybe, except that felt too close to self-pity. Despair seemed too melodramatic. Guilt too simple. Raymond couldn't say exactly what he was feeling, but it wasn't good.

Cheated. That was it. Or as close to identifying it as he could manage. He felt cheated. He couldn't say why or when or how though. The feeling was just there, free-floating, equally troubling and confusing, stubborn as fact.

Raymond continued down Memorial past corner streetlamps decorated to double as candy canes and turned right four blocks later onto 17th Avenue.

Stretching above and across the façade of the front entrance to Mercy General was an immense blinking outline in red, green, and white of Santa in his sleigh. The firing sequence of the lights created the illusion of him slowly waving.

Raymond followed the ramp in the hospital garage for five floors before he found a place to park. Ten minutes later, he stepped off the elevator at the entrance to the ICU. There were banks of pink poinsettias flanking its doors and a sound system piping in a sedated version of "A Holly Jolly Christmas."

Raymond did not recognize the security guard outside Tina Brackett's door. He had right-angled posture, a fresh military brush cut, and a brown and gray mustache the size and texture of a new toothbrush head. According to the patch above the left uniform pocket, his name was Glenn. He looked at Raymond and popped a breath mint.

Raymond asked where Ken Brackett was, and Glenn informed him that Brackett had checked out eighty-three minutes prior to Raymond's arrival.

"Subsequent to Mr. Brackett's departure, I had to contain Reverend Carlon Leaf. He was attempting to breach the Unit. He had tactical support in the form of three members of the Church of Eternal Truth's Steering Committee."

"What did Leaf want?"

"He was planning to lay hands on the girl," Glenn said. "A healing session. Reverend Leaf claims to have successfully performed a similar procedure on a number of his flock who attended the grand-opening at the Happy Farms restaurant at the Vista Mall and became ill."

Raymond remembered the good Reverend. In addition to healing sessions and local stomp-and-shout services on late night cable, Carlon Leaf's current crusade was seasonal and involved a series of billboards strategically placed across St. Carlton and along the interstate. They enjoined viewers not so much to put Christ back into Christmas as to keep Santa out of the show, the rationale being the demonic conspiracy Carlon Leaf had discovered residing in the name itself. According to Leaf, take *Santa* and the third letter at its heart and cut and move it to the end and see who you meet.

Raymond suddenly remembered something else.

"Was Arthur Cavanaugh's wife one of the three with Leaf?" Raymond paused for a moment, trying to remember her first name. It was the same as a month.

"June," he said.

Glenn consulted his clipboard and shook his head no.

Well, at least they'd caught a break there,

Raymond thought. Arthur Cavanaugh had been less than overjoyed when his wife suddenly left the Catholic Church to become a member of Carlon Leaf's flock, and while Cavanaugh still had as little as possible to do with Leaf, he had begrudgingly accepted his wife's presence at Eternal Truth after Cavanaugh's campaign manager at the last election ran the numbers and pointed out that June's defection from the Pope and his minions had actually ended up helping Cavanaugh garner crossover votes from the hard-line evangelical bloc.

"The Reverend Leaf promised to return," Glenn said.

"I'm confident you'll continue to hold the line," Raymond said. For a second, he thought Glenn might salute him, and before Glenn had the chance, Raymond stepped inside Tina Brackett's room and closed the door behind him.

The lighting in the room was soft and low, and Raymond was grateful for that. The uneasy feeling that had been building ever since he left Eileen Connelly's that morning had followed him into the room. Raymond stood at the foot of the bed and waited for his eyes to adjust to the light.

It was easier at first to concentrate on the objects at the periphery of his vision - the wall of get-well and Christmas cards, the Commander Sunshine banner, the autographed celebrity shots, the small artificial Christmas tree in the corner, the flowers, and the fuzzy pastel-colored menagerie of stuffed animals, all of which softened the starker reality of the medical equipment that monitored and sustained the life of the young girl before him.

And it was easier to look at the equipment than it was the young girl connected to it, to think of function and efficiency, of forces marshaled and brought to bear. The brain-shunt to relieve the inter-cranial pressure from the build-up of spinal fluids. The nasogastric tube snaking into the stomach. The stoma appliance for the colostomy after the bowel perforation. The dinamap monitoring the blood pressure and pulse. The oximeter on her finger for oxygen-level readouts. The bladder catheter. The endotracheal tube and ventilator. The portable x-ray unit to check for fluid build-up in the lungs. The hypothermia blanket for fever. The heart monitor. The IV equipment and the bags of glucose and saline solution and hyperalimentation fluids. In the room's soft light, the equipment seemed almost talismanic.

Raymond took the last step and forced himself to look at the girl herself, no props this time, just Tina Brackett, a still point in the center of the bed, wan and tiny and fragile, heartbreakingly beautiful in the way only sick children can be. She was a template for every adult fear of mortality, the end-of-the-night and zero-at-the-bone moments when every distraction fell away, leaving you with a single unalterable truth.

Raymond could not help resenting Tina Brackett for reminding him of that truth. The longer he looked at her, the more helpless he felt.

The prognosis for her condition remained unchanged. Raymond had talked to the doctors, reviewed each wrong turn her luck had taken after she'd eaten the tainted chicken - the severity of the initial symptoms of the toxemia, the body-wracking bouts of vomiting, diarrhea, and fever, the subsequent dehydration and electrolyte imbalance spawning one complication after another, the girl's previous medical history coming into play, a heart weakened by an earlier bout of rheumatic fever and an immune system undermined by allergies, everything going haywire with the antibiotic treatment, cause and effect blurring in a nightmarish mix of respiratory and heart problems that culminated in anaphylactic shock and cardiac arrest, then the slide into a coma when the spinal fluid began backing up in her brain, the final twist coming from the massive doses of steroids administered to counteract the allergic reactions and buttress a compromised immune system that produced yet another complication by weakening and tearing the tissue in Tina Brackett's intestines and leaving her with a perforated bowel and more surgery.

Raymond bent over the comatose girl, her skin so pale it was almost as if he could see through to the shadow play of organs and the cat's cradle of veins beneath it, and as he put his fingers to her forehead, brushing back the dark brown bangs, he let something close to hope fill him.

Everything could still turn out all right. All Tina Brackett had to do was get well. Her recovery was the answer to everyone's problems.

Raymond stood in the darkened room and began spinning scenarios for dramatic reversals and miraculous breakthroughs - Tina Brackett's coma a fairy tale sleep, a spell magically broken; Tina stubbornly clinging to life, fighting back through sheer force of will, tortuously lifting a finger and tapping Raymond's wrist, the Morse code for a happy ending; Tina's eyes suddenly springing open on Christmas Eve, church bells chorusing in the background, all the world's pain, frailty, and despair made coherent by and in her recovery, the tainted chicken and its effects and Tina Brackett's suffering hitched to a higher end, instructive and uplifting, Pandora's Box holding a present after all.

Raymond stepped away from the bed, bowed his head, and began rubbing his temples, the spell broken. The impulse to hold onto the scenarios remained though, the all too human pull of the melodramatic, the desire for larger than life resolutions that never fit the terribly small facts of our days.

He told himself to stop.

He was doing the same thing to Tina Brackett that Kate did to their son, Andrew, by letting desire bully belief, substituting a pretty but fraudulent wish-fulfillment for the coarse weave of plain truth, and daily turning back the odometer on the long shot so that your destination came to feel like yet another fresh start.

None of it changed a thing.

He could not save Tina Brackett or she him. She remained marooned in her pain, Raymond a reluctant witness. Tina Brackett did not deserve what happened to her, and there was no way to negotiate a way around that. A sick child was always the ultimate violation, and any response proved inadequate. The girl lying before him mocked every human pretension, emptied every impulse to nobility or vanity. She became a raw spot on the otherwise comfortable body of lies Raymond lived in and created for others.

Raymond Locke, though, had run out of bandages.

In the face of what had befallen Tina Brackett, anything seemed permissible. She let everyone off the hook. Raymond did not have to manufacture excuses or justifications for the dubious taste and questionable ethics of the PR campaign they'd built around her. Tina Brackett sanctioned her own exploitation. Her suffering was pointless and arbitrary and unjustifiable. It mocked and leveled anything resembling a moral distinction.

Raymond turned his back on Tina Brackett and fled the room.

He was cutting across the fifth floor of the parking garage when a battered yellow 70's Chevy Nova swung up the ramp, momentarily catching him in its beams. His shadow stretched and ran, folding itself against the gray concrete on the far wall. Raymond stepped back as the car roared by. A portion of the tailpipe had broken loose, dragging and jumping along the floor in a stutter of sparks. The vanity plates on the Chevy read *SAYM 2 U*.

The passenger side fender was bent out at an angle and just missed catching Raymond's leg.

The Nova stopped. It began to back up.

When it was alongside Raymond, the passenger window came down, and Ken Brackett said, "I didn't recognize you. I thought you might be him." He swung the door open. Raymond hesitated, then got in.

The floor was covered in fast food bags and containers and crumpled balls of newspaper. The heater left the air sour and overcooked. Taped on the lip of the dashboard was a series of index cards with block printing. Something dangled on a thin chain from the rear-view mirror.

"Him?" Raymond said.

Ken pointed at the balled newspaper around Raymond's feet. "The guy who jumped and beat Luis Murano. It was in the papers. The uncle's restaurant is only a couple blocks from here. The guy who did it is still at large."

"That's my car over there," Raymond said.

Ken drove by and continued on up the ramp leading to the next floor.

Raymond leaned forward and studied the index card hanging over the glove compartment. NECESSITY IS THE MOTHER OF INVENTION, BUT TO ACT, YOU MUST ALWAYS ORPHAN YOURSELF. PAGE 138, BOOK TWO, THE GUIDE.

Next to it was a card reading NOTE TO SELF: REMEMBER TO MONITOR YOUR EXCULPATION RATIOS!!

Ken parked and turned toward Raymond. His eyes, mismatched, were red-rimmed, their corners tightened by the drawstrings of his squint.

"You saw her, right?" he said. "Tina. You just came from her room. I can tell."

Raymond nodded.

"Then you understand." Ken wrapped his hands around the steering wheel. "It's how the Leash works, the way it can get tangled so that there's nothing we can do except what we know, and then we have to act even though we don't always know what we do until we do it. Afterward, we have to live with what we did even if it doesn't fit what we thought we knew."

"I'm not sure I'm following." Raymond spaced out the words. "I'm guessing, Dr. Tolson Whormer, right? Remember, I don't have Book Two yet."

"It's like this. Are you close to your parents?" Ken ran his hands over the wheel. Outside, the lights on the stanchions of the parking garage were pale yellow smears.

Raymond hesitated, then said, "They've been dead for over thirty-six years now."

"Your son then," Ken said. "Would you do anything for him?"

The car windows had begun to fog. Ken's and Raymond's breath skeined on the glass.

"Anything?" Raymond said. "I don't know. I guess. Within reason."

"Don't bullshit me," Ken said, thumping the steering wheel. "*Within reason* has nothing to do with family or love." He nodded to himself. "Or for that matter, the Leash."

Or this conversation, Raymond thought. It was time to look for an out without worrying inordinately about the amount of grace accruing to it. He wanted to get home and take a long hot shower and wash off the smell of the day.

Ken leaned over the wheel and traced his initials in the condensation on the windshield.

"Know whose car this is?" he asked. "Three guesses." He mumbled something about travel magazines and a garage and the smell of aftershave lotion and a woman standing in a doorway.

"That's the thing about Home," Ken said. He drew a line through his initials with his index finger. "You're constantly having to recalibrate your Hexaemeronic Shadows and maintain the focus and clarity of the Duality Corridors."

Ken sat facing the windshield with his eyes closed. "She waved, Ray. He didn't even see her in the doorway, but I did, and she *waved*."

Ken had put them back in Wilkesboro and in the garage off the kitchen, sounding alternately angry and stunned as he talked about his parents, his mother coming from money and the a priori privileges of small town social standing, her father the mayor and owner of a series of lucrative stone quarries. Ken's father was the proverbial dark horse in the race for his mother's hand, a good-looking quiet man with an easy laugh and a modicum of ambition, content to follow the unspectacular trajectory of a civil service career in the post office, a man given to long silences which lengthened proportionately to the number of anniversaries he chalked up with his wife. For her, silence existed only as a pause for breath between the next round of invective and complaint over what life and her husband had delivered. Depending on whom he asked, Ken was a blessing or an accident.

His father had established the routine of sitting in the garage in the car for a half hour to an hour each evening. He kept a cache of travel magazines and discarded, undeliverable letters from the post office in the trunk and read them while sitting behind the wheel. Ken would often join him, perching on his father's lap, surrounded by the scent of his aftershave and cocooned in his silence.

Ken was nine, just touching ten, he told Raymond, when his father brought out the duct tape. Ken helped him stretch it around the windows and the frame of the garage door. Then they got in the car. His father slipped the key in the ignition and turned the engine over. He picked up one of his travel magazines and began reading. Ken steered. His father occasionally tapped the gas to keep the car from stalling out.

"That's when I saw her," Ken said. "She'd parted the curtains on the door leading into the kitchen and was watching us. My dad had left the garage light on. She could see the duct tape. The Nova was running. She knew what was going on, and what does she do? She smiles and waves. I didn't know any better. I waved back."

Ken paused, and Raymond added nothing to the silence. He'd been snagged by a reluctant empathy when Ken had served up yet another victimized slice of his life. The jumble of rage, grief, and despair that comprised Ken's personality, though, left Raymond on guard. He didn't want to accidentally say anything that would tip Ken in Walker Anderson's or Arthur Cavanaugh's direction.

After a while, Ken said, he'd begun complaining of a stomachache and feeling dizzy, but his father had simply patted him on the head and let him turn the pages of the magazine. Ken remembered looking at pictures of the Painted Desert and Petrified Forest in Arizona. He eventually closed his eyes and drifted off.

He wasn't sure how long he'd slept, but he was jolted awake by a laugh, which erupted from deep within his father's chest.

The car had run out of gas.

His father wouldn't quit laughing. It was a laugh Ken was to hear many times afterward over the years, right up to the afternoon when his father died of heart failure while he sat in his easy chair watching *The Price Is Right*.

"Do you see now what I mean, Ray?" Ken let go of the steering wheel and leaned toward Raymond. "This car. The duct tape. A father's laugh. Your mother waving. You get leashed. And then everything becomes a Hobson's choice. You can't get around it."

Ken paused, then said, "I don't have to tell you how important it is that you rechart your Neotenic Field and open the Neroian Window in the face of that. Otherwise, something like that could mess you up pretty bad later in life."

Raymond nodded, then reached for the door handle.

TWENTY-NINE

After leaving the hospital, Raymond drove home. He kissed his wife. He washed up and changed. He came back downstairs. He did not think about Eileen Connelly and the child she'd given up for adoption. He did not think about Arthur Cavanaugh and Lamar Ditell and the long string of personal vendettas between them. He did not think about ten year olds in a coma. He did not think about Ken Brackett and his hard-bad-and-no-luck life.

Instead, he read his son a story. He worked on tone and inflection, trying, as the pediatric therapists emphasized over and over, to give Andrew the opportunity to inhabit the words and to live for a while in his father's voice.

The story dealt with Rodent Kings and warring Rodent Clans. There were meadows and forests and brooks. There were feast days. There were swords and shields. There were stirring speeches. There were pitched battles. There were acts of valor. There were fallen comrades. There was the triumph of Good. There were the defeat and banishment of Evil. There was an ending filled with the blessings of Love and History.

Raymond sat on the floor with his back to the couch. Andrew sat two feet away with his legs tucked under him. He was wearing old jeans and a bright red sweater. He looked at Raymond and the book with his head canted at an angle toward the kitchen where Kate was finishing up fixing supper. Andrew's hair had yet to grow in from his self-inflicted haircut. His scalp was pale and pasty looking beneath the fuzzy brown shadow of a hairline.

Kate called them to supper. During the meal, they took turns asking Andrew what he wanted for Christmas. Andrew made low humming sounds and alternately counted the total number of bites that he took to finish the meal. Kate changed the subject and told Raymond she'd run into Frank Atwell at the post office earlier in the day and that they'd have to have him over for dinner soon. Raymond agreed. Kate added that Frank's color had not been good.

The evening unfolded along its own and familiar family lines. On one level, Raymond enjoyed the routine. It was a quiet comfort. On another, it quietly oppressed. Most of the time he could tell the difference between the two. Tonight, though, wasn't one of them.

It felt like his life was sitting in plain sight and simultaneously hiding from him.

After dinner, Raymond opened a bottle of red wine and poured a glass for Kate and himself. They headed for the living room where Andrew was playing with a wooden set of alphabet blocks. He was building a tower. He called out the letter twice each time he stacked a block.

At least it wasn't the Echolalia Syndrome. That number had always been the most distracting and unnerving of Andrew's autism. Raymond had never gotten used to it. Raymond would always fall into a slow-boil hybrid of frustration and panic whenever Andrew took and repeated Raymond's words, echoing him again and again, word for word, in a voice that was as dispassionate and precise as the one that gave directions for transactions on his ATM.

Andrew finished playing with the blocks and then put them one by one into a mesh bag. Kate and Raymond helped him get ready for bed. They came back downstairs and poured another glass of wine, and then they cleared the table and did the dishes, Raymond washing and Kate drying.

The evening continued to unfold along its own lines.

They brought the bottle of wine with them into the living room. They settled on the couch. Kate kicked off her shoes, and Raymond did the same. They dropped their feet on the coffee table that fronted the couch. The Christmas tree burned in parabolic strings of light. The east window Xeroxed its image.

Kate nestled closer to Raymond, and he dropped his arm over her shoulder. Her hair was loose and carried the faint seasonal smell of cinnamon. She shifted, moving closer, and he felt her breast move beneath her sweater.

Kate picked up the remote and pointed. As if on cue, *It's A Wonderful Life* appeared.

"I don't know how many times I've seen this," she said, "but it always feels like the first time."

She lifted her glass. "So, a little more wine, Maestro."

It had become the type of evening Raymond had been looking forward to, Kate next to him, the smell of her hair, a mix of long and short kisses, the house bright with the season.

"Coming up is one of my favorite parts," Kate said. She tipped back her glass. They watched Mary and George Bailey's love at first sight encounter at the graduation of George's brother, Harry. Their dance at the gym. Then the prank with the gym floor retracting to reveal the swimming pool beneath it. A prank that became a kind of baptism of luck and love.

Kate fell asleep right after Mary sang "Buffalo Gals" and right before news of George's father's stroke.

Raymond had another glass of wine. Kate slept deeply, warm and contoured to his left side. The remote was loosely cradled in her hand. Her right was resting on Raymond's thigh.

He kissed the top of his wife's head and continued to watch George Bailey's life unfold.

The longer Raymond watched, the more agitated and upset he became. He wanted to yell at George Bailey to run and get out of town and not look back. He still had dreams to chase and birth. A moment later, he wanted to grab hold of Bailey and counsel him to do exactly the opposite. He had the love of a good woman and a family, and each grounded him and made fundamental sense.

Everything, though, came down to *duty*.

At the heart of Bailey's life was duty. Duty that always and inevitably trumped dreams and desire.

Duty and love. Love and duty. Each throwing the other's shadow.

George Bailey waking up each day to find

everything in his life barreling to a point and a truth no one wanted to look at too closely. A truth that limned all other truths.

The point in your life when you realized you were worth more dead than alive.

Raymond looked at his sleeping wife. He listened to her breathe. He thought about their child asleep in his room above them. He thought of his wife delivering that child into the world, and he thought of that child earlier tonight with eyes averted and counting the number of bites in his meal.

He turned back to the television and watched George Bailey's salvation unfold.

It was the ultimate in wish fulfillment. You had to see it to believe it and believe it to see it.

Bailey's salvation became a perfectly orchestrated PR campaign for the cosmos and everyone's place in it.

Or almost everyone's.

The power and sweep of the cosmic PR campaign made it easy to overlook that.

Still, Raymond couldn't help but be caught up in its pull and the sweet promise in George Bailey's redemption, a reassuring summing up, every fear and doubt assuaged, your entire existence justified and validated. Faced with oblivion, you discovered you *mattered*. What could be sweeter or more satisfying than that? You got a pass, a formal stamp of approval from the universe. What else could anyone hope for?

Raymond watched Bailey finish touring the world that would have existed without him. Then he watched Bailey come to his senses, realize his mistake, and step back into the light and the warm and loving bosom of his family and neighbors.

Raymond took his own tour.

He sat in his living room with his sleeping wife next to him and followed the arc of his own love and duty. He imagined Oblivion. Then he revisited the world without him.

Without him in it, the world was just and beautiful.

Without him in it, the world made sense and turned clearly and smoothly on its axis.

Because without him in it, the world was not a safe harbor for all the miscreants, criminals, fools, deviants, and sinners he'd fixed things for. Morality was not a mirage. The social contract was not a punch line. Your word was not written in disappearing ink.

Because in a world without him in it, Justice was served, and everyone got what he or she deserved.

Raymond Locke and Public Domain were not there to help you get away with it.

Raymond Locke, though, was in the world, and in that world, when you were faced with a persistently unpleasant truth, all you had to do was change the channel.

And then lean over and kiss your sleeping wife.

THIRTY

The package came in just as Raymond was about to leave for the office. He signed for it on the run and then dropped it in his briefcase. With morning traffic, it took twenty-five minutes over snow-and-ice-scabbed streets to reach Korvaus Street and the red brick building in the middle of the 600 block.

The brickwork in the building's façade had not so much faded as become clouded. The rehab mania had yet to arrive, and Korvaus had a badly used post-war feel to it, the buildings on either side of the street tightly packed and strangers to anything resembling sandblasting or new paint.

The home office of WMMK was on the third floor, the studio on the fourth. WMMK had a nondescript and anemic playlist and a stable of utterly interchangeable easy-listening disc jockeys. The station had one primary moneymaking venue, a popular talk show segment called *We're Only Human* hosted by Tony Shephard. Improbably, Tony Shephard, the show, and its tag line - *Stories from the Heart of the Heartland and from the Heartland of the Heart* - had become a staple for listeners in the tri-state area.

Raymond had cultivated a long working relationship with Tony Shephard, *We're Only Human* a convenient vehicle for recycling the problems and personal lives and personalities of Public Domain's clients because Shephard had no real interest or inclination to explore issues. His on-air persona was congenial and mellow. He was the Heartland's pal and confidante, encouraging and supportive, his voice a pleasantly banked campfire around which people gathered to tell their stories.

Tony Shephard was chunky and bearded and balding, and Raymond found him in the station's lobby area. He told Raymond Lamar Ditell was on the fourth floor getting prepped, but Ken Brackett hadn't shown yet.

"Is there going to be a problem with that guy?" Shephard asked. "Ditell's a little antsy about going on-air with him."

"He'll be okay," Raymond said, purposely leaving the pronoun vague. After Ken's meltdown in the parking garage, Raymond wasn't so sure about Brackett, but Raymond had pulled a lot of strings to get the booking on *We're Only Human*, and fifty positive on-air minutes with Tony Shephard could do a lot for Lamar Ditell's case in the court of popular opinion.

"This Brackett guy," Shephard said and sneezed. He pulled out a wadded handkerchief and went at his nose. "He's not questing, is he?"

Raymond frowned. "What?"

"I had to fire the booking agent for the show," Shephard said. "He kept slipping these Fulfillment Magi onto the schedule. I suddenly find myself booked with gurus and spiritual guides and healers, everything from the curative powers of crystals coated in Vitamin E to someone who claimed to be a raccoon on Noah's Ark in a previous life to using zip codes as the key to unlocking Eleusinian Mysteries."

Shephard paused to sneeze again, then gently probed the lymph nodes in his neck. "I asked the booking agent what he thought he was doing, and you know what he said? 'It's 1986, and the whole country's starting to quest. People are tired of excess. They're bankrolling spiritual journeys."

Shephard shook his head. "I told him he could do his questing at the unemployment office. So, Raymond, please tell me with Brackett there will be no Break-on-through-to-the-Other-Side moments, okay?"

"Brackett's daughter is still critical, so he's been under a lot of stress. I'll talk to him, Tony, and I'll have him on-track by airtime. You can stick with what I scripted."

"I like what I'm hearing," Shephard said. "I'm figuring Brackett's good for a Profiles-in-Courage riff, quiet dignity in the face of adversity, trials and tribulations, test of faith, the audience thinking 'There but for the Grace of etc.', your basic uplift package."

Raymond nodded, then took off his jacket, draping it over his left arm and loosening his tie. "Why so hot in here?"

"It's an old building. The thermostats are basically decorative." Shephard sneezed again. "Now a cold. Shit. I'm going to score a couple aspirin from the receptionist, then go upstairs and hold Ditell's hand until Brackett shows."

Ten minutes later, Ken Brackett appeared. Raymond watched him walk quickly down the hall toward the sign-in desk. He wore his Happy Farms work clothes, a pair of slate-blue pants with matching shirt and black steel-toed shoes. He appeared to be talking to himself.

Raymond intercepted and steered Ken into an unused break room. Its layout did not encourage employees to kick back or linger. Two of the walls were dominated by banks of vending machines. The other two were a jumble of clippings, photos, notices, classifieds, and announcements three or four layers deep and reminded Raymond of the tattered billboard he passed on the way to work each morning. The break room's floor was covered in stained industrial green carpeting, and the building's malfunctioning thermostats left the air with the damp weight of a tropical greenhouse.

Ken dropped into a seat at the table. He pulled over a paper napkin and began doodling. His arm was crooked in the awkward writing posture of the left-handed. He stopped and shook the pen and then shook it again before tossing it in the direction of the trashcan.

Raymond opened his briefcase and slid over a new black pen. He went to the vending machines and bought two soft drinks and sat down next to Ken who had immediately gone back to doodling. Raymond noticed that the skin around the nail of Brackett's left thumb was wet, raw, and bleeding.

"Nothing more natural than to be a little nervous before air-time," Raymond said.

"Ken's not nervous," Ken said.

Raymond tried to remember if Brackett had

referred to himself in the third person before. "That's good," Raymond said finally. "It can happen to anyone though, even seasoned professionals. Nothing personal behind the remark, Ken."

Ken touched the tip of the pen to his index finger and squinted. "That's a funny way of putting it, Raymond. You're talking about me, right? What other way, but personally, would I take it?"

Raymond sat back, letting things rest for a moment. Brackett brought to mind the child, embedded in everyone's memory, who'd been the all too easy target of grade school malice and mayhem, the victim of any number of cruel pranks and playground mockery. He struck Raymond as someone who'd become used to looking over his shoulder and expecting the worst. Even sitting still, Ken Brackett radiated an air of furtive defiance underwritten by a couple decades of curdled resentments.

Ken chugged his soft drink and crumpled the can. As he was setting it down, he glanced over at Raymond's open briefcase.

"Why didn't you say anything?" he asked.

Raymond shifted in his seat. "I'm not following."

"Of course not," he said, "and you never will again. Not after you finish it."

Ken leaned over and lifted the package from Raymond's briefcase. "I saw the return address and knew right off." The package was wrapped in what looked like butcher paper.

"You understand what it means to get this on your *first* try?" Ken asked. "What that says about you?"

Raymond finally figured out what was in the

package.

"Can't believe it. I really can't. To get *Book Two* of *The Guide to Unleashing* on the first try." Ken shook his head. "What did you write in the petition to Dr. Whormer?"

"*I'm Ready.*"

"And then what?" Ken said.

"That's it," Raymond said. "Just *I'm Ready.*"

"I always suspected you were," Ken said. He placed his hand on the package and left it resting there like someone being sworn in at court.

"You're part of it now," Ken said. "Something larger than those who remain Leashed will or can ever know." He leaned closer and gave Raymond a smile full of cloudy fillings. "Another return address you might recognize," he said. "1600 Pennsylvania Avenue."

Raymond waited.

"Air Force One has been making regular runs to Vancouver to meet with Dr. Whormer since the inauguration," Ken said. "Of course, they always file two sets of flight plans as cover."

"You're not planning to bring this up with Tony Shephard, are you?"

Ken smiled and shook his head. "Always with the joke." He paused. "Reagan. Oliver North. Weinberger. All three met with Dr. Whormer. The Leashed will never understand Nicaragua or the fact that Iran was a necessary Proto-Nexal Ceiling."

"I suppose not," Raymond said.

"You know how far John Tower and his little Commission are going to get in their investigation of

Reagan and North and the others? I'll tell you," Ken said. "They'll gather all the facts and miss the truth. Tower and his pals will hand down some indictments, and the Leashed will go to sleep believing Justice has been served."

Ken sat back. He pointed at the package. "You want to know what Justice is? Chapter Five, page 78. Check it out."

Raymond opened the package, then *The Guide*, and found the chapter and page Ken mentioned.

"Three-quarters of the way down the page." Ken waited. "What's it say?"

Raymond cleared his throat. " 'Justice is a puppet in a Halloween mask.'"

"Let's call that a bingo," Ken said. He got up and went to look for a restroom.

Raymond squeezed the bridge of his nose, then rubbed his temples. The heat in the building and Dr. Whormer's wisdom left him headachy and slightly nauseated.

He slid over the napkin Ken had been doodling on. The sight was not reassuring. Inked in its center was a series of childish-looking stick figures stacked, limbs akimbo, in a tall conical pile. It resembled a funeral pyre awaiting the match.

Ken drifted back to the break room. Tony Shephard strode in a minute later carrying a yellow tablet. He stopped abruptly at the end of the table. "Almost air-time," he said. "Are we ready to lift the hearts and thaw those winterized tear ducts of the listeners? If anyone can do it, it'll be you, Trina, and Lamar Ditell. I was looking over my notes, and I choked up. Me, Tony Shephard, the guy who's heard all the stories this city has the breath to tell."

"Tina," Ken said. "My little girl's name is Tina, not *Trina*."

"Of course. Knew that. Misread my notes." Shephard glanced at Raymond and then began ticking off items on the tablet, a rough working outline of the interview, a list of highpoints and transitions. Raymond watched Ken to see if he picked up on the forced heartiness and enthusiasm in Shephard's voice.

Even before the elevator doors opened on the fourth floor, Raymond had begun cataloging all the ways things could go wrong. The chemistry of the day was off. It felt as if something was on the verge of imploding. There was the real but unfocused sense of things threatening to spin out of control or the disorienting smear of something suddenly arising on your peripheral vision.

The sound engineer set and adjusted the mikes for Lamar, Ken, and Tony Shephard, and then Raymond joined him in the sound booth. The engineer keyed the show's theme, and Tony Shephard, after apologizing for his cold, introduced his guests.

Everything Raymond expected to happen didn't. Neither Ken nor Lamar Ditell had a meltdown on-air. Ken made no mention of Tableau Injunctions or the Insult of Being or secret Air Force One junkets to Vancouver. He did not mention a father so beaten down that he couldn't work out the logistics of a successful suicide or a mother whom Brackett had once described as "a woman with Rita Hayworth hair, a voice like an acid bath, and the soul of a truck."

Lamar Ditell, for his part, did not get sidetracked into diatribes on what the union movement had done to the American character or the insidious effects of D.C. regulations on business and industry or on any other of the heated and overcompensated grievances that arose from the fact that he stood no taller than fifty-eight inches.

Raymond's worst fears never materialized. Improbably, Tony Shephard managed to broker a Kumbayah moment.

Lamar Ditell and Brackett flawlessly hit Shephard's cues, conjuring up the image package Raymond had built the campaign around: a decent man with a hard-luck life who stoically refused to complain and shouldered the burdens that self-same life had delivered and the compassionate CEO who had never lost sight of his humble Midwestern roots.

Raymond marveled at the on-air decency, empathy, and respect they were able to manufacture for each other. For a moment, he could almost believe it himself.

Ditell had to leave right after the interview. Raymond made some calls to the office, then asked Ken if he wanted to grab some lunch before returning to the hospital. All the way down in the elevator, Ken hummed an insistent, asthmatic tune that Raymond didn't recognize.

When they hit the lobby, Raymond heard shouting. Lots of it. He recognized one of the voices.

Lamar Ditell was dancing around and shaking his fist at an olive-skinned man in black jeans and a white band-collar shirt under a dark overcoat. A security guard was futilely trying to get between the two.

Most of Ditell's high-pitched verbal assault was scrambled by his outsized anger except for his calling the man a cocksucker and a son-of-a-bitching bastard over and over.

The man stepped away from the security guard and Ditell, and Raymond saw it was Luis Murano from the *Courier*. He turned and pointed in Raymond's and Ken's directions. His right hand was in a white cast that ran as high as the middle of his forearm.

"You're going to thank me, Mr. Brackett," Murano said. "I'm not going to let them get away with what they did to your daughter and what they're trying to do to her now. Both of you." Murano went on to say that he was not done with his investigation, not by a long shot.

"Those responsible will pay, Mr. Brackett. I'll expose them all," Murano said. "And that's not a threat. It's a guarantee."

Raymond glanced over at Ken. He'd begun clenching and unclenching his fists. He turned and looked over at Raymond, then Lamar Ditell and continued to hum the low, atonal tune he carried down with him in the elevator.

THIRTY-ONE

When it came to his son, the trick, Raymond believed, was to marshal and ration hope, to keep just enough alive to avoid outright despair and on the other hand, to corral the delusion that some miracle or miracle cure would suddenly manifest itself and ransom Andrew from his condition.

That's why he had tried to talk his wife out of taking Andrew Christmas shopping with them at the Vista Mall earlier in the afternoon. He was simply trying to be realistic. He said Andrew would find it too difficult to accommodate the size of the crowd, all the lights and noise, the seasonal three-ring circus.

Kate insisted. We're a family, she'd said, and it's Christmas.

But that meant the harness. If there was one thing Raymond hated, it was the goddamn harness and everything it carried with it.

Andrew didn't like to be touched. At best, he could manage it for very short periods, but even then, the circumstances were slippery or arbitrary. There was no telling what would or would not set him off.

The harness was made of soft leather and covered Andrew's torso like a flexible web. It had a metal snap and eye in the back of the lead.

Most of the time Andrew didn't seem to mind the harness. Raymond, though, hated it because people ended up staring at them as if Raymond were exhibiting and parading an exotic pet. Even worse were those who could barely hide or disguise their pity.

This afternoon, Kate, Raymond, and Andrew had barely made center court at the mall when they ran into the photo shoot with Santa, and Andrew began screaming. One of the elves came over with some kind words and a candy cane, and Andrew tried to bite his hand. Kate stepped in, but Andrew had continued to thrash and flail and scream.

They gave up and left. All the way home, Andrew rocked in the back seat and sang over and over in a dirge-like rhythm, *Flying Night, Holy Bite, Joy to the Whirl, Hard the Marble Angels Sink, Gory to the Newborn Wink.*

Back at home, Andrew spent the first twenty-five minutes in his bedroom hitting its west wall with the oversized red plastic bat. Then he came downstairs and announced he was hungry and wanted a hot dog.

"How about something else?" Kate had said. "You can't have hot dogs for lunch and supper every day."

"No," Andrew said. "Hot dogs."

"Andrew, please," Kate had said.

"Andrew, please," Andrew echoed.

"I'll call Makenzie," Raymond said, "and see if she's available this evening to babysit."

Kate waited a moment before nodding. She left for the kitchen. Raymond made the call, then checked the water level in the tree stand and plugged in the lights.

An hour and a half later, Kate and he made a second run at the Vista Mall. As they flashed under the mercury lights studding the beltway, Raymond glanced over at his wife. For the first time in a long while, she looked more tired than he felt.

"It'll be all right," he said, though what exactly that *it* referred to, Raymond could not say. The *it* felt as windblown and free-floating as one of the snowflakes sweeping toward the car's windshield.

Inside the mall everything was stitched in color and glowed, blinked, twinkled, and burned. Kate and Raymond agreed to meet in an hour and then went their separate ways to shop.

The PA system reminded everyone of the number of shopping days before Christmas, the voice pleasant and measured but still managing to convey an undercurrent of quiet threat, of doors about to close forever.

Raymond fingered the Christmas list in his coat pocket and let himself get pulled along by the crowd. The evening seemed to contain every fragile, tawdry, sweet, and extravagant promise of the season. Raymond ended up back near center court and the tiered fountain whose waters were dyed holiday colors by a strategically banked series of lights. Off to his left was a large crèche, the principals fixed in their traditional poses but at the same time heavily stylized, holding the sleek sexlessness of mannequins. Each of the faces was a smooth pink oval.

Opposite the crèche was Santa's stopover. A line of kids snaked up a wide curved ramp to an elevated platform and imposing throne-like chair holding a heavily padded, red-suited St. Nick. A small army of college students dressed in elf costumes kept the kids moving. Lining the ramp were oversized plastic candy canes, and at its top two signs, one reading NORTH POLE OR BUST!, the other, MEMORIES ARE MADE OF THIS.

Raymond took the escalator to the second floor, and for close to an hour, he moved among the thronging crowds, shortages of advertised sale items, the omnipresent Muzak, the overworked and surly salesclerks, the absolute barrage on the senses of every conceivable variation of display and decoration, the collision of colors, and the sheer presence and pull of so many *things*, Babel-like in proportion to the aisle and counter spaces in store after store.

He ended up buying Kate a pale blue mohair sweater and a string of pearls and matching earrings and an expensive bottle of perfume named Late Rain. For Andrew, an Etch-A-Sketch, Lego set, gyroscope, sketch pad and box of colored pencils, Nerf Blaster, and a jigsaw puzzle of a tiger in a thick green patch of jungle.

Along the way, he lost track of the time. He couldn't remember with any certainty when or where he was supposed to meet Kate. The harder he tried, the deeper his bewilderment and frustration.

He thought he spotted Kate outside Dresses Etc., and he hurried to join her, moving through the aisles, excusing himself as he tried to catch up, but when he did, it turned out the woman was not Kate and in fact did not resemble her at all.

He fled back to the mall concourse. He tried to remember what Kate had been wearing and couldn't. In the press of shoppers, he caught three variations of her perfume. He kept seeing the shade of her hair, its style.

He told himself he was overreacting, but that didn't do any good. A sense of something caving in under its own weight dogged him.

He kept looking for his wife.

Before taking the escalator, he stood at the balcony rail with his armload of packages and watched the movement on the first floor. He kept hoping to see Kate kicked loose from the churn of winter overcoats and jackets, mufflers and hats below.

He didn't spot her. He couldn't spot her.

He dropped the package with the gyroscope at his feet and only with difficulty managed to reclaim it without losing the others.

He moved again to the balcony railing. Off to his left two sets of escalators ferried people between floors. Below the handrail the glass panels were blistered in artificial snow and edged with stenciled red and green Christmas trees.

He checked his watch.

He looked for his wife.

People.

People everywhere.

But no Kate.

And Raymond cradling his packages and standing at the balcony rail with a burgeoning sense of loss.

The fact that it was irrational made no difference.

No Kate.

He couldn't, and then he could, imagine the life that was left from her absence.

A life and a world where she, like his parents in the air crash, simply disappeared, no rhyme or reason, a blunt erasure, irrevocable and absolute, and the immense wind tunnel roar of abandonment that you lived in afterwards.

He told himself to calm down. He was tired, that's all.

He needed to recapture his focus and concentration. He was letting things get away from him. Lately, it felt as if he were always a half step behind where he needed to be.

Raymond took the escalator to the first floor. He moved to center court. He stood next to the fountain, its basin filled with coins that carried the accumulated wishes for love, health, and fortune, and he waited for the crowd to part and Kate to once again appear.

THIRTY-TWO

Winter was the only season that was sufficient unto itself. Above Alamonte Avenue, the December sky set its own terms and refused to negotiate. It owned St. Carlton's skyline and the horizon.

Raymond took a window seat at the diner. He checked his watch and ordered coffee. The inside of the diner was crowded and uncomfortably warm, and the upper reaches of the windows were beginning to run with condensation. He closed his eyes for a moment and rubbed his temples. Behind him were the smell and sound of bacon hitting the grill.

Fifteen minutes and one coffee refill later, Raymond watched Larry Hahn and his six-nine frame start across Alamonte and get caught by the light, Larry, not surprisingly, hesitating and momentarily setting himself up as a future hood ornament on the yellow cab bearing down on him before he decided to sprint the rest of the way across.

Hahn tucked his briefcase under his arm, emptied the change in his pocket in the red Salvation Army bucket mounted on a tripod at the corner, received his blessing from the soldier ringing a bell, and headed for the diner.

He slid into the seat opposite Raymond and asked the waitress for a glass of water.

Raymond waited.

Larry looked out the window. At the television mounted on the wall above the cash register. At the diner's doorway. At the glass of water the waitress deposited before him.

"Over here," Raymond said. "My eyes. Why don't you try looking into them?"

"If I had something, I would have called." Hahn took a long drink of ice water.

"Would you, Larry? Or maybe you've just been playing the odds."

"On what?"

"On hiding from and escaping the blow-back if everything goes to hell with Happy Farms. On thinking I'd become stretched so thin and become so distracted that I'd forgotten our arrangement." Raymond leaned forward and tapped the tabletop. "I haven't forgotten. Remember, eyes and ears, Larry, that's what we agreed on."

Hahn lowered his head and swallowed. Raymond watched his Adam's apple jump. The waitress came up and refilled his coffee. Hahn waved off more water.

"I wish I could forget," he said. "You, the Bushel of Love Daycare case, those kids, everything."

"I didn't twist your arm, Larry," Raymond said. "It wasn't my wife eyeing the real estate in Birchfield Heights. You took the money."

"There are too many days," Hahn said, "when I don't want to live with myself."

"Welcome to 1986, Larry." Raymond tapped the tabletop again. "Now, to the point. Arthur Cavanaugh."

Hahn let out his breath. "Okay. A lot of closed

doors lately. More than usual. And I'm on the wrong side of them. Cavanaugh hasn't included me in any of the meets."

"Tell me who then."

"Walker Anderson. Pretty much every day, for the last week and a half," Hahn said. "Anderson stays anywhere from forty-five minutes to an hour."

Raymond understood the meetings, figuring Cavanaugh was helping his former protégé, the two of them brainstorming on ways to drive Ken Brackett out of Public Domain's arms and into Anderson's. If Anderson ended up representing Brackett, the settlement was potentially Fort-Knox-sized. Cavanaugh, for his part, could then enjoy watching Lamar Ditell get crushed, hopefully once and for all. If things also went Anderson's way, Cavanaugh could count on some sizeable campaign contributions for his next run at the Mayor's office.

The frequency and length of Anderson's meetings still bothered Raymond some. They seemed excessive right now.

Something else occurred to Raymond. "Did Eric Donner ever show up for one of the closed doors?"

"I don't know because I don't know who he is." Larry took another swallow of water.

Raymond described Donner, ending with the ponytail and the part-time mascara.

Hahn shook his head. "I never saw him around the office." He started scratching his cheek.

"Okay," Raymond said.

Hahn started to slide out of his seat and reached for his briefcase.

"*Okay* as in what else?" Raymond said. "I think there is."

"Jamal Bell," Hahn said. "That's the *Okay*."

Raymond tried to work out the math on that one, but he couldn't make it add up to anything approximating sense. Jamal Bell was another of Cavanaugh's crew. Bell, though, worked murders.

"Come on, Larry," he said. "What the hell's Jamal Bell doing meeting with Anderson and Cavanaugh?"

"I told you," Hahn said. "Closed doors."

"When did it start and how many times?"

"This week," Hahn said, then held up three fingers.

It was Raymond's turn to look out the window.

"If you're fucking with me here, Larry," he said finally, "you will regret it for a couple lifetimes. I promise."

A moment later, Raymond set a folded newspaper in the middle of the table. "Merry Christmas. Best to Susan and the girls." He slid out of this seat and left.

Raymond drove back to Public Domain. He was barely in his office ten minutes before Daniel Pierce knocked and stepped inside. Raymond dropped the mail he'd been sorting back on his desk. Pierce turned down a seat and moved to the window, then asked Raymond to fill him in on his meeting with Larry Hahn.

While he did, Raymond tried to remember how many times Daniel Pierce had come into his office instead of setting up the meeting in his own or the conference room.

One, he thought. When they'd been trying to cap

the Bushel of Love scandal.

"This Hahn, he has no idea why Jamal Bell is meeting with Anderson and Cavanaugh? Pierce asked.

"That's what he claims."

"You believe him?"

Raymond nodded yes. "Hahn's too afraid to lie," he added.

The afternoon light angling through the window left the four-block view of downtown smudged and Pierce's profile a pale silhouette.

"I don't like the tendency here," Pierce said. "Jamal Bell should not be on the radar." Pierce turned away from the window. "Maybe Bell and the meet have nothing to do with Happy Farms or Lamar Ditell."

"I'd feel better if Walker Anderson weren't part of the mix too," Raymond said. "He's spending a lot of time with Ken Brackett. That doesn't feel like a coincidence."

Pierce didn't say anything to that.

Raymond's office followed the basic design and décor of the rest of the floors at Public Domain. The furniture dark and heavy. The carpet a soft neutral beige-brown and overlaid in the working areas with textured Persian rugs. The original oak wainscoting and molding. Three strategically-placed mirrors, one behind Raymond's desk between the two bookshelves and another two flanking on the east and west walls so that when clients sat before Raymond at his desk, their images were on display from any direction, reinforcing either their vanity or their guilt, whichever they'd brought to Raymond and Public Domain to stroke or erase.

Daniel Pierce studied the series of photos lining the middle shelf of the case to the right of the desk. The first of Raymond's aunt and uncle on the steps of the shingled row house in Gary. Raymond and Kate's formal wedding shot next. One of their first apartments. Kate in her cap and gown when she'd graduated with her Master's in Nursing. One of the Victorian on Hermitage. Kate seven months pregnant. Raymond holding Andrew in the delivery room. One at Andrew's christening. Then at his first and second birthdays.

Raymond watched Pierce taking in the chronology of the photos and where it stopped and the fact that the shelf below had room for more.

"Takes a lot to make a family work, doesn't it, especially today," Pierce said.

"Things are all right at home, Daniel."

Pierce turned away from the photos. "I'm glad to hear that. Never had the knack for the home life myself. And I have four ex-wives and three kids and some hefty monthly alimony checks that'll testify to that."

Raymond repeated that things were all right at home.

Pierce nodded once.

"Some concerns," he said. He waited a moment before continuing. "Who'd you bring in?"

"What do you mean?"

"The Luis Murano incident," Pierce said. "I'm concerned about loose ends, anything that could be traced back to Public Domain."

Raymond frowned. "Are you talking about the attack in the parking lot? His hand in the car door?"

"That was some cloudy thinking and poor judgment on your part, Raymond. All you ended up doing was providing Murano with some extra motivation when he already had a surplus as it was." Pierce looked directly at Raymond. "There was no need to use the attack to send a message. Pure overkill there. You should have just contracted to hurt Murano enough to take him out of action for a while. Keep it nice and simple."

"I had nothing to do with the attack on Murano, Daniel. Nothing whatsoever."

Pierce brought up stress. Exhaustion. Cloudy thinking again.

Raymond accepted the verdict on the first two, but categorically denied the third.

"The fact remains that the attack was packaged as a message," Pierce said. "No money taken. The broken hand. The saint's medal gone and replaced by a slug."

"I agree," Raymond said. "But you're asking the wrong person. Maybe you should check in with Eric Donner."

"I already did," Pierce said. "He said I should check in with you."

"Maybe you should check in on Donner's drug use," Raymond said. "He's become too unpredictable and unreliable. Bringing him in on the Happy Farms account was a mistake. I don't care who his parents are or what their personal and professional connections can do for Public Domain."

Pierce waited a moment before responding.

Eric Donner had made no attempts to hide or dress up the fact that he'd landed the job at Public Domain because of his parents' influence. He, in fact, had always seemed perversely to revel in it. Donner's mother and father catered to a smorgasbord of vanities, addictions, and neuroses belonging to a large number of dysfunctional high-end denizens of Chicago's Gold Coast as well as their pals in New York, D.C., Atlanta, Phoenix, and L.A. His parents ran a private clinic north of Chicago fronting the Lake, his father specializing in cosmetic surgery and his mother in rehab and holistic therapy.

"There are certain considerations attached to those connections that can't be ignored or discounted at present," Pierce said.

"I'm telling you upfront," Raymond said, "Donner may end up costing us the Happy Farms account. Frank Atwell tried to warn me about Donner a couple times. I'm starting to understand why."

"Right now, Luis Murano is the problem," Pierce said. "And he needs to be solved. He's making a lot of unwelcome noise."

Pierce started across the office for the door.

"So what it comes down to," Raymond said, "is you're giving Eric Donner a free pass on this thing."

"Someone could say I'm doing the same for you, Raymond." Pierce left the room without breaking stride.

Raymond went back to his desk. He took out a tablet with lined paper and began sketching out the current dimensions of the problems Lamar Ditell and Happy Farms faced.

He worked through lunch and late into the afternoon. He filled page after page with notes that became distressingly convoluted. He searched for the single thread that when plucked would unravel everything. There always was one. Raymond had counted on that with each of his accounts. Happy Farms was no different. The thread was there. He just hadn't found it yet.

It was a matter of time. Time and the luck he'd always counted on.

Raymond turned in his chair and looked at the empty shelf below the photographs of Kate, Andrew, and him, and his chest seized when he thought of how absolutely lonely his son was, Andrew spinning in a private orbit, and Raymond wanted, right then, nothing more than to be able to fill that empty shelf with photos that celebrated all the mundane triumphs of an utterly ordinary boyhood, a life among others that was validated on the simplest terms.

He got up, leaving his desk for the office window where he looked out on a long winter sky slowly draining the day's light. The remaining clouds held the color and texture of smudged pencil marks.

Out of nowhere, a dark shape ran straight into his reflection, and without thinking, Raymond cried out and stepped back.

He moved back to the window.

On the ledge below was a dead bird. It was soft gray with a white underside and a pale green iridescent band around a neck that had become twisted at an odd angle from the impact. Raymond thought it might be a carrier or a homing pigeon. At least, it resembled one. He looked for a small tube on its leg, but with the soiled light, he couldn't say for sure whether it was there or not.

He went back to his notes. He searched for the thread among them he had not been able to locate earlier, but he was tired, heavily tired, and that slowed everything down. He tried to remember his last good night of sleep.

He ordered out coffee. It didn't touch his exhaustion.

He leaned back in his chair. He rubbed his eyes and closed them, telling himself a couple minutes, that's all.

Sleep ambushed him, and the dream, when it arrived, unnerved and then frightened him. It felt like he'd been dropped into deep water without knowing how to swim.

Because Raymond understood even while in the midst of the dream that something was wrong.

For starters, he very seldom remembered his dreams.

Second, it wasn't his dream.

The dream belonged to Ken Brackett. He had told Raymond about it at the hospital earlier in the week.

Raymond was dreaming the details exactly as Ken Brackett had recounted them. He wasn't sure whose dream that finally made it. All he knew was he didn't want it.

He kept telling himself to wake up.

It didn't work.

He was left dreaming Ken Brackett's dream, and in that dream, there was an immense newly harvested wheat field with a brush-cut of gold stubble, and it wasn't clear if the sun was coming up or going down, but the light remained soft and diffuse and the sky empty of clouds, but suddenly it was raining, raining dead birds, waves upon waves of them, falling through the pale light and massing in piles across the field.

There were piles of cardinals. There were piles of blue jays. Then piles of doves. Sparrows. Hawks. Owls. Grackles. Bluebirds. Robins. Canaries. Crows. The sky becoming an ornithological apocalypse.

The sky continued to swell with wave upon wave of birds, and those birds continued to fall in waves, and their fall was soundtracked in the dream by cries that broke in a long, shrill crescendo.

Then the sky went empty, and everything was still.

And Raymond was left in Ken Brackett's dream that right then held the same charged quiet that existed just before someone cleared his throat and spoke.

THIRTY-THREE

Southeast St. Carlton was a patchwork of blue-collar neighborhoods defined along fading ethnic and racial lines. Those lines had been originally established and resolutely reinforced when the city's steel mills, shipping, and manufacturing base were thriving during the 40's and 50's. By the 70's, those self-same lines had begun to smudge, and by the early 80's, they had completely blurred so that what had been the Hungarian Club on Maynard was now a Korean Martial Arts Center, the Irish bar on Jarrell was now across from a Mexican bodega, and the Greek diner on Spencer now was cheek to jowl with a Vietnamese grocery and an Indian restaurant.

What remained the same though were the houses. Blocks and blocks of one-story boxy GI-Bill specials with one of two alternating floor plans and asbestos siding. Blocks of shingled two-story houses with attached garages and small sloping front lawns fronting wide sidewalks and streets lined in old maples with tangled networks of limbs and branches in need of trimming.

The neighborhood reminded Raymond of the one he'd grown up in Gary. Any of the brown-shingled row houses could have stood in for his aunt and uncle's. He could have walked through any of them blindfolded. Or stopped and knocked on any door and found his uncle getting ready for second shift at U.S.

Steel, his aunt packing her husband's lunch, and a boy daydreaming upstairs at a second-story bedroom window.

Raymond parked curbside at 518 Garrison. He went up the shoveled and salted sidewalk to the front door and pressed the bell. He waited, then pressed the bell a second time. He knocked. He waited, then went through it all once again.

A petite woman in jeans and a bulky red sweater stepped out on the porch next door. She smiled, then said, "Luis isn't home."

Raymond pointed to the car in the driveway. "Isn't that his?"

Inez Murano, Luis's mother, looked younger than her file photo at Public Domain. She nodded, then said, "He walked to the gym. Ferelli's. It's two blocks down and then one south on Houston." She smiled again. "You just missed him."

Raymond thanked her and went back to his car. He sat behind the wheel for a moment and surveyed the neighborhood. It was early dusk, and the strings and clusters of Xmas lights bled into and across the surrounding yards swollen with new snow and dotted with waist-high plastic Santas and Virgin Marys. Most of Luis Murano's relatives lived within a four or five block radius of each other. Grandparents on both sides of the family. Aunts and uncles. Cousins and their spouses and offspring. Raymond had run background checks on them all, but had been surprised and disappointed that nothing of any real significance or weight fell out.

A handful of parking and speeding tickets. Some

penny-ante income tax moves. A few extra-marital affairs duly confessed to and forgiven by Church and spouses. A couple drunk and disorderlies. A pot bust. A little pony and sports betting action.

Nothing, finally, that went anywhere.

Raymond started his car.

Ferelli's, as it turned out, was not a Health Club. It was not a Fitness Center. It was not a Spa. And not a Strength and Weight Management Clinic.

Ferelli's was a gym.

It was mats, speed bags, jump ropes, free weights, and a boxing ring. It was fluorescent lights and the layered smells of sweat and liniment, and disinfectant. It was musty air and ancient metal lockers and SRO testosterone.

Raymond found Luis Murano sitting on a bench in the locker-room. He was wearing rubber flip-flops and a towel wrapped around his waist.

Raymond loosened his tie and started to introduce himself, but Murano held up his hand and said, "I know who you are."

A stocky middle-aged man in a faded green T-shirt and gray sweatpants brushed by Raymond and sat next to Murano. "I had to hunt down some rubber bands," he said. He had a pair of bushy sideburns a decade out of fashion and a nose that had been broken and now looked like the spine of an old used paperback.

He went into the pocket of his sweatpants and then unfolded the white plastic sleeve from a loaf of Wonder Bread. He shook the crumbs out and then said to Murano, "Give me your right."

Murano held the hand with the cast running to mid-forearm. The man wrapped it in the Wonder Bread sleeve and secured it with three rubber bands.

"Go with the dry today," he said.

He left the locker-room and was back almost immediately, handing Raymond two heavy white towels. He pointed to a locker. "You can use that one. Don't worry about a lock. Nobody'll bother your things." He paused, tilting his head, taking in Raymond and the suit, and added, "The dry will clean you out." He nodded in Murano's direction, turned, and left.

"That's Pete Ferelli, the owner," Murano said. "The gym's been in the family since WWII."

Raymond changed, wrapping one of the towels around his waist, and followed Luis Murano to a wooden door just off the entrance to the locker-room. Outside the door was a deep bucket filled three-quarters of the way with water and holding a large ladle. Murano picked up the bucket with his good hand, and Raymond followed him into the dry sauna.

The room was a closet-sized rectangle with wooden seats built into its opposite walls, a cement floor, and a heater with a basket of stones positioned at its top. The lighting was dim, and the air smelled of cedar and eucalyptus.

Raymond and Murano sat facing each other. Murano had the bucket resting between his feet, and he started ladling water onto the pile of stones. Within seconds, the air was a fierce wall of heat.

"I've been expecting you," Murano said. "This talk."

"I didn't have anything to do with your hand," Raymond said.

"I didn't say you did."

Shit. What was wrong with him? Raymond knew better than to give up an opening like that. He might as well have sent Murano an engraved invitation.

Murano ladled more water on the stones. The room ballooned in heat.

Raymond's pores opened, and he could smell his insides. He closed his eyes for a moment.

He opened them a moment later to Murano pointing the ladle at him. "I'm close, you know."

"The famous 'mystery witness'?"

"He's coming around," Murano said. "He's afraid of Lamar Ditell, what Ditell might do to some of his family and friends who also work at the Wilkesboro plant. It's taken some time to win his trust."

Raymond waited for two beats and asked, "What would it take to lose it?"

Murano poured another ladleful of water on the stones and sat back.

It was enough of an opening.

Raymond made his pitch. Murano listened without interrupting. It appeared he was not so different, after all, from the other journalists Raymond had worked with on other accounts. Under the right circumstances, their ethics took on a certain elasticity. *Supple*, one of them had put it. Raymond was irritated with himself for ever letting Eric Donner work on reining Murano in. He should have stepped in and done it himself before they hit the phase where "mystery witness" became a bargaining chip.

"A novel," Raymond said. "I never met a journalist who didn't claim he or she had at least one in them. All they needed was a little time and money to midwife it. I'm betting you're no different, Mr. Murano."

"So you're prepared," he said.

"Two book deal. Guaranteed. Hard and softcover. Hefty publicity budget. Author tour." Raymond paused, then ticked off three New York publishing houses. "Your choice. Door's open at each."

"I imagine it would be quite a thrill to see your work translated to the Big Screen."

"Not on the table at present," Raymond said, "but I imagine we could set a place for it down the road."

Murano leaned forward, one-handed the ladle, and poured more water. The stones hissed, and Raymond braced for the rolling wave of heat. Once again he got a whiff of what his sweat carried.

"The thing about a novel that's important to a lot of readers," Murano said, "is its setting. They like exotic locales, but without being on the ground, it's difficult to get all the details right. Verisimilitude's important."

"London, Paris, Venice, Athens, or the Islands," Raymond said. "Any of them work for inspiration and verisimilitude?"

Murano nodded slowly, considering each, and then made a show of furrowing his brow. "A novel, a really *good* novel, takes time though."

"I think you'll discover that any one of those three publishing houses would be willing to put up a sizeable advance for a really *good* novel," Raymond said, "one that would let a writer live comfortably for a year to a year and a half while he wrote that really good novel."

"It's definitely tempting, a prospect like that," Murano said.

Raymond impatiently waited for the *but*.

"Not sure I want to try my hand at a novel," Murano said. "Or that I'd be any good at it. I'm afraid I'll always be a journalist at heart." He looked down at his broken hand and adjusted the rubber bands holding the Wonder Bread bag covering it in place. "Given a choice, I'll take facts over verisimilitude any day."

"Okay, no fiction," Raymond said. "Marilyn Salgin then."

"I don't," Murano said, then stopped, puzzled.

"Marilyn Salgin," Raymond said again. "Nominated for an Oscar as Best Supporting Actress in *Secrets and Laments*. Won a Golden Globe for *The Thursday Motel*. Just finished the wrap on her latest, *The Empty Mirror*." Raymond paused. "Marilyn has led what is known in the business as a colorful life. She's ready to tell her story."

"Let me guess," Murano said. "No one's been assigned her biography yet."

Raymond smiled and nodded. "She's also between husbands right now, so you'd have to watch out for yourself. Marilyn has a soft spot for writers. Husbands two and four fell into that category."

"I can certainly see the appeal of a project like that, working so closely with a celebrity of Ms. Salgin's status, but I'm afraid that's just not me. I'm an investigative journalist and have always been partial to exposes." Murano leaned toward Raymond. "I just happen to believe people deserve truth of a little higher order than the one shared between the sheets by Ms. Salgin and any of her husbands and lovers, colorful as they all may be."

"What people deserve and what they want are not necessarily the same," Raymond said.

Murano picked up the ladle. "You're right. And I think Lamar Ditell is going to find that out very soon himself. Tell him and Happy Farms: No Sale."

The dry heat seared the insides of his nose and tightened his chest, and Raymond worked on evening his breathing. "I wish you'd reconsider the offer," he said finally.

"You mean the bribe," Murano said.

"*Offer. Bribe.*" Raymond held up his hands. "Five letters each. In the end, they come from the same alphabet."

"So does *Justice*," Murano said. "So does *Truth*."

"My point exactly." Raymond almost appended *Kid*. Then he remembered that he was not quite ten years older than Murano.

Murano ran his hand over his head, the thick black hair becoming darker and slick with sweat. He smiled.

"You showed up today, and you know what I thought?" He looked at his hand, then Raymond. "I thought you were going to tell me you were ready to step forward and cooperate with my investigation, that you'd finally hit your limits and couldn't continue working at Public Domain and for Happy Farms anymore." Murano paused and shook his head. "I thought you'd had an attack of conscience and wanted to make things right."

"You're one of them, aren't you? A true believer. Everything black and white. No room for doubt. Judge and jury in one. And no idea how deluded and dangerous you are."

"There's a little girl in a coma," Murano said. "She did nothing to deserve that."

"There's an earthquake in Chile too. A driver who's just gone left of center into oncoming traffic. A couple in a divorce lawyer's office. A radiologist looking at some bad news x-rays. A president who's a former actor and confuses breaking the law with playing secret agent. A dead-zone named Chernobyl. " Raymond sat back against the wall. "You can afford to burn with a self-righteous purpose and champion Truth and Justice because you can't admit just how terrifyingly little either of them has to do with anyone's life, including your own. The world's broken, my friend, and so are you, me, and everyone else in it."

"I can't accept that."

"Of course you can't," Raymond said. "You still think this is some two a.m. dorm room discussion."

"We're not talking about an isolated case of food poisoning here. There are larger ramifications. I told you I'm close. You can pass that on to Ditell."

Raymond stood up and took the ladle from Murano and emptied what was left in the bucket on the stones, and as the air began to burn, he turned and left the sauna.

THIRTY-FOUR

Sex in the morning had its own syntax, following in its sleepy fumbling the grammar of desire rather than the rhetoric of seduction, from bodies easing into a slow unfolding after the pull and tug of nightgowns and pajamas, of the shifts of sheets and blankets and the compacted smells of bodies each held, then the sudden presence of warm unencumbered flesh, and the long ache running under it in the pre-dawn light, the slow sleep-heavy kisses and his wife Kate reaching down, taking him in hand, guiding him, the welcoming warmth of her thighs, the slow churn of hips, the eventual orgasms that shredded their breaths, and the gradual return to sleep.

The disembodied noise awoke Raymond before the bedside alarm did.

Kate remained locked in sleep.

He turned back the covers and sat on the edge of the bed.

He listened.

He noticed the bedroom door was slightly open. A sliver of pale yellow light ran at an angle along its base.

The sound was soft and insistent, steady as a pulse or a slow rain.

Raymond slid to the floor. He got on his hands and knees. He looked under the bed. He waited for his eyes to adjust to the thin available light.

He discovered the source of the sounds.

It was his son's fingers on the buttons of the remote control for the television.

There among the haphazard shoes, dust clots, and boxes from the overflow of the closet shelves, Andrew lay flat on his back under the bed with the remote pointed at the middle of the mattress above him and his fingers rhythmically running across its buttons over and over again.

Raymond whispered his son's name. He asked him to put down the remote. Andrew ignored him, keeping his gaze and the remote pointed at the mattress above him, his fingers telegraphing repeated pattern on the remote's buttons.

Raymond watched his son's silhouette and continued whispering his name and asking him to stop.

After a while, his words disappeared into the sound of his son's fingers on the buttons.

He stopped speaking when Andrew swiveled his head in Raymond's direction. There was nothing he recognized in his son's eyes. For his part, right then, Raymond only had the compass points of guilt and despair and the truncated hope that he could still tell them apart.

Raymond got up off the floor. He walked to the bathroom and took a shower. Andrew was gone by the time he finished, the bedroom door shut tight again. Kate remained wrapped in post-coital sleep.

Raymond dressed in the dark.

The incident with Andrew had the feel of a math problem with unwieldy fractions that had no common denominator. Raymond had no idea how Andrew had gotten into the bedroom without Kate or he noticing or how long Andrew had lain under the bed or even at what point Raymond had exactly become aware of the sound of his son's fingers on the remote.

There was a nest of messages for him at the office. Most were from Gerald White, the Head of Security at Mercy General, and the messages pointed to one thing: Raymond needed to get over there as soon as possible.

Twenty-five minutes later, Raymond found Gerald White in the waiting room at the south end of the corridor leading to the ICU. There were three other people in the room, all with the shell-shocked postures and undifferentiated gazes of those closing out a long vigil.

Raymond and White moved across the room to the curved bank of floor-to-ceiling windows overlooking the downtown skyline of St. Carlton and a low sky spitting snow.

"It started off bad and only got worse," Gerald White said.

Tina Brackett's heart had stopped twice in close succession during the night, the first time for fourteen seconds, the second for eighteen. A little over an hour after Dr. Schonefeld, the attending physician, got Tina stabilized, Lamar Ditell showed up at the ICU.

"No idea who put the call in," White said. "Might have been Dr. Schonefeld himself. Any case, it was someone on Ditell's nickel."

According to White, a lot of what happened next shouldn't have. "Two things," he said. "A fire alarm going off near the X-ray Department and a shift change. One distraction too many. That's how they got by my people."

In addition to Lamar Ditell, *they* were Luis Murano from the *Courier* and Eric Donner and Ditell's Amazonian wife, Carly Waite aka *U.*

There had been a lot of shouting and cross-referenced threats. A couple of overturned chairs. Some spilled coffee. White eventually cleared the waiting area outside the ICU. None of the principals, however, would admit to throwing the literal or figurative first punch.

"No idea what set any of it off?" Raymond asked.

White shook his head. "Best I could do was contain it. Sorry." He shook his head again when Raymond asked about Ken Brackett. "Holed up in the room with his daughter. Refuses to speak with anyone."

Raymond ducked down to the hospital cafeteria where he bought a large take-out coffee and five glazed doughnuts, hoping they'd be enough to get through the door of Tina Brackett's room and an opening shot at placating Ken.

When he got back to the sixth floor and the ICU, Raymond detoured into the restroom and found Eric Donner at the sink holding his right hand under a stream of water.

"Somebody bit me," Donner said.

He probed the flanged web of skin between thumb and index finger. "Based on the bite pattern, I'd put my money on Brackett." He went back to studying his hand. "Ever get a look at that mouth of his? All those rat teeth and cloudy fillings."

The fluorescent lighting running along the top of the large rectangular mirror backing the row of sinks leached the color from Donner's face. Donner's pupils were staging their own disappearing-act, and he kept running the back of his hand across his forehead.

"You know what a Blue Tag is?" Donner asked.

It sounded vaguely familiar, but Raymond finally shook his head no.

"I don't either, but that's what Murano kept saying. The thing is, Lamar Ditell and Murano were already into it heavy when *U* and I got to the ICU. Ditell kept shoving Murano and saying Brackett and his daughter were off limits. I don't know where security was. Brackett must have heard the shouting and came out to see what was going on."

According to Donner, Luis Murano kept brandishing a miniature tape recorder and firing off questions, working from the inventory of charges against Happy Farms and Lamar Ditell he'd been maintaining since the outbreak occurred. Doctored, misplaced, or shredded records. Irregularities in the inspection process. Alleged payoffs to USDA officials. Violations of health and safety regulations in the processing plants and growout farms. A clear and definite pattern of food poisoning outbreaks over the last three to four years that had originally gone undetected because they were small-scale and therefore off everyone's radar.

Murano pushed things into the red zone when he brought up accusations that Ken Brackett had been bought off for an undisclosed sum by Ditell and

Happy Farms and then segued that into another overlapping pattern of manipulation and intimidation of line workers at the Happy Farms plants by management, acting directly on Ditell's orders.

"Did Ditell take the first swing?"

Donner shrugged. "All I know is things fell completely apart after Murano brought up the infamous mystery witness again. I don't think Brackett much appreciated Murano's claim that he'd let himself become Ditell's stooge, bought off at bargain basement prices."

"You never told me what you were doing at the ICU in the first place."

Donner glanced at the line of closed stalls to his right. "Returning *U* to Lamar Ditell. I'd brokered a reconciliation. The three of us were supposed to go out for a celebratory brunch at Edward's on Ninth afterwards. I already had a photo shoot booked."

Lamar and *U* had been approaching critical mass for a while now, and *U* had announced she was planning to make good on her threat to leave Ditell again. There'd been rumors too that she was shopping a behind-the-scenes story to the tabloids on the manufactured reunion that Raymond had engineered and its current malfunctioning.

"And you'd convinced her to stay with Ditell?" Raymond asked. "How?"

"Hey with the right combo of pharmaceuticals, I could achieve world peace."

A laugh, off to Raymond's right, and the fourth stall door slowly opened and *U* stumbled out, dressed and moving across the room like a disheveled parody of herself in the "Addicted To Love" video.

She stopped next to Eric at the sink and gave a short whistle-stop tug on his ponytail and stage-whispered, "Eric, Angel, I can't find my panties. Any idea where they are? I'm experiencing a distinct draft."

U then turned to the mirror and began working on her make-up, pursing her lips and experimenting with different shades of lipstick, most of them on the dark end of the spectrum. She eventually held up a tube tipped in a glossy indigo, then reached over and turned Donner's face toward hers and ran the color over his lips until they were fully covered. She stepped back a little unsteadily to survey her work.

"Give Mom a kiss," she said.

THIRTY-FIVE

The doughnuts worked.

Five glazed got Raymond into Tina Brackett's room, but once there, Raymond wished he'd rethought the move and waited until later. Ken took the bag of doughnuts and left Raymond with the coffee, then moved back to the chair he'd pulled next to Tina's bed. The television was on, but the volume turned so low that the voices were reduced to pure sound. The window blinds were drawn, and the remaining light in the room was low and dim, no different from the heavy sky Raymond had driven under earlier. The room had a slightly burnt smell that Raymond could not trace back to anything in particular. It reminded him of a set of brakes going bad.

"Two times," Ken said.

He looked down at the bag of doughnuts in his lap. "Thirty-eight seconds total. How many and what, that's what you think about." He lifted his head and looked at Raymond. "How many brain cells die in thirty-eight seconds and what they carried that's gone?" Brackett paused again. "Of course, if you're in a coma, it's hard to get an answer for either."

"You need to remember Dr. Schonenfeld is a good man, top of his field," Raymond said. "Tina's in good hands."

Brackett kept his gaze on the white bag of

doughnuts and the Rorschach-blot grease stains darkening its sides. Tina lay off to Brackett's right in the dim light, and something about the scene triggered a left-field memory of a college art history class and a painting, but Raymond could not remember exactly which one, just the deepening sense of dread its lines and colors had evoked in him at the time.

"You're telling me Tina's in good hands," Ken said without looking up. "But what I have on mine isn't *good*. It's *Time*. That's what I have, time on my hands, and what you can't spend, you end up killing, so finally time on your hands is really not different from blood on your hands, but it never washes off, never." Ken paused and glanced at Tina. "Chapter Five, page thirty-seven of Dr. Whormer's *Guide*: 'Time, is, was, and always will be the first crime and Eden the original crime scene.'" Ken nodded. "You think about it, and you'll see it's the basis of every Aglossiatic Concourse you pass through in your lifetime."

Ken was wearing the same clothes as the last time Raymond had seen him. He needed a shave. His voice sounded like a late night disc jockey's at the far end of the dial.

Raymond held out the cup of coffee, but Ken waved it off. "I'm already awake. You drink it."

Ken opened the bag, took out three glazed doughnuts, and stacked them on top of each other, positioning them so that he had something approximating a sandwich. He squeezed, crushing and compacting them, and finished them off in less than a half-dozen bites. The remaining glaze ringing his mouth resembled drying glue.

"Two times," Ken repeated. "I feel just like I did with the cigar box. Not with finding it. I mean later when I figured things out."

Ken took the fourth doughnut out of the white bag. He pointed over Raymond's shoulder and waited until Raymond had turned in that direction too and run into Oliver North being interviewed in a televised news special.

The volume was too low for Raymond or Ken to make out what North was saying. They watched his lips move, and Raymond was left with the unsettling feeling that North was speaking from a place beyond words, that behind the face that North wore with its deceptively bland All-American mix of arrogance and deference, he was speaking a private language, one that had little to do with the world most people walked around on.

Ken continued to point at the television with the hand holding the doughnut. "Everybody's divided. Some call North a traitor, some a hero, but they're all wrong. He's the *NMU*."

Ken stopped and tilted his head, studying Raymond. "I thought you said you had read Book Two of *The Guide*."

"Not read. Reading." Raymond hoped his features had been able to bypass the lie and toss together a convincing facsimile of a sincere expression. "With Tolson Whormer, there's a lot to take in. I'm taking my time, working slowly through what he has to say."

Ken took a large bite from the doughnut and nodded. "I hear you, Raymond. You try to hurry through Books One and Two and overreach, you can end up missing or blurring some fundamental distinctions. I don't need to tell someone like you the problems that arise from not being able to keep the difference between a Blastorporal and a Blastular Panel straight. That's a train wreck waiting to happen."

Ken finished the doughnut and immediately went after the last one. "The *New Man Unleashed*," he said. "You don't get to be a *NMU* by cutting corners." He wadded the white bag and dropped it on the floor. "Forget *Hero*. Forget *Traitor*. He's beyond labels. Dr. Whormer makes that clear. 'The *New Man Unleashed* will have no center because he *is* the center: Chapter Five, page 63.'"

"What does Oliver North have to do with the cigar box you were talking about?"

Brackett picked up his daughter's hand, holding it in front of him in the same way he had the doughnut. "Nothing at first glance. But once you understand that Justiciary Threads nine times out of ten will lead you to an Impanation Reversal, you're on the way to a DM. or Defining Moment, which in turn is a doorway to your true Destiny."

Raymond mentally flipped a coin. To err on the side of generosity and empathy, he figured if anyone sat long enough in a darkened hospital room next to his comatose child, they would after a while start talking about and believing in Impanation Reversals and Blastoporal Panels and their relation to the development and destiny of the New Man Unleashed.

On the other hand, batshit crazy was batshit

crazy, and right then, all Raymond wanted to do was get out of that room and away from Ken Brackett and the nest of resentments, grievances, grudges, insults, indignities, and affronts that Ken called his life.

An opening, that's what Raymond needed to make a clean exit, but before one appeared, Ken had begun talking about the cigar box again.

"A Mother, that's what we're talking about here," Ken said, "but you mention my name, any time, and you know what she brings up? I'll tell you. *Disfigurement*. She never forgave me because she had to have a Caesarian. I never asked to come into the world, but it's my fault she's *scarred*. She never let me forget that."

According to Ken, the Caesarian paved the way some twenty-nine years later to his finding the cigar box on the top shelf of his parents' bedroom closet. At the time, his father had been dead less than six months, and his mother wanted Ken to clean out the closet and pack up his father's things. Ken was working on the line at Happy Farms, Tina was about to start kindergarten, and Ken's wife Leah had yet to die in the fire that would destroy their house on 1313 Sandstone Lane.

"Cleaning out a closet," Ken said. "Packing things up. Something simple."

Ken found the cigar box partially covered by a hat he didn't remember his father ever wearing. Inside the box was the unwound watch his father had been given for twenty years of service at the post office, and underneath it was a letter addressed to Ken dated eight months earlier. In it, his father explained he'd decided to give suicide another try but had not yet determined how or when, something Ken would know by the time he found the letter.

"He was still working on the details when he had the heart attack," Ken said, "and died in front of *The Price Is Right*."

The rest of the letter was a long apology to Ken's mother, the gist of it being a summary of his father's shortcomings and his abiding regret that he'd never been able to give Ken's mother what she deserved. He concluded by saying he was counting on Ken to make up for that. No, more than counting on. His father made it his formal last request.

Which Ken went on to honor.

And continued to honor while his own life followed its own slow implosion. Money problems. Marital tensions. The grind of line work at Happy Farms. The house fire. Leah's death. The adjustments to single parenting. Moving back into his childhood home. Ken honoring his father's last request through all of it, Ken putting up with a mother whose personality had all the charm of barbed wire, Ken putting up with her neediness and her increasingly strident demands, Ken putting up with it all right up until the point where his mother had two strokes in quick succession that robbed her of coherent speech and over half of her muscle control and Ken could then dump her into a nursing home and hide behind short, obligatory weekly visits.

Except, in this case, last requests became synonymous with last laughs.

Ken's mother's.

"It was the *d*'s, *n*'s, and *t*'s that finally tipped me," Ken said. "I took a sample, this old To Do list she'd put up on the refrigerator, to this guy I went to high school with who worked for the State Police lab and did handwriting analysis, and he confirmed it."

His father had not written the note that ended up in the cigar box, Ken said. His mother had.

Raymond didn't want to run down the full implications of that one. The obvious was monstrous enough.

"I did everything everybody expected of me my whole life," Ken said. "Everything I was supposed to. What say you draw a line under it and add it up and see where and what that's got me?" Ken paused and picked up his daughter's hand again. "You ever add up your life, Raymond?"

One of the ICU nurses stepped into the room. "I'm here to check Tina's vitals. I'm afraid I'll also have to ask you, Mr. Brackett, to lower your voice some. Even with the door closed, we can hear you at the nurses' station. Your daughter needs her rest."

"Rest? She's in a fucking coma, lady."

"Language, Mr. Brackett." She moved to the other side of the bed and flipped through Tina's chart. "It's been documented that often while even in a coma, patients can hear what's being said around them."

"Let me ask you something," Ken said. "Anyone ever tell you that you look like Kelli McGinnis, you know, in *Top Gun*?"

She looked over at Ken and smiled and stood a little straighter. "Actually, no."

"Good," Ken said. "Because you don't. Anybody

does, you'll know they're lying."

Ken waited until the nurse left before turning to Raymond and asking him once again if he'd ever added up his life.

"I don't know," Raymond said finally. "I'm probably like most people when it comes to things like that. Maybe a little, once in a while, I do."

"Earlier you told me Tina was in good hands," Ken said. "What about me? Would you say I'm in good hands?"

"I guess it would depend on how you define 'good.'"

Ken laughed and shook his head. "Is that what you guess, Raymond? Something like that? That's the best you can do? Dr. Whormer says, 'To Define is to always and inevitably leash and be leashed.'"

Raymond looked down at the floor for a moment, then back at Ken. "Lamar Ditell is trying to do right by you and Tina. The compensatory package he's put together is very fair."

"What say we take a stab at defining 'fair,' Raymond?"

"I know you've been talking to Walker Anderson. I know Walker, and I'll tell you upfront: be careful of any good faith gestures on his part." Raymond waited a beat, then added, "We both know what Dr. Whormer has to say about them." Actually, Raymond had no idea in hell but figured Ken would go on and provide the usual Whormer punch line.

"'A Good Faith Gesture is the Wet Dream of the Impotent.' Chapter Four, page 35, *Book Two*." Ken looked over at Tina, then back at Raymond. "Walker

Anderson told me you call your clients puppets."

Ken waited a moment before adding, "Good hands or not, sooner or later, you're called to your pain and the necessity of rescuing grievance from grief."

Raymond saw it once more. Ken Brackett needed hostages. You would always need hostages if your life held a mother who forged last requests from suicidal fathers, if it held a wife who died in a house fire, if it held lawyers who cheated you after those losses, if it held a job that robbed you of whatever dignity you could lay claim to, and if it held a ten year old child whose heart had stopped two times in the middle of the night.

Raymond saw something else.

The low light. Ken's posture as he leaned close to Tina with her head turned on the pillow, her unearthly pale skin and frail shoulders and thin hair.

Raymond saw the painting from his college art history class in his mind's eye. Munch. Edvard Munch. *The Sick Child.* The child in bed and looking over the top of the bent head of the person next to her, looking toward an indeterminate black shape, something like a curtain, filling part of the far wall. Raymond remembered the professor pointing out that the child and the other figure were holding hands and that Munch had painted them without fingers, one set of hands disappearing into the other in the face of all that was inconsolable.

THIRTY-SIX

A muffled concussion that reminded Raymond Locke of an abruptly slammed door or a fastball finding the heart of a catcher's mitt, then a moment later, the rear of the car dipping and starting to swing to the left, Raymond readjusting his hold on the steering wheel and trying to compensate for the drift and the day's quota of black ice, and it was due as much to blind luck as his driving skills that the car followed its long slide into the guardrail and stopped at the top of the curve on the I-494 Beltway that overlooked northeast St. Carlton.

One glance in the side-mirror told him how far gone the left rear tire was. He got out and tied his handkerchief to the radio antenna and got back in the care and set the flashers. Then he waited for a State Trooper or Good Samaritan.

Across from I-494's four lanes was the abandoned billboard that greeted him each morning on his commute. It towered on pylons above the warehouse district, and from where Raymond sat, the billboard looked as if it had broken free and was floating in the gray afternoon light.

Raymond had no idea how old the billboard was or how many layers of ads covered it, but lake-effect weather and the wind-driven day whipped, lifted, tore, and peeled endlessly at the layers of tattered images and shredded slogans.

A hamburger, a baby's foot, a blue door, a wing of a plane, an apple, a dollar sign, and an open mouth. All surrounded by *I 's l r e. No 's he t m . Bu l Y ur Dr ms. Ev y o y R d s!*

A shift in the speed of the wind and the hamburger became a man's head, the baby foot a keychain and keys, the door staying a blue door, the wing becoming the roofline of a house, the apple a swim-suited breast, the dollar sign becoming more dollar signs, and the mouth remaining open.

The lettering in the slogans continued to jump and blur in an unruly and mismanaged alphabet.

Flux. Fragments. Flutter and pulse. One becoming another.

It was as if a small rectangle of sky had torn open, accidentally revealing, like a parted curtain, the backstage machinery of the universe.

Raymond looked away, dropping his hands back on the steering wheel. He checked the rear-view mirror.

He counted his breaths.

It was irrational, he knew, but *there*, the same feeling he'd had this morning when he'd looked under the bed and discovered Andrew holding the remote control and the same feeling he'd had in the ICU while he stood in the dim hospital light in front of Ken Brackett and his daughter, the sense that things were somehow connected in a way beyond sense itself. That perception, though, yielded no comfort or enlightenment. It denied all access. It simply was.

One becoming another becoming something else.

Over and over again.

Raymond counted his breaths. The traffic streamed by. It took a while, but eventually blue and white lights flashed in his rear-view mirror.

THIRTY-SEVEN

While Kate reheated supper leftovers, Raymond hunted down a corkscrew and opened a bottle of red wine. The furnace rumbled and stuttered. Andrew kept walking in and out of the kitchen to a Pavlovian soundtrack only he heard.

"When'd you put this up?" Raymond pointed to a note posted on the face of the refrigerator next to the holiday schedule for Andrew's pediatric therapist and a take-out menu for a new Thai restaurant on Coldwater Avenue. The note was a reminder for Raymond to return Frank Atwell's call.

"Three days ago," Kate said. "I thought you'd seen it."

"Frank say what he wanted?"

"I think just to talk. He sounded kind of low."

"Probably the holidays. He misses Judy."

"I told him you'd call back." Kate half-turned from the stove. "You know that's the third time it's happened in the last two weeks, me putting up a note about Frank."

Raymond set out plates and silverware. Kate's cooking had always been blunt and utilitarian. Her mother had been alternately an indifferent or distracted teacher in the kitchen, and after Kate and he were married, the stress and pressures of studying for the Masters in Nursing, then a difficult pregnancy followed by Andrew's eventual diagnosis and the coping and adjustments it required coupled with the demands of Raymond's job at Public Domain left the menu around the Locke household close to that of most Midwestern Rotary Club luncheons. Tonight, supper was a pink slab of ham, instant mashed potatoes, canned green beans, and iced tea, dessert a slice of thawed lemon meringue pie.

Raymond took the plates into the dining room, Kate bringing along two glasses and the bottle of wine. Raymond worked his way through most of the meal, but it was only after the second glass of wine that he began to get out from under the unease that had followed him home after the flat tire on the Beltway.

He tilted his head and looked through the archway separating the dining room from living room. "Tree looks nice," he said.

"I had to take off all the strings of white lights," Kate said. "Or at least the ones that blinked. They upset Andrew."

Christmas had always been a difficult time for Andrew. The decorations and ornaments required a delicate balancing act. Kate kept adjusting their number and type because it was difficult to predict their effect on Andrew. He might be supremely indifferent to them or delighted or become highly agitated or shut himself down and withdraw completely. Anything was possible.

"He's okay with the star this year?" Raymond asked.

Kate nodded. "I'm not sure about the crèche though."

"Well, the tree looks nice," Raymond said. He

poured another glass of wine. Kate waved away the offer for hers.

Andrew stutter-stepped into the dining room, moving his arms in an oddly stylized manner. Every so often, he struck and held a studied pose and then moved on, repeating the arm movements.

"Walk Like A Remission," he said, his voice empty of inflection.

"*Egyptian.*" Kate said. "Walk Like An Egyptian. Not Remission, honey."

"Not Remission, honey," Andrew said. "I'm walking like a not Remission honey."

"Egyptian," Kate said.

"What?" Raymond said. "What goes here?"

Kate got up and started following Andrew around the table, imitating him, jutting her arms in a *Z*. They were a mother and son pair of moving hieroglyphics.

"What Egyptian?" Raymond said.

"Andrew, your father needs to watch more television." She laughed and continued to follow Andrew around the table. "Andrew, what do we want?"

"I want my MTV. I want my MTV. Money for Nothing and Walk Like A Remission." Andrew's voice moved at half-speed and flattened very syllable.

After a couple more circuits of the table, Kate plopped down in her chair. She smoothed back her hair with both hands. "I'll have that second glass of wine now."

Andrew moved into the living room, and a moment later, the television came on, its volume spiking.

"I meant to ask," Kate said, "about the remote. I looked for it all morning while I was cleaning and couldn't find it. Have you seen it?"

"I'm sure it will turn up."

The television volume jumped again, and Raymond heard the commercial for and the all-too familiar lead-in for *Nightshade Theatre*: a long scream, a guttural howl, and the gothic organ riffs, then Gary Ghoulmaster intoning, 'Live from the Grave, it's the Ghoulmaster bringing you the *Best of Nightshade Theatre*. Tonight's feature is a Ghoulmaster favorite. *Hell's Elevator*."

In his more mundane incarnation, the Ghoulmaster, aka Paul Crosley, was currently in the process of drying out at the Nu-Day Clinic, so Channel 5 had been recycling old shows and calling them the "Best of" as a holding action until Crosley was ready to climb back into his casket. Paul Crosley had drunk his way through most of the opportunities, career and otherwise, his life had held, and he owed his continued existence as the Ghoulmaster because the show had developed an improbable cult status among kids and among those in the kitsch appreciation and arrested development communities. Raymond had been getting Crosley out of alcohol-fueled jams for the last five years, something made a little easier than it should have been by the fact that none of the Ghoulmaster's audience and fans had ever seen him out of costume or knew his real name.

Kate took a sip of wine, then said, "I talked to my father this morning."

No, Raymond thought, you *listened* to your father.

274

Leonard Simco was not big on two-way conversations. Any conversation with Kate's father was a camouflaged monologue. The listener's job was to agree with or to what Leonard Simco said.

"Holiday plans," Kate said. "He was wondering when we were going to visit."

"I thought you'd told him it would be after Christmas."

"He meant exactly when," Kate said. "A specific date. They have to make their own holiday plans too, you know."

Raymond and Leonard Simco had never gotten along. At best, they barely managed a fragile détente and that built only on the love each had for Kate. Her father had made it plain from the start that he thought Kate could have done much better than Raymond in the marriage department, and Raymond, for his part, had made it clear that Leonard was not going to micromanage Raymond's and Kate's marriage as if it were a branch of the insurance empire Leonard oversaw from Toledo.

Raymond had used some of his Public Domain connections to run a background check on the Insurance King of Toledo, and one of his biggest life-disappointments was benchmarked when the check came back clean. Leonard Simco was guilty of nothing more than being an inveterate bore and a terminally flaming asshole.

Leonard had pulled Raymond aside at Andrew's fifth birthday party after Andrew became over-stimulated and trashed the backyard table holding his presents and cake before anyone could stop him.

Leonard had pointed one of his ever-present cigars at Raymond and said, "I had a couple people research that autism thing, and the kid didn't get it from the Simcos or my wife's family. There's nothing like that on our side of the fence."

Raymond's first impulse had been to hit Leonard, but when he finally settled on threatening to tell Kate what her loving father had said, Leonard had laughed at Raymond and said, "Go ahead, my friend. Tell her. See who she believes when I tell her I never said anything like that."

"Kate loves me," Raymond said.

Leonard laughed again. "Tell her then. See what happens. I'm betting on a kill-the-messenger scenario."

Raymond dropped it.

Tonight, Kate sat back from the table and started listing dates for the visit. "Dad said any of those would work."

"Pick one that's good for you and Andrew."

"There are three of us in the family, Raymond."

"I can count, Kate. All I'm saying is I might have to join you two later."

Kate closed her eyes for a moment. "It can't all be about the job, Raymond. It's Christmas, after all."

"Things are a little more complicated than they were a couple days ago." Raymond checked the wine bottle and refilled his glass. "Tina Brackett's heart stopped twice last night."

Kate closed her eyes again and didn't say anything.

"Ken Brackett trusts me," Raymond said. "There's

a lot at stake right now."

"Listen to yourself." Kate abruptly got up from the table and went into the living room to join Andrew. Not long after, the channel changed to a Charlie Brown Christmas special. Andrew surprisingly didn't protest the change.

"What do you expect me to do?" Raymond asked the empty chair across from him.

From the living room, Lucy berated Charlie Brown over the condition of the Christmas tree they were going to use for the pageant.

Raymond sat at the table and finished his wine. He'd do what he'd always done, he told himself: Try to insulate his life at home from the world and what people did to and with each other and expected him to fix. He'd do what he'd always done: as long as Kate was determined to stay home with Andrew, Raymond would invoke the pragmatic trinity of sacrifice, duty, and necessity and try to provide a future for a son that didn't have one, or at least one that wasn't straitjacketed by his condition. He'd do what he'd always done: check any self-doubt or moral qualms at the door when he left home each morning for work and plead the Fifth on the nights his conscience cross-examined him.

That's what he told the empty chair across from him.

The phone rang, and Raymond got up and headed for the living room to get the call, but Kate picked up first.

"I'm sure you are," Kate said, "but is it important you talk to him right now?" She turned to Raymond and held out the phone. "It's someone named Larry."

Raymond waited until Kate had joined Andrew on the couch before speaking. Across the room, the Christmas play continued to tank for Charlie Brown and the gang.

"I can call back later or meet you at the diner tomorrow morning," Larry Hahn said.

"It's okay, Larry."

"You said, eye and ear. That's why this call and at home."

"I said it's okay, Larry."

Hahn explained that he was working late and thought he was the only one in the office, but it turned out that Arthur Cavanaugh, Walker Anderson, and Jamal Bell were having a long after-hours conference. Larry, however, had only been privy to the parting salvos as it broke up.

"Bell was there again?" Raymond said. "Nothing's changed, right? He's still exclusively working murder cases?"

"He was there and yes," Larry said.

"What did you hear exactly?"

"Cavanaugh mentioned the managing editor at the *Courier* and something about 'timing' and the Christmas season. Jamal Bell was talking about something being 'do-able.'"

"Anything else?"

Hahn waited a moment before saying, "Your name. It came up. I think Walker Anderson."

Across the room, Linus explained the true meaning of Christmas.

"My name what?"

"Your name," Hahn said. "Then all three laughed."

THIRTY-EIGHT

Division Street ran on a diagonal through northwest St. Carlton. Raymond pulled under a streetlight and double-checked the address he'd been given, then eased out and drove another three blocks under a snow-choked night sky.

He parked across from the Keyhole Club whose neon-splattered marquee offered *Exotic Dancing Nitely* and promised prospective patrons a glimpse of Heaven, but after Raymond paid the cover charge and entered, the Club's décor and atmosphere were decidedly less celestial and more along the lines of the purgatorial. At bottom, though, the Keyhole Club lacked the energy to be truly sleazy. It was the equivalent of Gomorrah as underachiever.

A long and wide wooden bar dominated one wall. In the center of the Club was an elevated square stage with runways coming off each corner. The stage and runways were covered in Plexiglas and lit from beneath with a milky blue glow. The show was either between sets or had not yet begun. The weather had seriously thinned the evening's crowd. The empty tables left the general mood of the evening in a three-way tie among desolate, forlorn, and desperate.

Raymond crossed the room and walked up four steps to a grouping of tables running parallel to the Club's back wall. Ken Brackett was sitting at the table closest to the pay phone and bent over an oversized paperback he was highlighting with a yellow marker. Raymond looked down at the comb lines running through the lacquered black hair, Ken's head bobbing as he read. He wore a baggy parka with a green and brown camouflage print. At his elbow were a diet cola and a plate of nachos pooled in orange cheese.

Raymond sat down, resigned to letting the evening play out along familiar lines. He'd wondered how long it would take for Ken to reach this point. He'd seen it over and over again with Public Domain clients: a kind of sexual kamikaze run set off by the stress of the weight and magnitude of their personal and professional problems.

Raymond had been watching for similar signs in Brackett. Ken's wife, Leah, had died three years ago in the fire that had also destroyed their home, and Raymond remembered nothing in Ken's file that suggested Ken had been seeing anyone since his wife's death. He'd moved back into his childhood home and taken care of Tina and his mother. The background check had unearthed no indications of one-night stands, clandestine affairs or sessions with paid company. Raymond knew that didn't necessarily mean that none of them had occurred, but it appeared to reinforce the idea that Brackett had probably kept his pants zipped since his wife's death.

Three people wandered into the Club, followed a few seconds later by four more, then two, all of them shaking snow from their coats and heading for tables close to one of the runways.

A barmaid came over to take Raymond's order, and when he said he'd have a bourbon and water, she told him there was a two-drink minimum. Raymond nodded okay and took out his wallet.

Ken shook an empty cola can in her face.

"You know I'm going to have to charge you drink prices for that." Her voice was flat, her words a toss-up between question and statement of fact.

Ken squeezed the can, mangling it, and set it on a stack of cans at his elbow. "Coin of the realm," he said. "*Trust* stamped on every piece." He managed to turn the phrase into the equivalent of a piece of wire without insulation, one carrying enough voltage to convince the barmaid to drop the attitude and quickly bring their drinks.

"A little *F&C* tonight," Ken said, tapping the cover of *The Guide.* He got up and headed for the men's room.

Raymond turned over the paperback. Its back was dominated by an author photo of Dr. Tolson Whormer standing next to an empty cage and holding a stick. The front cover was white and simply read *The Guide* in black and in the lower right corner *Book Two* in red. Above the Table of Contents was the full title: *The Guide To Unleashing: The Four Step Plan To Freeing and Caring For Your Inner Orphan.* It was followed by a bare outline. *Introduction: The Hand That Feeds You Leads You; Step One: Acknowledging Your Leash; Step Two: Testing Its Length; Step Three: Determining Its Strength; Step Four: Unleashing Yourself For Life; Afterwards: Biting The Hand That Feeds You.*

There was no Glossary or Index, and within the text itself, Dr. Whormer did not seem to be a fan of paragraphing. Ken had developed a complicated system of highlighting using three different colored markers - red, yellow, and blue - with some sections a hybrid green. Raymond could see no pattern in any of the highlighting. A whole page might be highlighted in blue and then on the facing page, the first half in yellow, the second in red. On other pages, individual words might be highlighted. Some pages were left in their original condition. Raymond felt an echo of the same sense of unease he'd had watching the billboard and its wind-tattered flurry of images when he'd had the flat tire on I-494.

Ken came back to the table just as a microphone squealed and the emcee moved to the middle of the stage and introduced himself as Don. He wore a tight black suit on the other side of wrinkled and a skinny black tie over a white shirt. He needed a shave.

He surveyed the audience. "Welcome to the Keyhole Club, gents. We have a special treat for you tonight. A little time-tripping for your viewing pleasure."

Don pointed over his right shoulder, and a spotlight fell on the first runway.

A black-haired woman stepped into the square of pale blue light. She was wearing high heels, seamed stockings, garter, and torpedo bra. "Welcome to the 50's," Don said. "Think martinis. Moonlit drives. Slow dances. Meet Susan. She knows what men like. She's all woman, and she'll always be the girl of your dreams." The soundman segued into the lead-in to the Platters' "Smoke Gets In Your Eyes."

Don then pointed over his left shoulder, and a

willowy barefoot blonde stepped into the square of sunshine-yellow light. She wore a headband and beads and a buckskin fringed garter belt. Don introduced her as Feather and a "real piece of love child." The soundman came in with the opening to Steppenwolf's "Born to be Wild."

Moving his arm clockwise, Don pointed to his right and a square of pale green light. "Watergate and gas rationing got you down? I'm betting Candi will get you up." Candi wore platform shoes, sprayed-on short-shorts, and a tight tube-top. She had layered light brown hair. The soundman hit the opening of "Staying Alive."

"And now I'd like to welcome you to the 80's and Taylor. She's the original Material Girl, and anyone can see she's got the goods." Taylor stepped into a soft red square of light to the opening strains of Duran Duran's "Hungry Like the Wolf." She had an explosion of permed black hair and wore a tight torn T-shirt, leggings, and a thong.

"Okay, you've met them," Don said. "Now here's your chance to *really* get to know them." He pointed over his right shoulder again. "It's back to the 50's with Susan."

"This was a good idea, us getting together here," Ken said. "It's important to re-establish your *F&C* on a regular basis. Keeps things in perspective."

"F&C?"

"Focus and Clarification." Ken lifted his arm and pointed it in a compass sweep of the Club. "Look around you, Raymond. You are looking at the Ground Floor of Being."

Below them, Susan, moving to Fats Domino's "Blueberry Hill," ditched the torpedo bar and held both arms straight up. There were whistles and cheers. The drift of cigarette smoke. Glasses raised.

"Humiliation, not Trust, is the real coin of the realm," Ken said. "Fear of it. The desire to inflict it. It's who we are. The thing in and of itself. You can touch it here." He tapped the cover of *The Guide*. "We're looking at Step One. You have to acknowledge the Leash."

Susan stood at the edge of the runway and turned her back to the audience, spreading her legs for balance, and slowly bending over until her hands touched and flattened against the floor.

"An endless cycle of Leashing and Unleashing to no end," Ken said. "Look at her. Look at them. It's like tying and untying a shoe over and over but never taking a step."

Ken went back to the plate of nachos. He scooped cheese and pointed below. "All of them unable to cross their Humiliation Thresholds and lost to themselves. The strippers viewing the customers as a bunch of losers with hard-ons who are so stupid that they forget it's all an act. The customers viewing the strippers as sex puppets who'll move any way they want for something as simple as cash. Each of them thinking they're in control. They feel, but can't see, the Leash."

Raymond sipped his bourbon and water. It left a flat ashy aftertaste. He noticed the ice cubes in his glass were the same color as Ken's fillings.

"You keep a journal, Raymond?"

Raymond shook his head no.

"Ever keep one?"

No again.

"Me either." Ken looked down at the plate of nachos and the thick puddle of yellow-orange cheese. "In fact, I don't think I've ever met a guy who has. Ever wonder why that is?"

Below them, Feather started her routine, eyes closed and torso slowly undulating to the Zombies' "Time of the Season."

"Your wife keep a journal, Raymond?"

"I don't think so." Raymond finished the first bourbon and water and pulled the second closer.

"Imagine that she did," Ken said. "What do you think she'd put in it?"

"Daily things," Raymond said after a while. "Kate is practical. A nurse at heart. She's good at taking care. She'd probably be writing about things to do with Andrew, our son, who has special needs." That's as far as Raymond would go. He took a sip of the second bourbon and water. It wasn't any better than the first.

"Till death do you part," Ken said, nodding. "Special needs. I hear you."

Below, Candi started her routine to the Eagles' "Take It Easy."

"You have a life," Ken said. "You think it's yours." He watched Candi work the refrain and then started nodding again.

"After the fire," Ken said, "I found Leah's journal. What are the odds, something like that? I mean, the fire wiped out everything in the house."

Ken said the journal was singed and water-damaged in places but still readable. Ken thought it a miracle of sorts. He'd recovered part of the woman he loved and then had to bury. A woman whose features shadowed their daughter's.

Ken paused for a moment, his face a roadmap of rage and pain.

"Sexual fantasies," he said. "That's all she put in the journal, her sexual fantasies. Detailed fantasies. I wasn't in a single one of them. The mailman was. The bag-boy at the Buy Rite was. Our next-door neighbor. Strangers, I'm referring to absolute and total strangers, were. Some guys I knew from work. But not me. I read all the entries. All the details. What and where and how. My wife writing about secretions. Other men's dicks. Positions. Devices."

Ken ran down. He squeezed the bridge of his nose and slowly let out his breath. He went back to studying Candi as she finished up her routine.

Raymond tried his best to provide solace and hopefully get the subject changed. "They were fantasies, Ken. You said so yourself. Don't make too much of them. That's the whole point of fantasies. They don't have to be real."

"How you live," Ken said. Raymond waited for him to continue, but he didn't. The emcee introduced Taylor, and she stepped into the opening of "What a Feeling" from the *Flashdance* soundtrack.

"I should probably get back to the ICU," Ken said, looking at the floor. "So why the call?"

"What do you mean?"

"I mean, why did you call?"

"I didn't call," Raymond said. "You called me. I got the message."

On the periphery of Raymond's vision was a small knot of a navel. When he lifted his head, he ran into a see-through bra and a pair of tightly packed breasts, and then a wide angular face palletted by some heavy-duty makeup and framed by a shoulder-length fall of hair dyed a shade of red that Raymond associated with derailed trains and chemical spills.

"I didn't," Ken said.

"My name's Yvonne," the redhead said. She winked. "You can call me Yvonne."

"Wait a minute," Raymond said. "If you didn't call."

"I just said I didn't."

Yvonne leaned over, pushing away the remains of the drinks and Ken's nachos. She ran a stubby index finger along the length of Ken's jawline. "Oh Baby," she said.

Ken crossed his arms. "I told you before. No table or lap dances. I'm not paying for this."

"Don't worry about it, Honey-Baby," she said. She put her hand on Raymond's thigh and swiveled, wedging herself between Ken and Raymond and then lifting her arms and dropping them over their shoulders, pulling them close to her. "It's all taken care of," she said and smiled.

A couple seconds more might have made all the difference, but by the time Raymond pushed back his chair and yelled at Ken to cover his face, the bartender had already tossed down his rag and bellowed to the monolithic bouncer in the doorway that someone had a camera down front.

Yvonne had disappeared as suddenly as she'd appeared.

Raymond was still blinking away the after-image from the camera flash when Ken and he got to the front door of the club and the bouncer who was blocking the path of two men standing before him.

The bouncer kept looking back and forth between them, one fist balled at his side, the other hand open, demanding the film. "This club has rules," he said, pausing to work on his glower. "No cameras on the premises is one."

"We're the Press," one of the men said. "This is news."

Raymond immediately recognized the voice. It belonged to Luis Murano. Standing to Murano's left was a tall man who'd slung the camera over the shoulder of his long overcoat. Murano called the man Steve and showed the bouncer their Press credentials.

"I don't care," the bouncer said. "No cameras on the premises, so give me the film."

"You set us up, Murano," Raymond said. "Those calls."

Murano turned so that he was facing Raymond and Ken. "I never made a call to either of you. I *got* a call. A tip. An anonymous one, saying you and Mr. Brackett would be here." Murano paused. "Still I was surprised to find you here. I knew you were low enough for something like this, Locke, but honestly, I didn't think you'd be dumb or careless enough to bring Mr. Brackett to the Keyhole."

"You're talking about me as if I'm not here," Ken

said.

The one Murano called Steve smiled.

"I told you," the bouncer said. "There are rules."

Luis Murano turned and made a small bow in the bouncer's direction. "You can ask Mr. Locke," he said. "I respect rules. In fact, according to him, I'm a True Believer when it comes to them."

Murano nodded to Steve who shrugged and handed over the camera. Murano opened its back and took out the roll of film, then gave the camera back to Steve.

Luis Murano held up the roll of film between his thumb and index finger.

Steven buttoned his overcoat and looked around. "I'm gone," he said and started for the door. The bouncer remained focused on Murano and let him by.

"No," Raymond said, again a couple seconds too late.

"Yes," Luis Murano said. He smiled and with a quick flick of his wrist tossed the roll of film over the bouncer's head. Steve one-handed it at the door and hit the sidewalk running.

THIRTY-NINE

The fallout from the photo-shoot at the Keyhole Club was swift. It carried weight and ran on its own clock. Raymond Locke could not lighten or re-set it.

Earlier in the morning, Kate had walked into the kitchen just as Raymond was making coffee. She laid the *Courier* and the *Herald* on the counter and walked off without a word to get Andrew ready for the day. Before Raymond had made it out of the house, the phone calls had started coming in, the answering machine picking up one after another as reporters, television and radio people, friends, and family tried to cadge additional details.

There was nowhere to hide.

The photo had run front page in both the *Courier* and *Herald*, Yvonne giving an exaggerated lascivious wink and smile, Raymond wedged on her right, Ken on her left, their expressions holding an unruly hybrid of surprise, guilt, despair, and rage.

The *Courier* compounded the effect of the front-page fiasco by running a smaller version of the photo in the C Section and framing it within a collage of Christmas shots around St. Carlton, a cross-section of conventional and sentimental nods to the spirit of the holidays - children building snowmen; a rink thronged with skaters; a giant evergreen ablaze with lights; Arthur Cavanaugh, the Prosecuting Attorney, and his abundantly procreative Irish-Catholic brood sitting with bowed heads before a holiday dinner; an old man shoveling his driveway; a Salvation Army Santa ringing a bell on a street-corner; customers log-jammed at department store registers - all of them implicitly foregrounding Raymond's and Ken's guilt and depravity. The collage was followed by an editorial giving a gloomy update on Tina Brackett's condition, then moving on to ask a number of leading questions concerning Ken Brackett's character and ethical orientation, italicizing the same questions about Raymond and Public Domain, before attacking Happy Farms once again for its unwillingness to cooperate in the paper's investigation of the food poisoning incident at the franchises.

Raymond had been at the office no more than fifteen minutes when Daniel Pierce called and told him to be ready to fly to Wilkesboro to meet with Lamar Ditell. Within a half hour, Raymond and Pierce were strapped in the Bell Ranger copter. On the way, Pierce was no more communicative than Kate had been at breakfast. Pierce kept his hands folded in his lap and his head turned so that the light from the east caught his compact blunt features and remained silent for the entire flight.

At the Ditell compound, Lamar moved among the child-sized living room furniture he'd bought to compensate for his self-consciousness about his height, marching in an exaggerated stutter-step, hands knotted at the small of his back, head and shoulders leaning forward, his movements reminding Raymond of the mechanical pirouettes of the shooting gallery.

Every so often, Ditell stopped and said, "I don't fucking need this." He then glared at Pierce and Raymond, his tiny anger-creased face resembling a malevolent raisin.

Lamar Ditell paused during one of his circuits through the room and picked up the *Courier* and *Herald.* "How and why?" he said, waving them in Raymond's direction.

Raymond was ready with an explanation. He'd pulled an all-nighter working out various scenarios behind the photo-shoot, testing all angles and possibilities until he came up with the most plausible.

Raymond explained that Arthur Cavanaugh was at the center of it all and then went on to connect the dots. Cavanaugh and Lamar were long-standing enemies. Cavanaugh had political ambitions beyond the DA's office. He had had a legitimate shot last election at a bid for mayor, but Lamar Ditell had done everything in his power to sabotage it. Then, tables-turned, Lamar and Happy Farms end up in trouble with a food poisoning incident, and a ten-year-old girl in a coma. Enter Walker Anderson, Cavanaugh's former protégé at the DA's office, now in private practice. Anderson has no more love for Lamar Ditell than Cavanaugh does. Anderson also likes the public spotlight. He could be center-staging it if he could convince Ken Brackett to let Anderson represent him in a case against Happy Farms. Brackett, however, won't fully commit. Anderson and/or Cavanaugh work out the Keyhole Club angle to drive Brackett into Anderson's open arms. Anderson is then in the public spotlight and in line for a very nice chunk of the settlement the suit against Happy Farms would bring. Cavanaugh, in turn, has crushed his enemy and cleared the pathway for his next run for mayor.

Raymond had no ready answer though for Lamar Ditell's next question. "That sounds about on the money, how Cavanaugh and Anderson worked it, but what are you going to do about fixing it?"

Lamar then turned in Pierce's direction. "This fucking thing keeps coming back on us, and it's gonna keep coming back on us, and that's not acceptable on any level."

Pierce nodded. He avoided looking at Raymond.

Raymond did not need spelling lessons. The same held true for his reading skills. The handwriting on the wall was becoming very clear and legible.

During his years at Public Domain, Raymond had fixed the problems the old and new money people managed to cause for themselves and others. He'd sat before one of the twenty-two fireplaces in the Queen-Anne mansion at 1861 North Ridge Avenue, the residence of the Archbishop, and worked out the particulars for keeping Bishop DeMarco within the fold after his mistress committed suicide. He had taken an express elevator to the thirty-fifth floor of a new postmodern apartment complex overlooking the Lake to confer with one of the head buyers in wheat futures when the man's own future had been called into question by a couple of paternity suits. A foray to Wisconsin Avenue and the Georgian Revival home of a former railroad magnate whose heir had tried to ventilate his lover's windpipe with a broken Heineken bottle after a colorful spat in one of the gay bars on South Royal. Raymond had helped wash the hands of the spouse of an owner of a chain of video stores after she'd drafted herself a personal loan from the proceeds of a city-wide charity she'd chaired for disadvantaged youths. He'd smoothed things over for a mover and shaker at the main office for Midwestern Savings and Loan when his sixteen year old son and his pals had decided to spice up their Saturday night cruising routine by chasing down and clipping the indigent and homeless with their Vettes and Porsches. He'd put a thumb on the scales of justice for the owner of a meat packing shipping concern who'd commissioned an arson job that had ended up horribly botched. He'd reupholstered the reputation of the brother of the founder of Midwestern Furniture after the Bushel of Love Daycare scandal broke.

Raymond had always managed to erase or re-route consequences. He revised and replaced the scheme in the scheme of things.

He reminded himself that he'd always been lucky. It was his backhanded legacy, bequeathed to him after he beat the odds as an infant and survived the plane crash that killed his parents and 185 others. Since then, he had trusted to his luck to take him where he needed to go and then went to work from there, taking what luck had given him and making it his own.

He'd been in tight places before, but the Keyhole Club incident had turned the usual dynamics inside out. Raymond had lost his behind-the-scenes protective coloration and become publicly tied to a client. For the first time, Raymond unexpectedly found himself part of the problem he was supposed to solve.

The Bell Ranger had barely gained altitude for the return flight to St. Carlton when Daniel Pierce cleared his throat.

"An example," he said. "That's what we're looking at."

"Wait a minute," Raymond said. "You heard what I told Lamar. Cavanaugh's behind the Keyhole shoot."

"Absolutely," Pierce said. "The pieces fit."

"I don't understand then. I'll start working..."

"Timing," Pierce said. "That and the fact you'll never be able to prove Cavanaugh and Walker worked the Keyhole Club thing out."

"There are still some angles," Raymond said.

"We've lost Brackett now," Pierce shifted in his seat and looked out the Ranger's window into an afternoon sky wadded in gray clouds.

"And we need an example," he said again.

Raymond saw it then.

Public Domain's January Stockholders' Meeting in New York. All the current and subsequent fallout from the Happy Farms account.

Daniel Pierce was covering himself. If the stockholders decided to raise the banner of corporate ethics and social responsibility and demanded accountability, Pierce could serve Raymond up and keep his directorship intact. Pierce had managed to smoothly and carefully step aside from the whole mess, playing both sides against the middle, fixing it so that Raymond could take the fall for anything that went wrong with the Happy Farms campaign from here on out.

An example.

Raymond had become a scapegoat for all seasons.

FORTY

After the return from Wilkesboro, Raymond didn't bother going back to the office. He went straight to the parking garage, intending to leave for home early, but ended up sitting behind the wheel, keys in hand, watching his breath materialize in the cold air and drift, patterning the windshield. He was exhausted on what felt like something approaching the molecular level.

A slow-boil anxiety. A slow-cresting panic. That's what he'd been expecting as a response to the meeting with Ditell and Pierce. He'd become an official *example* and was suspended without pay until further notice. Pierce assured him it would be temporary. Raymond had heard Pierce deliver that line on more than one occasion and understood all too well the weight it did and did not carry.

He had to come up with an angle. Something he could work with. He had become his own client. He needed to start and work from there.

He fixed things.

Now he had to fix himself.

As he slotted the key in the ignition, he spotted movement in his rear-view mirror, and then a fist materialized and tapped on the glass of the passenger-side window, followed by Larry Hahn's gaunt features tilted horizontally as he bent over and looked inside.

Raymond unlocked the door, and Hahn slid

inside. He sat with his shoulders and knees hunched.

"I called the office," he said. "They told me you'd left early. I took a chance, hoped I might catch you here."

Hahn made a show of rubbing his hands. "You mind turning the car and heat on? It's cold."

Raymond started the car and rested his hands on top of the wheel, crossing them at the wrist.

He waited.

"You'll want to hear this," Larry said.

Raymond figured Susan Hahn had exceeded her Christmas allowance, and Larry was angling for a bonus for some tidbits from the DA's office.

He was not, however, ready for what he heard. With the Keyhole Club debacle that made two times in the last two days he'd been surprised and unprepared. He didn't like the feeling. Hahn was not offering tidbits.

"You can't be serious," Raymond said after Hahn once again told him that Arthur Cavanaugh was going to bring Lamar Ditell up on a charge of attempted murder.

"Cavanaugh's serious," Hahn said, "and there's precedent."

Hahn went on to contrast the civil suit brought against Ford Motors by Grimshaw with the criminal one levied against the company after the deaths of three Indiana girls, both cases centering on the infamous Pinto and the questionable engineering and placement of its gas tank, the civil suit succeeding in garnering compensatory and punitive damages, but Ford finessing its way out of the State's charge of reckless homicide in the three girls' deaths.

The groundwork, though, Hahn said, for similar future cases had been laid. Cavanaugh could also go after Lamar Ditell with two Supreme Court cases involving Dotterweich and Park, both of them chief executive officers of their corporations who'd been charged with violations of the Federal Food, Drug, and Cosmetic Act. The court ultimately found in each case that not only the corporation but the manager of a corporation could be prosecuted and that Dotterweich and Park had a position of authority and responsibility in the situation out of which the charges arose and thus could be held personally accountable.

"Lamar Ditell is very vulnerable," Hahn said. "There are enough narrow liability statutes that can attach criminal responsibility to Ditell even if he didn't have personal knowledge of the wrongful act. With the Park case I was telling you about, it was enough for the corporate executive officer to be in a responsible position over the employees who actually committed the crime."

Raymond closed his eyes for a moment. The attempted murder angle explained Jamal Bell's presence at all the meetings with Cavanaugh and Walker. Bell was there to help finesse the details.

"In the public's eyes, Lamar Ditell has become synonymous with his product," Hahn continued. "He wanted high visibility, you and Public Domain gave it to him, and now he's got a problem, a big one. Think about it. The man was at the Grand Openings of the Happy Farms franchises personally handing out samples. Every one of those samples was a loaded gun."

Raymond thought about it. The image that Ditell had funneled millions into Public Domain's coffers to create and lodge Happy Farms in the public's mind was now going to damn and incriminate him. Lamar Ditell in his trademark porkpie hat, bow tie, yellow shirt, and brown suit mingling with the crowds at the grand openings of the franchises, shaking hands, passing out discount coupons, encouraging everyone to try free samples of the chicken that would go on to poison close to a third of them.

Raymond let out his breath. "How soon is Cavanaugh planning to move on this?"

"Some time early in the new year. He's waiting to see what else Luis Murano and the *Courier* investigation turn up. Murano's still working on that witness. There's enough evidence at present for Cavanaugh to begin mobilizing the office. He wants to be ready when and if anything else breaks."

"What are the odds Cavanaugh can pull this off?"

Larry waited a moment before answering. "I've seen grand juries hand down indictments on far less."

The wind ran from the east and marshaled thin skeins of snow down the center aisle of the garage. When he looked up, the rear-view mirror held a pair of eyes Raymond didn't recognize.

Larry Hahn cleared his throat. ""I should be going."

"I can't get the money, Larry."

Hahn frowned and forced a smile. "Tomorrow, then. At the diner on Alamonte."

"I didn't say 'don't have.' I said 'can't get.'"

"Wait a minute. What I just brought you, there's a price tag. I took a big chance here, and I need the cash, Raymond."

Raymond let his hands fall from the steering wheel. He looked over at Hahn. "Okay, Larry. This then. You got away with it. No more meetings. You're in the clear. Or as clear as it will ever be for either of us."

Hahn shifted in the seat so that he was facing Raymond. "You mean you're cutting me loose from the Bushel of Love thing? I don't believe that. Why now?"

"No more calls. No more favors," Raymond said. "My word on that. It's done and over. You're safe."

Raymond lifted his hand. "*Te absolute sunt.*"

"I don't understand," Hahn said. "What did you say?"

Raymond leaned over and opened the passenger door. "Just go," he said. "Go home to Susan and the girls."

.

FORTY-ONE

The first time it happened was an accident. The 500 block of Spencer Street was congested from a funeral procession, so Raymond took Harrison and simply had not been paying attention.

He was driving for driving's sake, simply to be in motion. Something he couldn't name had wrapped itself around his life. He wanted movement.

He eventually left Harrison for Rowland and the old warehouse district, block after block of sheeted steel or brick buildings with battered and rusty tin roofs, fading names and company logos on the streetside doors. Lots of concertina wire and junkyard dogs.

A dull pressure in his head.

The afternoon sky looked painted.

He needed to regain his bearings. Sort his thoughts. Something had wrapped.

The *Courier* headline above the Keyhole Club shot: *Tis the Season for Strip Clubs*!

The point of his job was to anticipate, avoid, exploit, or neutralize surprises.

Surprises were truth-heavy and unwieldy.

Raymond left Rowland and took Trent, passing into the no-man's neighborhood between the warehouse district and port system. Dirty-spoon diners and corner bars. Mom and Pop grocery stores. More bars. A few tenement houses. All on the downside of flush now but at one time prospering when shipping and manufacturing were running three shifts.

There was the question of money.

Even before the suspension without pay, there'd been the question of money. It was a constant. Kate going back for her Masters in Nursing. Buying more house than they needed or could afford at the time. Kate's pregnancy and later decision to stay home with Andrew. Some trapdoor investments on Raymond's part. The monthly assisted living bill for his aunt. Andrew's treatment and care, short-term and forever.

Always the question of money and no satisfactory answers.

Off to Raymond's left, the shipyards. A row of cranes and stacks of multi-colored cargo containers. The immensity of the Lake, a dull-nickel in the December light.

What he was looking at: a ten-year-old girl in a coma. Lamar Ditell passing out samples of Happy Farms Snuggets at the grand-openings of the franchises. With Tina and Ken Brackett backdropped as innocent victims, Arthur Cavanaugh would have no trouble convincing a grand jury that indicting Lamar Ditell would send a message to every CEO in the food industry across the country that they could be held personally accountable for the quality and safety of the food that landed on the public's plates.

And in the face of all the allegations of corporate malfeasance and irresponsibility, Public Domain's stockholders would demand justice and Daniel Pierce's head. Pierce would placate them by handing over Raymond's instead. Raymond's neck was already in place and laid out on the chopping block after the photo-shoot at the Keyhole Club.

On the periphery of vision, the billboard with the layers of tattered images.

An escape hatch. There had to be one. He needed to find it and quick.

Tight places. Raymond understood them.

He remembered starting at Public Domain and going to Frank Atwell, his mentor at the agency, for advice about getting his clients out of those tight places.

Chase the implications, Frank had told him. *Eyes wide open. Remember, why and how are always joined at the hip.*

Raymond went past the entrance ramp for I-494 and continued on under the overpass, staying in motion, taking the long way home. He stayed on Wood and drove into the ethnic and racial jumble of south St. Carlton.

To his right, Douglas Street which would have taken him into Luis Murano's neighborhood and Ferrilli's Gym.

Further on, a cluster of churches. A high school. Convenience stores. A few half-hearted strip malls sandwiched into blocks of working class homes.

The first time was an accident. Raymond had been distracted and not paying attention.

The second was on impulse.

Wood became Dennison and widened to four lanes.

The third time was calculated. Raymond timed his approach, maintained an even speed, and passed under the yellow at the exact moment it disappeared.

Raymond unbuckled his seatbelt.

The fourth time, he ran a full red.

Each time he tried to narrow the margin between deliberation and chance. He worked on matching it to his breathing and the pressure of his foot on the gas pedal.

The fifth time, he sailed through the intersection with his eyes closed.

On each occasion, he waited for the blue and white strobes or the cry of sirens or the blare of horns that became the screech of tires and tearing metal and exploding glass. He waited, but none of the moments materialized.

The sixth intersection was the busiest and trickiest because of extra lanes and arrows for left-hand turns. He pulled into the parking lot of a convenience store near the intersection. He parked facing the street and left the car running and sat and studied the intersection, timing the sequence of the lights and analyzing the movement of traffic, trying to nail down the pattern and jotting his observations in shorthand on the palm of his left hand.

If he hit the intersection at a little over fifty miles per hour, only ten miles over the limit, just as the left turn arrow for the east-west lanes was disappearing, he had a two second free zone, an absolute blank spot in the traffic's movement, when the light would be his alone. He needed to be in the forefront of the north-south traffic or at least have the lucky break of a last second open lane for it to work.

He pulled into traffic, driving south four and a

half blocks and spotting an empty church parking lot, then swinging in and positioning himself so he was facing the two northbound lanes. The car was idling a little rough, and he tapped at the gas. Behind him, at the other end of the lot was a beaten-up basketball goal, net missing, the faded white backboard canting slightly off-center, a thin black cross and *Score One For Jesus* hand-painted across its top half. Raymond turned on the radio and watched the street, waiting for his opening.

When it came, he hit the gas and moved into the left-hand lane headed north. He kept it at forty miles an hour for a half block, then eased up to forty-five, hanging between two groups of cars. Four blocks away, the green for the north-south traffic disappeared, and the east-west left turns clicked on.

He pressed down on the gas. Raymond began threading his way through the first group of cars that were just starting to slow for the light. He ignored the long blare of horns erupting around him. He cut back and forth between lanes in a rhythm that arose like that of an old song he'd suddenly remembered.

From the radio came the time and temperature, then *Fly Lakeland Commuter. The Sun Doesn't Melt The Wings We Wear.*

Raymond pressed the gas feed.

Less than two blocks. Three cars in front.

The light red. Suspended above the intersection. Ripening.

Raymond starting to pull around the last cars.

A moment ripped from his movement: the man in the car next to him turning his head, looking at

Raymond and saying something, the lips moving silently behind glass, Raymond not sure if he were looking at a curse, warning, or something else entirely.

Then, open space.

Hands involuntarily tightening on the wheel. The light holding. Red. A decision beyond words. A sweet taste rising in his throat and flooding his mouth. Movement.

The needle's eye.

He glanced in the rear-view. Less than a half-block behind him, the intersection swarmed with cars.

He pulled over and rebuckled his seatbelt.

He hit the turn signal, merged with the after work commute on McNair, and drove home.

FORTY-TWO

Raymond took off his overcoat. He registered without exactly registering what was lined up on the landing just inside the foyer because Kate started in with the names.

"Melanie and Lucy," Kate said, ticking each name off on a finger. "Janet and Sylvia and Barbara."

"I'm sorry, what?" Raymond said.

Andrew walked by carrying a large mesh bag of wooden alphabet blocks. He emptied it in the middle of the living room floor, then stood and surveyed the jumble of letters. He wore a pair of red sweatpants with black piping running down the outside of each leg and a blue sweater with a yellow rocket moving diagonally across his chest. The lights from the Christmas tree washed over the right side of his face. His hair had not yet grown in from Kate's emergency haircut, and his scalp was a stark white under the brown fuzz and bristle.

"Sylvia, Melanie, Lucy, Janet, and Barbara," Kate said. "I'm waiting."

Raymond hung up his coat. Twenty minutes earlier, he'd run a light with his eyes closed. He told himself he was home now. He watched Andrew lay out a string of blocks.

He tilted his head, looking at the dining room. The table was set for one. He checked his watch. "You two already eat? Why didn't you wait?"

Kate repeated the string of names. Her tone, flat and direct, gave no clue to the intent behind them or at least none Raymond could decipher.

"Is that some kind of riddle?" he asked. "I'm lost here."

"Yes," Kate said, "You are."

"Everybody rides," Andrew said. "Everybody rides. They do, yes." He kept laying out the blocks.

"You're upset," Raymond said. "I can see that."

"Melanie, Lucy, Janet, Sylvia, and Barbara," she said again. "Tell me who."

Raymond looked over at the landing and frowned.

"What there is is what," Andrew said. "Color-fast. Tumble dry. I want my MTV. Crunchy and delicious. Excuse me while I fix the sky. If you have to ask. God test ye murky gentlemen."

"You want to know who they are?" Kate said. "They're my *friends*, Raymond. They're people I can count on. I'm part of their lives and they mine."

Kate took a step closer. She softened her tone. "Okay. Your turn. The names of five of your friends. People you can count on and can count on you."

"Why are you doing this?"

"Okay," Kate said. "Four then." She paused. "I'll make it even easier. Three. Give me the names of three people you consider friends."

"Power away stains," Andrew said. "Express yourself with American Express."

"Two," Kate said. "Counting down. Can you even name two?"

"Look, I know you're upset about the Keyhole Club photo," Raymond said. "I am too. But it's not the way it looks. There's a lot more going on than you know."

Walnut. Burnt-almond. Dusky-beige. Raymond had always thought of Kate as inhabiting those colors. Her eyes. Hair. Skin. A woman not of contrasts but subtle variations. He could still see the woman he'd fallen in love with each time he looked at her. That had never changed.

"A glass of wine," Raymond said. "Sounds like both of us could use one. I'll open the Merlot."

He started for the kitchen but stopped after Kate said, "You talk in your sleep."

"What's going on here, Kate?"

She pointed at Raymond, then dropped her hands to her hips. "What's going on is I'm married to a man who, among other things, talks in his sleep. You do, and you have ever since I've known you. I used to think it was kind of endearing. You had to be asleep before you'd admit to any vulnerability. It was like a secret we shared but never had to acknowledge."

"Kate," Raymond interrupted. "I love you." Though it was the truth, even to Raymond's ears, it came out sounding like a twelfth-hour plea bargain.

"No. I've already heard enough," she said. "Every night for over a month now, I've lain next to a man who keeps telling me how much he loves me and then had to listen to him curse in his sleep. That's what my husband does now, curses in his sleep. Strings of curses so horrible and angry and vile that I've had to get up and leave the room."

"Just listen for a moment, okay?"

Kate shook her head. "I've listened to what you've

become, Raymond, and it scares me."

"It's stress talking. Pressures from work. Nothing more than that," Raymond said. "I'm still me." People don't change, he told himself. Not at bottom. The job had taught him that. He cleaned up the messes his clients made, and they went back to their lives until the next time they needed his services. He had a lot of repeat customers.

"I'm me, Kate," he said.

"I want you to quit," she said. "Walk away from Public Domain. I'll go back to work. You can freelance until you land something with another agency."

"I can't, Kate."

"Can't or won't?"

"Both."

Given his ties to the Happy Farms account, if he walked right now, his career, in essence, was over. His credibility and reputation would be shot, and he'd be perceived as a major-league fuck-up, the guy who choked big-time. He'd be indelibly marked in public relations circles. He'd have no clout even for freelance work, at least not the type he was accustomed to, and even if he was picked up by another agency, no one would trust him to handle the big accounts. He'd live in the shadow of the Happy Farms scandal and its botched PR campaign for the rest of his professional life.

There'd be nothing resembling a new or fresh start until he found a way to get out from under the photo-shoot at the Keyhole Club and the potential future fallout from Arthur Cavanaugh's attempted murder ploy with Lamar Ditell.

The problem was, right now, he had no idea how to do either.

"So what you're telling me," Kate said, "is it's more of the same."

Raymond pointed at the landing, finally acknowledging the luggage lined against the wall. "Any chance of changing your mind?"

"It's just for the holidays, Raymond."

"You sure?"

"Let's leave it at that for now, Raymond."

"Let's not." He took a step closer to Kate. "The job, everything I do, everything I did, it's for you and Andrew. Why can't you see that?"

Raymond touched Kate's cheek. "Don't do this. Please. Not now."

Before she could respond, Raymond heard his words returned to him, verbatim, but empty of any inflection whatsoever.

Don't do this. Please. Not now.

Of all Andrew's symptoms, Raymond had never gotten used to the Echolalia Syndrome, that and what the pediatric specialists had called Autoerotic Linguistic Patterning, Andrew's studied retreat into private language shorn of any immediately accessible context. This unnerved Raymond in ways that went beyond any other symptoms of his son's autism.

Raymond crossed to the landing and picked up the suitcases, testing their weight. They had not just been set out to make a point. They were already packed. Which made its own point.

Kate stepped up behind him. "Would you say that we're friends, Raymond? I mean something beyond or in addition to spouses and lovers."

"Jesus. How can you even ask me that? Of course we are."

"Was Frank Atwell your friend?"

Raymond frowned, puzzled. He nodded. "You know that."

"The phone messages on the refrigerator. Did you ever get back with him?"

"Not yet," Raymond said. "I plan to soon." He'd been thinking about Frank, thinking Frank might be able to help with some of the angles on shutting down or derailing the Cavanaugh murder charge.

"He called here eight times in the last week and a half," Kate said. "When were you planning to return his calls?"

"I told you," Raymond said. "Soon."

"Well, *friend*," Kate said, her voice breaking. "*Soon* is going to be a little too late."

FORTY-THREE

In the wake of Kate's and Andrew's departure for her parents' home in Toledo, Raymond came to feel as if cause had become severed from effect, and he floundered in the gap left between the two.

In the mean time, things occurred.

There were events, and there was sequence, but no chronology or coherence, nothing that bound those events and sequence together in a meaningful way. Things occurred or did not occur. He was awake or asleep, hungry or not hungry, afraid or not afraid that everything in his life was broken.

In the meantime, there was too much time and simultaneously too little. Too much, Raymond waiting, hoping and hoping again, for Kate and Andrew to return home. Too little, Raymond tamping down panic, as he tried over and over to chase down a solution to the very unsavory consequences looming from the Public Domain stockholders meeting in mid-January and Arthur Cavanaugh leveling the attempted murder charge against Lamar Ditell.

He bought a dozen lined legal-sized tablets and a fistful of different colored felt-tip pens.

He called his wife but kept getting his father-in-law who either immediately hung up on him or told him Kate was too busy with her family to come to the phone.

He went to the State Store and stocked up on

Beefeaters, then the grocery for tonic and limes. He leaned on a high-profile internist for whom he'd helped bury some potential malpractice suits and landed some prescription speed.

He watched weather reports, finding an inordinate and unexpected comfort in the meteorologists' predictions and the eventual outcomes. He carefully followed the movement of fronts and high and low pressure systems.

He left the television on to fill the otherwise silence of the house. The sink filled with dishes for meals he couldn't remember eating. He drank gin and tonics and fell asleep sitting up in the chair he'd dragged into the living room. He ate Dexedrine and churned through pages of tablets, charting possibilities and outlining schemes for getting out from under his professional problems.

He called Kate over and over. Or at least thought he did.

He was full of self-pity, desperation, rage, remorse, and yearning.

He went back through the tablets, crossing out and adding to the notes.

He tried to keep track of the days, but the Beefeaters and Dexedrine conspired against that, and at some point, the calendar was added to the things broken and lost in his life.

At some point, he went to Frank Atwell's funeral.

At some point, Christmas day happened.

At some point, Eric Donner called and said Ken Brackett had disappeared.

Raymond found himself walking into a room and

expecting to find Kate. Her absence felt like some violation of a fundamental natural law. He had always seen their love for each other and marriage in terms of absolutes: something unassailable, protected, complete, sacrosanct, bulletproof, indomitable, incontrovertible, and inviolate.

Kate, after all, rhymed with Fate.

Myocardial Infarction. That's what finally got Frank Atwell. He'd been dead three days before his landlord discovered the body. Raymond had gone to the funeral mass at St Mark's and listened to one Monsignor Lovetti deliver a eulogy for a man whom he obviously knew nothing about. Piles of platitudes. Ramped-up sentiments that could have applied to anyone's life or death. St Mark's cavernous interior holding a handful of mourners. Raymond, a few barstool philosophers from Frank's drinking haunts, a couple of former Public Domain clients old enough now to have outlived any repercussions from the scandals Frank had helped to defuse or bury. A showy funeral wreath from the office but no sign of Daniel Pierce or anyone else.

When he remembered to eat, Raymond found himself cooking Andrew's favorite meals. He climbed the stairs and stood in the middle of his son's room and breathed in what lingered of his presence. He kept finding small objects that Andrew had hidden around the house. He had no clear idea of their significance.

Eric Donner called again asking about Ken Brackett who'd gone AWOL a second time. Donner had inherited the Happy Farms account after

Raymond had been suspended, and he suspected Raymond of trying to undermine him. Raymond kept telling Donner that Ken Brackett was his problem now, not Raymond's.

Tina Brackett showed no signs of coming out of her coma.

Raymond made plans to drive to Toledo and reclaim his family, but his resolve faltered, then fell apart, when he admitted to himself that he'd just end up losing Kate and Andrew all over again after the first of the year unless he found a way to keep the suspension from becoming permanent.

So he ate Dexedrine and filled lined tablets and futilely called his wife at her parents' home and he left the television on to erase the silence and he stood at the kitchen door and watched fresh snow gather in the backyard and he thought about *Myocardial Infarctions* and remembered Frank Atwell and a drunken ramble about stories and he stood in the middle of his son's room and found himself crying and he cut limes and measured out the gin and the tonic and listened to the television and the rumble and stutter of the furnace and he noticed that the mail held more bills than Christmas cards and he passed out in the chair he'd dragged into the living room because he could not bring himself to sleep alone in the bed he'd shared with Kate and he erased the hangovers and the accompanying slow terrors and panic by eating more Dexedrine and scouring his nerve endings so that they ran clean and fast in pursuit of the solution he had yet to find for what his life had become and he watched weather reports and followed the churn and sweep of storm systems and he ate when he remembered to and he replayed Frank Atwell's funeral mass in his mind and the couple times he managed to get Kate on the phone for any extended period, their conversations were strained and full of non sequiturs and though he ended each of the calls with *I Love You* and *I Miss You* his words sounded as if he were reading them from a script to a bad movie so he would go back to the gin and tonics or Dexedrine and along the way the days he'd lost track of eventually deposited him in his son's room where Raymond found himself hefting Andrew's oversized red plastic bat and swinging it again and again into the bare west wall of the room, each hollow *thwack* or *thump* a mimic of his own heartbeat.

Then he was downstairs and in the living room and in his chair in front of the television, a lined tablet on his lap, a tall gin and tonic on the end table next to him.

A puppet bat flopped its way across the screen pulling a tattered banner that read *You're Watching Nightshade Theatre.*

He watched Gary Ghoulmaster flip open the lid of his coffin and sit up. "Keep your claws off that dial. You don't want to disappoint the Ghoulmaster by changing channels." The camera panned in so that Gary Ghoulmaster's face and its blue-cheese pallor filled the entire screen. "Remember, the Ghoulmaster loves you to death." He went on to howl and growl his way into announcing the conclusion to this evening's feature: *Lab Accident.*

A brief dubbed announcement followed, the

station manager informing viewers that tonight's show was another holiday installment of *The Best of Nightshade Theatre.*

Raymond picked up the gin and tonic and took a deep swallow. He looked down at his notes, then up and over at the television.

An elaborate state-of-the-art laboratory and a nubile blonde in a white coat. A chiseled-featured colleague with graying hair put his arm around her. She tilted her head, lifting her face to his.

What he appeared to be had become what he was, the blonde whispered tearfully.

Or maybe it had been, *Who he was had become what he appeared to be.*

Raymond wasn't sure which. He got up to make another gin and tonic.

When he returned, the nubile blonde assistant recoiled from the mutated remains of the creature that had once been her boyfriend, a genetic-engineering scientist whose experiments had pushed beyond the acceptable bounds of humanity and God and had reduced him to a low-budget special effect. The chiseled-featured gray-haired colleague pulled her close to him and whispered, "It was an accident, that's all, an accident. We have to remember that and continue our work. The project is too important to abandon."

The blonde lifted her head and nodded.

They kissed.

The camera panned to the remains of her boyfriend. Out of a soupy mix of what appeared to be green Jell-O laced with chunks of ground beef, a lone eyeball surfaced, looked around, and then winked, signaling, as the credits began to roll, the inevitable advent of *Lab Accident II*.

Raymond glanced down at his notes and then looked up.

It was right there.

An opening.

He'd been looking right at it for the last half hour.

A way out of the aftershock of the Keyhole Club photo shoot and the shitstorm that would follow Arthur Cavanaugh's charging Lamar Ditell with attempted murder.

As the credits for *Lab Accident* ran themselves out and Gary Ghoulmaster cracked open the lid of his casket and raised a claw of a hand to wave goodnight, Raymond saw it again.

The opening he needed was there. It was workable.

He watched Gary Ghoulmaster close the lid of his coffin.

Raymond had found what he needed to turn everything around.

FORTY-FOUR

*A*tlanta.

Raymond lathered his face, leaned toward the bathroom mirror, and began shaving, pausing every so often, to repeat the name.

Atlanta.

Three syllables. He spaced them out, listening to and weighing each, the syllables like tumblers clicking on a lock that was on the verge of opening.

Atlanta would be his ticket out. A new start. Once again, means connected to ends. Choices that felt like choices. Distinctions and drawn lines. Lies that could remain lies. Clean hands. The world in his hands. The left hand knowing what the right was up to. Words that fit what they meant. Talk instead of ventriloquism. Hands, mouth, his again. Whole.

It felt good.

Just as it did knowing that Kate and Andrew had started on their way home earlier that morning. Raymond had worked hard, very hard, at convincing Kate and Andrew to return. He had finally resorted to floating *Atlanta* and what it meant for their family, but he'd withheld the details that had made *Atlanta* possible. Even then, Kate had balked, her skepticism about promises of fresh starts underwritten by her anger and the battery of disappointments that had fueled her departure to her childhood home in the first place.

Raymond suspected, though, that Kate agreeing to return to St. Carlton had as much to do with her overbearing father as Raymond's power of persuasion. Leonard Simco's paternal love contained as many qualifying riders as the insurance policies his agencies peddled. Raymond was also betting that Leonard had been unable over the holidays to fully hide his feelings about Andrew's condition. He remembered all too well Leonard pulling him aside at Andrew's fifth birthday party and telling him: *There's nothing like that on our side of the fence.*

Raymond set the safety razor down and held his hands out before him. No shakes. He nodded to himself in the mirror. He'd cut the Dexedrine and gin. *Atlanta* precluded both. He needed to stay sharp and steady.

He imagined Kate and Andrew in the car, their progress marked on one of those cheesy maps used as transitions in old movies, a two dimensional car bouncing its way west along I-94, toy ships floating in Lake Michigan, a handful of Midwestern icons - toy bars, mills, churches - scattered across northern and central Indiana, the cities and towns marked by a constellation of large and small white stars.

Raymond finished shaving and dressed, getting ready for the drive to southwest St. Carlton and the Nu-Day Clinic.

Atlanta. Raymond had it in writing. Daniel Pierce had initially refused to meet with him. Raymond quickly changed Pierce's mind. An imminent attempted murder charge leveled at the head of the agency's biggest account tended to rewire SOP.

Particularly when Pierce had to answer to Public Domain's stockholders in mid-January in New York.

So Raymond delivered the news and watched Pierce absorb the consequences.

Raymond then explained he could and would fix the problem and went on to name his price: he wanted to head up the Atlanta branch of Public Domain. For now, the temporary suspension could stay in place. It worked as protective coloration. Raymond, however, wanted his salary reinstated and the promotion to officially go into effect by the end of January.

Pierce had agreed.

So Raymond went to work and created Vernon Masters.

Raymond created him out of the dust and rubble of the career of one Paul Crosley currently residing in C Wing of the Nu-Day Clinic.

Paul Crosley aka Gary Ghoulmaster.

Raymond had manufactured a bogus work record and personal history and had them planted in the personnel files at the Happy Farms main headquarters in Wilkesboro. He'd been sure to give Vernon Masters a varied work history at Happy Farms so that it appeared he'd been employed in any number of positions and shifts at the plant. That shrunk the possibility of identification problems from co-workers. The fact that part of Gary Ghoulmaster's on-screen persona and popularity was tied to the mystery of his off-screen identity let Raymond hedge some bets too.

The physical modifications were a mix of the straightforward and subtle. A new hairstyle and different color. Glasses instead of contacts. A half-hearted mustache. Staining rather than whitening the teeth. Lifts in the shoes. Monochromatic work uniform.

Paul Crosley had studied acting. And voice. So a new accent geographically distinct from the Ghoulmaster's was not a problem.

The way Raymond had scripted it: Vernon Masters, forty-one years old, Indiana born-and-raised, thoroughly blue-collar, army vet, no significant church or political affiliations, divorced, estranged from wife and child, a loner with no social life beyond a regular rotation among three bars in Wilkesboro, a man who nursed grudges, someone who refused to side fully with union or management, a man used to keeping his own counsel.

It hadn't occurred to Raymond, until he'd finished coaxing Vernon Masters into being, that he'd modeled Vernon on Ken Brackett. If not completely brothers, Vernon and Ken were at least first cousins under the skin.

On the drive to the Nu-Day Clinic, Raymond stopped at a Revco and made two purchases.

Southwest St. Carlton was a landscape with no locus, a Jackson Pollock canvas of commerce, everything veined in a tangled network of roads that indiscriminately spilled into and past subdivisions, shopping centers, commercial strips, schools, motel chains, churches, restaurants, doctors' offices, service stations, car lots, light industries, and a mammoth hexagonal mall, the clutter and sprawl broken only by taller buildings housing offices for banks, brokerage and law firms, and insurance companies that had moved out of downtown. The taller buildings were usually fronted in mirrored glass that gave nothing back to the landscape or sky but its own image.

Raymond spotted the landmark he'd been looking for, a large billboard advertising a pet obedience school with *Your Wish Is Our Command* in bright red lettering. A block later, he pulled into the parking lot of Nu-Day. There were mash-potato mounds of plowed snow perimetering the lot. They absorbed the sunlight pouring from a porcelain-blue winter sky.

Raymond walked up a sidewalk to the entrance of the clinic whose architecture was a paean to the plainer virtues of geometry, its face a series of flat tan rectangles spaced equidistantly between narrow recessed windows.

After signing in, Raymond walked down a long corridor to the C Wing and bypassed the Visitors Room, following another corridor to a room four doors down usually reserved for counseling workshops. Like everything else in the building, it was squat and angular and managed to be both sterile and cheery at the same time. The floor was buffed and waxed, the walls a pale institutional green. Counterpointing all the order was the equivalent of bulletin-board art. Soft-focus pictures of kittens and puppies and wooded glens and waterfalls abounded, all holding inspirational messages on the order of *Hang In There! Believe!* and *Dare To Hope!*

A heavy-set nurse who looked like she belonged in the serving line at an elementary school cafeteria led Paul Crosley in. She handed Raymond a clipboard, and he signed the attached form. Crosley and he moved to a table in the middle of the room. Raymond opened his briefcase and took out his notes. He slid the Revco bag across the table.

"You know this is the last shot we have of fine-tuning the details before you leave for Wilkesboro," Raymond said.

Paul Crosley nodded. He opened the Revco bag and took out the carton of Marlboro Lights and king-sized bag of Hershey's Kisses.

Crosley frowned. "Coffee?"

Raymond held up an index finger and left, hunting down a vending machine and returning with two blacks. By that time Crosley had a Marlboro burning and a line of silver Kisses spread before him.

"The right, not the left," Raymond said and pointed. "Remember to part your hair on the right."

"I'm not in character right now."

"You should be," Raymond said, "and from now on, you should stay in character until you hear otherwise."

At one time, Paul Crosley had the Magic. Raymond had done the homework and read the reviews. Twelve years ago, Crosley had been on the verge. He was a classically trained actor who'd paid his dues. He was looking at a future with some wattage. *The Tempest*, however, was the beginning of his undoing. As Prospero, Crosley had not so much drowned his book as marinated his liver in Jameson's. He missed rehearsals, was chronically late for performances, dropped lines. His personal life had become a tsunami of ill-conceived and executed decisions.

Raymond pulled one of the two lined tablets before him closer and started quizzing Paul Crosley on the names. He'd settled on five to six names from each of the three shifts at the Happy Farms plant in Wilkesboro and branched out to four of five regular after-work drinking buddies and acquaintances.

Paul Crosley parked his cigarette on the lip of an ashtray and hit every one, from the second shift supervisor to the bartender at The Sunset. When he was done, Crosley went down the line of Hershey Kisses, unwrapping each in succession and popping it in his mouth.

"Okay," Raymond said, nodding. "Okay."

"'Though this be madness, yet there is method in it'" Crosley said and dropped back in his chair.

Raymond cleared his throat and flipped deeper into the tablet. "These now," he said. "Live Hanger, Bone Popper. Pinner. Deboner. Lung Gunner. Skin Roller. Mirror Trimmer. Gut Drawer."

He interrupted Crosley halfway through his recitation. "The job descriptions, too rote with the delivery. Remember, a mix and match of the conversational and confessional. Make me believe," he said. "Run Lung Gunner by me again."

Over the next hour, Raymond watched and listened to Paul Crosley come to inhabit the role he had created and scripted for him.

Paul Crosley starring as Vernon Masters, a disgruntled line-worker at Happy Farms who had tried twice to report violations in the food safety inspection process at the Wilkesboro plant. Vernon

Masters would claim that he'd been ordered by the in-house Quality Control Inspector to help remove the Blue Tags on close to three hundred pounds of contaminated chicken a few days before the grand opening of the Happy Farms restaurant franchises. The Blue Tag removal was necessary to maintain quota and profit margins.

According to the script, management ignored and eventually buried everything Vernon Masters brought to them. Vernon protested. Management leaned on union people who leaned on Masters and explained the need for cooperation. Jobs were at stake.

In the mean time, the Happy Farms restaurants held their grand-openings, and within forty-eight hours, the first wave of symptoms crested.

At this point, Raymond wrote himself into the script and guest-starred in how things played out. His role wasn't much of a stretch.

In the story he'd scripted, Raymond, working for Public Domain, went to Wilkesboro and met with Vernon Masters and tried to buy Masters' silence on the line and shipping violations he'd tried to report and was threatening to do again in the face of the food poisoning incident. Masters, however, refused to be bought off, and Raymond had gone on to level his own threat, one he implied was along the lines of Luis Murano getting beaten and his hand crushed in his car door earlier in the month.

The threat had become unnecessary after Vernon's uncle, a good man who'd raised him had died of a sudden Myocardial Infarction. Vernon was the only surviving relative and had to travel to

Harrisburg, Pennsylvania to make all the funeral arrangements.

For a time, Vernon's grief had distracted him, but when he returned to work, his conscience as well as the perpetual chip on his shoulder once again bothered him, and he decided to do something about it.

In Act Two, Vernon would put in a call to Luis Murano at the *Courier*. He would become the whistleblower, the star witness, and inside source for a fat expose, someone willing to buck the corruption at both the management and union levels at Happy Farms. Someone willing to step up and bare all.

Raymond was counting on Luis Murano to latch onto Vernon Masters. Murano had yet to produce his famous mystery witness, and Raymond figured the witness had either been a bluff on Murano's part or the witness had gotten cold feet and changed his mind. Whatever the case, Luis Murano would have a hard time resisting Vernon Masters and his story.

Raymond would sit back while Murano ran his big Happy Farms expose, including Raymond's supposed part in attempting to bribe Masters and later threatening him. He'd let Murano wallow in his self-righteousness and wave the terrible swift sword of journalistic justice.

Raymond was also counting on Arthur Cavanaugh jumping in then with the attempted murder charge against Lamar Ditell.

At that point, the script called for Vernon Masters to come in from the cold.

A press conference. A lot of hype surrounding it.

At the conference, Vernon would reveal his true dual identity, explaining that he was both Paul Crosley and Gary Ghoulmaster, and then go on to come clean, confessing that after losing his spot as the Ghoulmaster due to some serious drinking problems, he'd been despondent and morally confused, and in a moment of weakness, he'd agreed to Luis Murano's proposition to impersonate a Happy Farms employee and offer up his perjured testimony to support Murano's investigation of Happy Farms as well as knowingly helping to buttress the case being made against Lamar Ditell by District Attorney Arthur Cavanaugh.

The script then called for Paul Crosley to break down and cry.

He would go on to explain he'd found his moral bearings again and simply could not live with himself anymore in the face of the gross miscarriage of justice that Murano et al had bribed him handsomely to perpetuate on an unsuspecting public.

Paul Crosley's staged confession at the press conference would shut everything down. Every legitimate shred of evidence that Luis Murano had gathered would be rendered tainted or at minimum, suspect. Arthur Cavanaugh's case would collapse.

The subsequent fallout would leave Lamar Ditell and Raymond untouchable and above reproach and Luis Murano, Cavanaugh, and their pal, Walker Anderson, with Grand-Canyon-sized credibility gaps and themselves the target of accusations of collusion and obstruction of justice.

The public would get a big second helping of

spectacle, centering this time not on chickens and food safety violations and food poisoning outbreaks but on the price of ambition, political machinations that rivaled any that sister-city Chicago could boast, and a pile of debased journalistic ethics.

And Raymond would get *Atlanta*.

Raymond gathered up the pens and tablets and dropped them in his briefcase. Crosley started another cigarette and shot the first lungful of smoke toward the ceiling.

"Remember, you drive straight to Wilkesboro when the paperwork is done here," Raymond said.

"Right," Crosley said. "Straight to the splendors of the Ridge Line Trailer Park. Lot #28."

"All necessary," Raymond said. "Exposition and protective coloration." The Ridge Line virtually guaranteed anonymity, given the constant turnover among residents, coupled with the mind-your-own-fucking-business attitude of those residing there who long ago ceased believing that their lots in life would ever change for the better.

Paul Crosley took another hit on the cigarette. "'The art of our necessities is strange/that can make vile things precious.'"

Raymond sat back and closed his eyes for a moment. "This arrangement an affront to your delicate sensibilities, Paul? Maybe you'd rather spend the next ten years or so as Gary Ghoulmaster and climb out of your coffin and into a bottle each night?"

"Hey," Crosley said, leaning forward.

"Hey, this," Raymond said and held up two fingers. "Two safe-deposit boxes have been opened in your name. You play the part we've scripted, and you get a key mailed to you when Luis Murano's first round of articles comes out. The second key for the final wrap and confession at the press conference."

Raymond reached across the table, took a Hershey's Kiss, and unwrapped it. "You play this right, you'll find a hefty bonus in that second safe-deposit box." Raymond popped the chocolate into his mouth.

"'I look down toward his feet,'" Crosley said, sliding back his chair.

"'But that's a fable,'" Raymond finished. He tapped the tabletop twice. "You're not the only one who took a lit class, Paul."

FORTY-FIVE

A held breath, one that you then slowly and carefully let out, that's what Kate's and Andrew's return home felt like.

The old ease between Kate and Raymond that had been automatic, something he'd taken for granted, was still there but damaged now in a way he was not sure how to go about repairing. Everything that had once been natural and routine between them felt vaguely accusatory and provisional.

Raymond had hired a service to come in and clean the house before Kate and Andrew arrived. The problem was they had done the job too well. Everything was in place, but it felt overly insistent, too calculated and artificial, as if someone had obsessively tried to clean up a crime scene.

Raymond unloaded the car, taking Kate's and Andrew's suitcases upstairs. Back downstairs, he found Andrew camped in front of the television, the volume too high and the screen full of frenetic cartoon mayhem. He walked into the kitchen where Kate was going through the refrigerator and shaking her head.

"I thought we'd just do take-out," Raymond said.

"No, a real meal tonight." She handed Raymond a list. "Andrew had enough junk food and snacks at my parents' and on the drive home today."

Raymond went back to the living room. He squatted next to Andrew. In front of them, a large black dog in a blue hat lit a bundle of dynamite and dropped it down an open manhole. A smaller dog popped up and tossed it back. The routine continued until a commercial for a line of mutant action figures came on.

Andrew was holding the remote, and Raymond took it and downsized the volume. "Hey, Champ, you want to come to the grocery store with your dad? Just you and me. I'll let you pick out the dessert for tonight."

Andrew took back the remote and cranked the volume. The black dog with the blue hat was back, this time with an airplane loaded with bombs. He began circling the smaller dog's house.

Raymond went on to the grocery store. The late afternoon light was graying, softening into dusk. Raymond parked and watched an empty shopping cart drift across the lot and come to rest against the driver's side door of a silver car. He went inside and got everything on Kate's list. In the checkout line, a tall man in a parka told the woman next to him that Oliver North deserved a medal.

Raymond made three trips carrying the groceries inside the house. The television was off. He watched Kate palm three aspirin. He helped her put up the groceries. He asked her what he could do to help with supper. She pointed towards the ceiling.

"Take Andrew outside for a while, okay?" She finished filling a pasta pot with water and set it on the stove. "He's having a rough time settling back in."

Raymond nodded and brushed back Kate's hair. He leaned in and kissed her temple. She stiffened, and he stepped back.

Andrew had taken his suitcase and thrown it and its contents into the center of the room. Clothes and toys were strewn everywhere, echoing the aftermath of a traffic accident. One small bedside lamp cast the only light. Andrew was on the far side of the room wielding the oversized red plastic bat on the bare west wall.

Raymond kept tossing out his son's name until Andrew stopped and looked his way but not directly at him.

"Let's go outside," Raymond said. "We'll build a snowman."

Andrew was wearing a pair of new jeans and a gray sweatshirt with two parallel rows of cats and dogs. Raymond coaxed him into a coat and some gloves and then hunted down a knit cap.

"This is the good stuff, Andrew," he said when they were in the backyard. He scooped up a handful of snow. "It's not too dry or powdery. Wet like this, it packs just right."

Andrew lost interest in the snowman before they were half done. He moved to the farthest edges of the yard and began to walk in a large circle. The snow was knee-deep, and as he moved, he pumped his legs like a drum major.

Raymond remained next to the abandoned snowman and looked across the yard at the back of the house and the brightly lit kitchen windows. There was a flash of light blue sweater, and then Kate was at the window overlooking the sink. For a moment, it was as if she were framed within a painting. Raymond felt the same kind of inchoate yearning he'd experienced when she left with Andrew for her parents' house.

Andrew continued to move in precise ever-smaller concentric circles. He counted each step. Raymond remained standing in the center of the back yard.

The sky cleared and ran with stars.

689," Andrew said when he'd completed his last circuit. He stood to Raymond's side, just behind his right shoulder.

Kate tapped on the window, and they went in and ate supper.

Later that night, Andrew asleep two doors down, Raymond rolled over in bed and turned his wife's face to his. "I've missed you," he said, " and I've missed us."

Her kiss was tentative but there.

"It's going to be okay," Raymond said.

"What is?"

"Everything." He rested his hand against her cheek.

"You like that word a little too much, Raymond." She shut her eyes for a moment. "'Everything is fine.' 'Everything will be different.' 'You'll fix everything.' 'Everything will be okay.'"

"Kate," Raymond said.

"I don't' want to hear about Atlanta," she said. "Not right now." She reached over and turned off the bedside light.

FORTY-SIX

It was Epiphany plus one, Raymond a day late for the customary family ritual of taking down the Christmas tree. The living room was cluttered with half-filled boxes of ornaments and decorations that, along with the artificial tree, would eventually end up in the attic.

The early evening light was sagging under its own weight, and Raymond went around turning on lights, then dragged the ladder over, repositioning it closer to the tree.

Andrew stood at the bay window overlooking the front yard and street. For close to the last hour, he'd watched the passing cars, counting each and naming its color. He turned and watched Raymond climb the ladder and claim the star at the tree's top.

Andrew went back to the window. "Twenty and silver. And Mother."

"Hey, Champ, that's the color of your mom's car all right, but it will be a while before she comes home." Raymond started down the ladder with the star. "Remember, she told you she was going to see her friend, Mrs. Ward, and would be home after our supper."

"Twenty-one and yellow," Andrew said.

Raymond, used to the doorbell, didn't immediately register the sound at first, but as the knocking increased in volume and frequency, he crossed the room and opened the door.

"You should open a door by the fifth knock or not at all," Ken Brackett said. He held up a fist with reddened knuckles and stepped inside. He wore a brown and green camouflage parka zippered tightly to the neck and a pair of dark blue khaki work pants. It looked as if he hadn't shaved for a couple days, but his hair was carefully combed with a sharp part and a small black bump of a pompadour.

"You're a hard man to find lately," Ken said. He surveyed the living room.

"I wasn't hiding," Raymond said, though right now that didn't seem like a bad idea. He didn't particularly like the look in Ken's eyes.

"Twenty-two and red," Andrew said.

Ken whistled. Andrew turned around. Ken squinted.

"Hey Andy," he said, "anyone ever tell you that you look just like your old man? DNA doesn't lie."

Ken tilted his head back. "Those are high ceilings."

"It's an old house," Raymond said.

"You forgot to ask me how Tina was."

"You didn't give me a chance to, Ken."

"She's still in a coma. You could probably pinch her anywhere really hard, and she wouldn't know the difference." Ken rubbed the back of his neck and then pointed at the fireplace. "You should probably clean that grate, Raymond. You're looking at a fire hazard." He swung his arm in a semi-circle. "Like you said, it's an old house. Place would go up pretty quick."

Andrew left the window. Ken stepped over and

lifted his hand and began rubbing Andrew's head.

"He doesn't like to be touched," Raymond said.

"News to Andy and me."

"Everybody rides," Andrew said.

"I hear you," Ken said. He dropped his hand and pointed toward the stairs. "Your wife taking a nap or something? What's her name? Karen?"

"Kate. And no, she's not taking a nap."

"We knew that, right Andy?" Ken looked over at Raymond. "How about some coffee? We have some things to talk about."

"I'm not sure this is the time."

"Hey," Ken said. "That wasn't a request." He dropped his arm around Andrew's shoulder, and they followed Raymond into the kitchen.

"It is true you got canned?"

Raymond had to remind himself to follow his own script. "Temporary suspension without pay. But it will probably turn permanent by the end of the month."

"Dire things on the horizon," Ken said. "That's what Walker Anderson said is in store for you, Happy Farms, and Lamar Ditell. Possible criminal charges is what he told me."

Things were playing out as they were supposed to in Wilkesboro. Paul Crosley aka Vernon Masters had called Raymond two nights ago and said he'd made contact with Luis Murano and that Murano was very interested in meeting him and hearing his story. Raymond figured Murano's editor at the *Courier* must have pipelined the news to Arthur Cavanaugh who in turn alerted his pal Walker Anderson.

"Walker said you tried to bribe a guy at the plant,"

Ken said. "Is that true?"

Raymond set out coffee cups. "You and Anderson on a first-name basis now?"

"He said you've been playing me from the start, promising things you couldn't and would never deliver."

Raymond opened the refrigerator and gave Andrew a juice box. "You can watch TV while Mr. Brackett and I talk."

Ken took his coffee and leaned against the counter opposite Raymond. He left his parka zipped. "Who is he? The guy you tried to bribe? Murano wouldn't name his source. At least not yet."

"Don't be too quick to sign on with Anderson, Ken."

"What's that supposed to mean?"

"That's all I can say for now."

"You got a secret, Raymond, that's what you're telling me?"

From the living room, the volume on the television spiked, Dan Rather doing the lead-in for the evening news, his take on the Tower Commission and its investigation of the Iran-Contra affair breaking off into a Ginsu knife commercial and then Scooby-Doo as Andrew punched the remote's buttons.

"One way or another, I'm due," Ken said. "I thought you understood that."

"I do and you are." Raymond heard the faucet dripping behind him. "That's what I'm trying to tell you."

Carefully, that was how Raymond needed to take it. He wanted to do right by Ken or at least as right as circumstances allowed. The guy already had more than his allotted share of bad luck. There was no reason to involve him in what was playing out with Paul Crosley in Wilkesboro. At the same time, Raymond was not about to lose sight of *Atlanta* and what it promised for Kate, Andrew, and him. He'd do what he could to steer Ken where he needed to go, but there was no way Raymond was going to jeopardize his chances of running the Atlanta branch of Public Domain.

"Just wait," Raymond said. "That's what I'm recommending."

"How long exactly?"

"Not long," Raymond said. "You'll see."

"That's not an answer." Ken set down his coffee cup and crossed his arms over his chest. "And I'd like one. A real one."

"Best I can for now."

Ken looked up at the ceiling, then back at Raymond. "What don't I know?"

From the living room came *Scooby Doo Where Are You?* Followed by Scooby's answering *Reareyeram.*

"Sounds like the Mystery's solved," Ken said. He smiled and picked up his coffee cup from the counter. Raymond stepped aside so Ken could set it in the sink.

"Appreciated the caffeine," Ken said.

There was something about the follow-up smile though. It was a couple degrees off-center.

Ken threw his arm around Raymond's shoulders. "You've been, however, seriously fucking with my Eutectoid Vectors, my friend, and that I do *not* appreciate."

Ken's fist was a blur. Raymond was on the kitchen floor before the pain completely found him. Ken compounded it with a couple kicks from his steel-toed shoes.

Raymond rolled onto his side and threw up.

Ken unzipped his parka. He touched the butt of the pistol tucked in his waistband. "What say we start over?" he said. "What don't I know, Raymond?"

FORTY-SEVEN

There might be seven types of ambiguity, but the same could not be said of fear. Fear did not respect distinctions. It leveled and absorbed them. True fear, at bottom, was its own reference point. It squatted in the center of the moment and drained the world of familiar lines.

Raymond Locke was afraid.

The beating and Ken brandishing the pistol had led to the front seat of the Chevy Nova, Ken behind the wheel, Andrew in the middle of the front seat, and Raymond slumped against the passenger door, his head bouncing against the window as he struggled to regain some focus.

Ken looked over at Raymond. "In the end," he said, "it is always the message that delivers the messenger."

With the pain xylophoning his spine and crawling over his ribcage, Raymond was unable to locate any clear context for Ken's remark.

The handcuffs also distracted him.

His right wrist was handcuffed to the molding of the armrest on the inside panel of the passenger door. Ken had removed the door handle and broken off the knob on the lock.

Andrew sat with his legs folded under him, the Etch-A-Sketch Raymond had given him for Christmas resting in the middle of his lap. He looked, if not exactly content, at least nonplused. He wore his bright red nylon jacket, and the gloves, attached by metal clips, dangled from its cuffs, and in the weak light from the dash it appeared as if he'd grown an extra set of hands.

Ken kept the heater cranked to compensate for the competing cold drafts whistling and streaming through the car. The floor of the Nova was littered with fast food discards, a jumble of cups, plastic silverware, Styrofoam containers, wrappers, and grease-stained bags leaking a stale impacted smell of yeast and meat.

They'd left the city limits behind, and Ken, hunched over the wheel, was sticking to back roads. A fine snow whirled and spun through the air, its movements both delicate and frenzied.

"You sure you don't want to run that story with Vernon Crosley and Paul Masters by me again?" Ken asked. "Maybe this time around, you can make it believable."

"The names," Raymond said. "You have them crossed. It's Vernon Masters and Paul Crosley."

"Oh right. But Crosley and Masters are really the same guy," Ken said, "and together, they're Gary Ghoulmaster who you hired to pretend to be Vernon Masters so he could set up Luis Murano and then Arthur Cavanaugh and Walker Anderson and get Lamar Ditell and Happy Farms off the hook for the tainted chicken that put my daughter in a coma." Ken punctuated each story thread with a nod. "That about it, Raymond?"

"It's the truth, Ken. That's what I set up."

"A truth that is made up completely of lies, right?" Ken started nodding again. "And all I have to do is let it unfold as you planned it, and Lamar Ditell will make sure I'm compensated for all my and Tina's suffering? You made sure we would be taken care of. Is that how it's going to be, Raymond?"

Raymond tried to keep his voice steady. "Look, I know how it sounds, Ken, but I didn't want to involve you. The point was you'd never have to know. The end result would be the same."

"And everyone lives happily ever after?"

"It happens, Ken. Sometimes it really does. Believe me, this time you can't and won't lose."

Ken's laugh would have given a hyena pause. He reached over and flicked the wipers up a notch. The snow had started to thicken, pouring around them, fast and fat and wet, the size of quarters. The landscape was flat and moon-coated, a mix of small subdivisions and empty fields.

"You want to hit replay on that story, Raymond, or maybe try something different this time, like maybe the truth?" More head shaking. "I mean, come on, you expect me to believe you got someone like Gary Ghoulmaster to go along with a scheme like that?"

"He's a drunk, Ken."

"He's an artist."

"Fine, then. He's an artist. He's also a drunk. And broke. And in chronic trouble with Channel 5. He jumped at the chance, Ken. I didn't have to twist his arm."

Andrew lifted the Etch-A-Sketch and held it against his chest and began humming.

349

Ken pulled the pistol from his waistband and held it up. "Charter Arms Pathfinder. Twenty-two. Six shot cylinder. Three inch barrel. One pound two ounces. Adjustable rear sight. Ramp front." He reached over the wheel and set it on the dash. "My old man's gun. One of his options when he was considering ways to kill himself."

Ken caught Raymond calculating the distance between where he sat and the pistol.

"You can try," Ken said, "but you'd come up short by 19 inches. I measured." He created something approximating a smile and pointed toward the ignition. "Same with the car keys and the one for the cuffs. No matter how you stretch, you'll always be at least a half foot short."

Andrew kept the Etch-A-Sketch pressed against his chest and continued to hum, the sound resembling a swarm of sluggish bees. He held his face pointed toward the windshield and started rocking slowly.

"I'm due," Ken said. "I won't be cheated. You and Lamar were going to hang Tina and me out, Raymond, and that is not acceptable."

"I'm not trying to cheat you," Raymond said. "I never have. What I was doing, Ken, was fixing my life." Raymond tried to catch Ken's eye, but he kept his gaze straight ahead. "But not at your expense or Tina's."

Ken knocked the heater up a notch. "So you're still telling me that you made up this whole thing with Vernon Masters? It's all a set-up?"

"Yes." Raymond started to elaborate again but checked the impulse. Keep it simple, he told himself.

Ken swiveled his head in Raymond's direction. "You know, Raymond, I don't think I should have to point this out, but coming up with something like that is kind of sick."

Right, Raymond thought, unlike the rational move of entering a man's home, beating him, threatening him with a pistol, and then while explaining the working principles behind Dr. Tolson Whormer's Eutectoid Vectors and Tableau Injunctions, kidnapping the man and his son, and finally handcuffing him to the armrest of a fifteen year old Chevy Nova.

"I set it up because I was trying to fix my life," Raymond said again.

"I hear you," Ken said, "but you start out to do that, you need to remember there's a world of difference between a Modal Replication and a Neroian Window. That's why we're going to Wilkesboro and talk to this Vernon Masters."

Andrew rocked and hummed between Ken and Raymond and set the springs in the seat of the Nova squeaking.

Raymond lifted his right hand and rattled the cuffs. "Turn around now, Ken. We just have to let things play out as they will."

"As they will," Ken said. "Okay." He reached up and over and flicked the large pair of fuzzy dice hanging from the rear-view mirror. Dangling between them was something on a silver chain.

"St. Francis de Sales," Ken said.

Looking at the Saint's medal swinging against the backdrop of the front windshield and the snow that furiously ran under the wind gusting through a landscape that was flat and open and lost in its own immensity, Raymond felt his fear return, and with it, he could not duck the thought, irrational as it was, that he'd become trapped not so much in Ken's car as in Ken's head and that they'd passed far beyond something as simple and recognizable as the city limits.

FORTY-EIGHT

They drove deeper into the night. They stayed on back roads. The snow pulled back and the clouds broke apart and stars spilled. The moon floated fat and half-full.

Raymond resisted the implications surrounding the Saint Francis de Sale medal dangling from the rear view mirror. The implications, however, continued to gather weight until Raymond finally had to acknowledge them. They made no sense though or at least not on rational terms. They only made sense if Ken Brackett had snapped and moved beyond what had seemed his idiosyncrasies and rough edges into something else entirely.

"Why?" Raymond asked. "Why did you do it, Ken?"

"You said you understood, Raymond, but you don't, not really." Ken shook his head. "A little, maybe, but not enough, finally."

"Okay, explain it to me then," Raymond said. He life-jacketed himself in the hope that there was still a chance that Ken might talk himself out and turn the car around. It wouldn't be the first time Ken required an audience to defuse the set of grievances and bad luck that underwrote his life.

"You said you read Dr. Whormer's *Guide to Unleashing*," Ken said. "The problem is you read it with your eyes closed. Now it's time you opened them."

Raymond worked on evening his breathing. Next to him, Andrew quit rocking and dropped his fingers onto the knobs of the Etch-A-Sketch.

"One day, Dr. Tolson Whormer will be recognized for his genius and vision. He's a true pioneer. He embraced what everybody else in the Recovery and Self-Help Movement was unwilling to admit: it's not enough to get well."

The other experts, Ken said, had it all wrong when they encouraged re-establishing ties with the Inner Child. By doing so, you were then obligated to care for and nurture it and ended up unwittingly reproducing the dysfunctional dynamics that produced all the problems in the first place. You became a parent to yourself and were still imprisoned within the debilitating paradigms of the family structure.

"'Home is where the horror is,'" Ken said, jabbing the air with his index finger. " 'The American Family deforms as it informs.'" He waved his hand over the steering wheel. "If you want to punch your own ticket, forget about the Inner Child and concentrate instead on the Inner Orphan. Without that, there's no real breakthrough. You have to orphan yourself or stay twisted."

Then, according to Ken, you Life Task became ferreting out Modal Replications, those moments where you discovered the dysfunctional paradigm of the Family duplicated within larger social structures, and you went on to Unleash yourself from each.

"Think about it," Ken said. "You take the workplace and the school and the judicial systems, and what are they but 'The Family living room writ large?' You're Leashed to a paycheck, report card, and law book. In each case, someone's Mom-and-Daddying it over you, pulling your strings and then telling you it's for your own good. Those systems don't serve you. You serve them. And once you buy into their terms, you're no different from the battered child who willingly degrades himself because he's come to confuse abuse with love."

Raymond glanced over at Andrew. His fingers were moving methodically on the knobs of the Etch-A-Sketch, the lines on the gray screen intersecting, then overshooting each other and wavering, like a crossword puzzle in the process of collapsing under its own weight.

"How about turning the car around, Ken?" Raymond asked.

Ken tilted his head and looked over at Raymond. "What's your take on the Fifth Commandment?" There was no traffic, and Ken let the Chevy drift left of center until it was straddling both lanes.

Raymond blanked. He wasn't sure if it was the one about Graven Images or Bearing False Witness.

"Neither," Ken said. "Number Five is the ringer God threw Moses. He played it smart and slipped it in the middle so that most people would end up waffling like you did if someone brought it to their attention."

Ken kept the Chevy centered and ran his hand repeatedly over his jawline. "Once you're at the end of your Leash, you're also face to face with who's been pulling on it. You see God for exactly what he is: a Modal Replication in its purest form. Every dysfunctional dynamic converges in Him.'"

Raymond dropped his head against the seat. Near the dome light was a large jagged tear in the material covering the roof of the car, the outer edges dangling like the flap on a hastily opened envelope.

"You can't be serious," he said slowly. "You're telling me you know God and that he's dysfunctional?"

"Actually, if you want to get technical," Ken said, "it'd be more to the point to say that God is codependent."

Raymond kept his eyes on the tear in the roof. This can't be happening, he thought. He had a wife, a child, a home, a job, a history. There were clear and recognizable lines to his life. Raymond had drawn them himself. There was no room inside them for a Ken Brackett. Yet, somehow, there he was.

"The whole point of a Commandment," Ken said, "is to let you know what's what. Do this. Don't do that. You listen, you get rewarded. You don't, you get punished. Simple and clean and clear, right, Raymond? You know where you stand. Everything makes sense." Ken paused and scratched his neck. His skin had the pale cloudy texture of transparent tape.

Ken then went on and explained how Dr. Tolson Whormer had exposed the con God had worked on Moses. Originally, there were supposed to have been Nine Commandments. That was the deal. But God had gone on to bait-and-switch Moses on an extra one with some high-pressure celestial salesmanship by setting up the meet on an isolated mountaintop and cranking up the pressure with the cheap sales gimmick of a burning bush. Moses ended up coming down the mountain with an extra Commandment and foisted it and the Mystery of God on his people and every subsequent generation.

The Fifth Commandment, God's ringer, then became the basis of every Modal Replication because it perfectly echoed the dysfunctional beat of the twisted heart in every family. In essence, the beginning and end of the Leash were the same.

"You see how it works now, Raymond?" Ken asked. "Once God billed Himself as Mysterious, He established Himself as Co-Dependent for eternity by tying judgment to personality and Holy-Ghosting His."

You were then left with the Insult of Being, Ken said, and woke each day to a world in which the good suffered and evil prospered, where justice was bought and sold a dozen times over before you finished your first cup of coffee, and grace and damnation felt as arbitrary as the direction of the wind. Pain, Humiliation, Justice, Love - it was all God's show, Ken said. He pulled the strings indiscriminately. He had to. He needed us to need Him. God, therefore, always promised more than He delivered and delivered more than we deserved. He literally loved us to death.

"But," Ken said, thumping the wheel, "you take away Mystery and God has nowhere to hide. Then you see how things work. *Secrets*, not Mystery, is where you find the truth. With Secrets, the only thing you have to worry about is how big they are and who gets to keep them. God isn't Mysterious. He just needs us to believe that. That's how he keeps us Leashed."

Ken leaned back from the wheel. "I've told you

this before. Don't look at me like that. I have good peripheral vision. You can't get a look like that past me."

To the west, floating on the edge of the horizon was a small bright cluster of light, and over the next fifteen minutes or so, an irregularly spaced string of cars and trucks appeared. Raymond yelled and waved at the approach of each one, but Ken slowed down and good-neighbored his driving style. Raymond's frenzied gestures were recast by the pull of the handcuffs and only convinced a few drivers to wave or blink their lights.

Then the radar blip of a town disappeared, and they were left once again with empty fields and the dark lines of windbreaks and the occasional farmhouse and barn, a landscape as smooth and flat as a slice of white bread.

Ken lifted the Charter Arms Pathfinder off the dash and pointed it in Andrew's direction. "You try something like that again, Raymond, and I swear I'll do him right in front of you. Do we understand each other?" Ken shook his head in disgust and placed the Pathfinder back over the steering wheel onto the dash.

Without quite understanding how it happened, Raymond's fear became indistinguishable from his rage, and he heard himself yelling, "No. I don't want to understand you, Ken. I'm sick of all this twisted shit you call a worldview."

"Watch the tone and tenor there, Raymond."

"No, this has gone far enough."

"I'm telling you, I don't like what I'm hearing. I'm about to demand a retraction."

Andrew kept his attention on the Etch-A-Sketch, turning its knobs.

The air carried a salting of new snow. The Chevy's headlights hit and bounced across large icy patches covering both lanes.

"Everybody suffers," Raymond said. "There's nothing unique about pain. It's time you accepted that. So why don't you stop this goddamn car and all the crazy talk about Modal Replications and God and keep yourself from doing something that will really fuck up your life?"

Ken slowly shook his head, the gesture suggesting the mix of disbelief and impatience you'd feel for a slow child who'd completely missed the answer to a simple math problem you'd painstakingly worked through for him.

"You should know by now, Raymond, that nothing stops in time," he said. "Nothing."

"It's a choice, Ken," Raymond said. "You have one. Come on, turn the car around, and we can forget the whole thing ever happened."

"A choice, huh? Maybe a Hobson's, but that's it," Ken said. "There's nothing free about free will." He went back to the nodding. "One Modal Replication will show you that. So don't fool yourself, Raymond. Nothing's free. You either pay for it, or you take it, or if you have the courage and conviction to fully Unleash, then you take it and make others pay."

Next to Raymond, Andrew kept going at the knobs of the Etch-A-Sketch. The lines careened, broke apart, and rejoined over again.

"Jesus," Raymond said. "I still don't know what's

going on here."

Ken one-handed the steering wheel. He shrugged. "That's what Pontius Pilate claimed just before he started washing his hands." Ken nodded twice. "But, sorry, no soap in this car, Raymond."

Raymond pointed at the Saint Francis de Sale medal. "Why? You never answered me. Why did you attack Luis Murano and crush his hand in the car door?"

"I stepped up and did what you didn't and should have." Ken dropped his free hand back on the Nova's wheel. "Murano wouldn't leave it alone about the mystery witness."

"What's that to you?" Raymond asked. "If there was fallout from Murano and his witness, it would be on Lamar Ditell and Happy Farms."

"Right there," Ken said. "You think you understand, but you don't. Not by a long or short shot." He glanced over at Raymond. "Murano was getting close. Too close."

Ken eased the Nova through a crossroads and then by a large stop sign. He turned right. Raymond saw a sign for Wilkesboro flash by but missed the mileage. Within less than a minute, they passed a combination service station and convenience store, a church, a post office, and a blink of remaining town and were back in open country.

"The mystery witness," Ken said. "You were supposed to be taking care of it, but you weren't doing enough. I had to make sure."

The arc of the Nova's wipers cut small windows onto the night and snow. Andrew remained silent and folded over the Etch-A-Sketch.

"You," Raymond said. "It was you." He hadn't seen it. Nobody had.

"I want to hear you say it, Ken. You took the Blue Tags off of the contaminated chicken and shipped it out, didn't you? You took a short-cut to meet a line quota and ended up causing the whole goddamn food poisoning outbreak in the first place." Raymond dropped his head back against the seat. "Or at minimum, you stood by and let it happen. It amounts to the same thing."

"No," Ken said.

"No, what?"

"No, it's not the same."

"What's that supposed to mean?"

Ken thumped the top of the steering wheel. "It means you have to be equal to your impulses, Raymond."

Raymond didn't think it possible, but Ken's tone had become even more disturbing. Each word was raw and wet, every syllable skinned of reason.

"Turn the car around, Ken. Please. We can work something out. You'll see."

"As usual, you have it backwards. You make it sound as if it's a question of living with myself. But I don't have to. That's the whole point of Unleashing: I live for myself now."

"Tina, then," Raymond said. "Think about Tina."

"Tina understands. It's like Dr. Whormer says. 'Children are, by nature, Conduits and Conductors.' I explained what I needed her to do." Ken rubbed his forehead and dropped his hand back onto the wheel.

The car shimmied on the ice. Andrew sat next to Raymond and continued moving the knobs of the Etch-A-Sketch with the precision of a metronome.

"Think Fifth Commandment," Ken said. 'I'm her father. Children are supposed to do what they're told. It's not my fault she's a picky eater."

"What in hell are you saying, Ken?" Something scuttled across Ken's features that Raymond couldn't recognize.

"I told her she had to clean her plate," Ken said. "I wouldn't excuse her from the table or let her watch television until she ate everything on her plate. Simple as that."

Raymond didn't have to ask what Ken had served for dinner.

"I told you, watch it with the eyes there," Ken said, pointing at Raymond.

"You really don't have a clue, do you, no fucking clue, just how far you've gone?"

Ken turned away, leaning over the wheel as if he were reading what he wanted to say off the windshield. "It wasn't something I decided," he said. "It was more like something I recognized. The meat was right there in the barrels. The line was down, and the USDA inspectors were on break. I looked at all those Blue Tags, and I saw how the whole thing fit together. Just like that. I didn't have to figure anything out. It was right there in front of me."

Raymond closed his eyes. The whole thing was too monstrous and unwieldy to be true, but it was. It made no sense, and it made too much sense.

"You almost killed her," Raymond said. "We're

talking about a child. Your own daughter for Christ's sake."

"I was owed." Ken remained bent over the wheel, squinting through the measured slash of the wipers and the snow whirling in the twin beams of the headlights.

"I was owed," he repeated and started nodding. "For my life. For every day of that life. Tina was simply the price tag I attached to it."

"What you did," Raymond said, but then let his words trail off. He looked down at his handcuffed wrists and then over at his son hunched obliviously over the Etch-A-Sketch.

Ken had put himself beyond his or anyone else's words. It had been his show from the start, but nobody had seen that. There was a brutal skewed logic to the way everything fit. Ken had taken the tags off the sick birds, then doctored the line quota figures and shipped them out. He waited for the grand openings of the Happy Farms franchises and for the initial symptoms of the food poisoning to manifest themselves, and then he prepared a blue-tagged supper for his daughter. He waited, again, this time for Tina to get sick, then delivered her to the emergency room and let things play out as they had. He waited for Lamar Ditell to do exactly what he'd done - mobilize Happy Farms' lawyers to begin drafting compensatory settlement offers and bring Public Domain and Raymond in to launder the images of everyone involved. Ken had recycled his crime in front of the whole country and used everyone around him to engineer his exoneration. He'd unleashed himself on them all.

The snow started to fall harder. Ken reached over and kicked up the wipers once again.

Something, Raymond thought. He had to do something.

Ahead, to the south and slightly west were the silhouettes of a farmhouse, barn, and silo. The upstairs and downstairs lights in the house were a pale burn against the snow and night sky.

Raymond leaned over, ripped the Etch-A-Sketch from Andrew's hands and threw it on the dash of the Nova.

Andrew pursed his lips and sputtered and began furiously rocking.

Ken looked over, puzzled, and then put the Etch-A-Sketch back in Andrew's lap.

Raymond threw it on the dash again.

"What the fuck do you think you're doing?" Ken asked.

Andrew suddenly quit rocking. His shoulders tensed. The sputter became a high thin wail.

Raymond waited until Ken had returned the Etch-A-Sketch to Andrew's lap. He then counted off five seconds, snatched it up, and tossed it further down the dash this time.

Ken started to reach over the wheel, but Andrew beat him to it, sliding down the seat and grabbing at the errant Etch-A-Sketch, pawing the Charter Arms Pathfinder out of his way in the process.

Ken saw what was happening a moment too late.

Raymond lunged for the pistol. His fingertips brushed its grip.

The Chevy hit a patch of ice. The tires whined and hissed and found more ice.

Andrew fell off the seat.

Raymond slammed against the passenger side window.

Ken yelled.

Raymond threw himself at the pistol sliding on the dash.

And then the night sky passed across the windshield like a page abruptly torn from a book.

FORTY-NINE

Raymond struggled to piece together a welter of sensations, but the world had tilted and taken on the bloated and unwieldy texture of dreams. Each breath was a confusion. He fought to map basic facts.

There was burning. Also wetness and weight.

A pressure in his ears as if he'd plunged too quickly into a deep body of water.

Dizziness. The taste of salt.

A pervasive ache in his chest and left arm.

The air webbed in white.

Andrew's bent head, his red parka a blot against the floorboards.

Ken's voice, his words running together.

A flashpoint of pain and Raymond slowly coming to inhabit his predicament. The Chevy in a deep ditch, trapped in an acute-angle nose-dive. Ken wedged in the space between the door and steering wheel, his face hidden by the hunch of his shoulders and the folds of the camouflage parka. Above him, an oval web of cracked glass and the segment of dashboard below pinwheeled in blood.

The muscles in Raymond's chest, shoulder, and left arm knotted and clenched and knifing in pain. Raymond remembered reaching for the Pathfinder and then the car leaving the road, his arm involuntarily flying up and at the on-coming windshield.

If he tilted his head toward the back seat, Raymond found that he was just able to see as far as the lip of the ditch. The sky above it looked as if it were being torn apart, the snow falling hard again, careening and eddying in the blasts of wind.

On the periphery of Raymond's vision, a brown and green patch of camouflage parka shuddered, and Ken Brackett pushed himself away from the corner and sat upright.

Ken's face was battered and torn almost beyond recognition, a mask that had been turned inside out and then repeatedly stepped on. He coughed and swayed, then blindly grabbed the Nova's wheel and pulled himself up and behind it.

Ken peered through the splintered windshield, mumbling to himself, and cranked the ignition. The engine momentarily caught and roared and just as abruptly stopped.

Ken's hands slipped from the wheel, and he fell back against the driver's door, facing Andrew and Raymond. His right eye was red and swollen, and flaps of skin the size of stamps dangled from his forehead and brow.

"We're not finished," he said, each word italicized by the labored wheeze of a broken nose.

"Certain verbs occur to me," Ken said. "I'm thinking *Surmount, Prevail,* and *Triumph* among others." He began picking glass from his face.

Raymond looked for the Pathfinder, but what he found instead was the weight and drag of his left arm. He had a hard time moving it. His wrist as well as most of the fingers on his left hand was broken, his index, middle, and fourth finger splayed and bent at odd angles from knuckles crushed flat as dimes.

Raymond looked at his hand and started choking great heaving gulps of cold air.

"I remember some lights," Ken said, "to the south, just before we hit that ice. A farmhouse." With each word the cuts scattered over his forehead re-opened. Ken wiped at them with the back of his hand and winced. "A second wind. I feel it arising. All I need is the Pathfinder and my flashlight. I will then liberate some wheels, and we will be in Wilkesboro in less than an hour to finish what we started."

Ken kept trying to push the flaps of skin dangling from his forehead back into place. The right eye below was now almost swollen shut. Ken jabbed at the air.

Raymond watched Andrew begin moving and looking through the trash on the floorboards for the Etch-A-Sketch.

"The gun, Andrew," Raymond said. "Look for the gun."

Ken grabbed the steering column and painstakingly pulled himself from the corner, edging his way up the incline of the seat. "That's right, Andy," he said. "Find the gun."

Raymond tried once more to lift his arm, stubbornly willing it to move, and managed to lift it a foot or so off the seat. The hand and its tangle of broken fingers bobbed in a syrupy palsy.

Ken continued edging up the seat, his face crosshatched with cuts and abrasions and his head wrenched at an odd angle to compensate for the damaged eye.

Andrew stirred through the debris on the floorboards.

"Gun rhymes with Fun, Andy," Ken said.

Raymond looked down at his useless hand and then swiveled, swinging his legs onto the seat, and kicked out, catching Ken in the chest and knocking him back against the driver's door.

Andrew came up with the Etch-A-Sketch. Its face was splintered and one of the knobs missing. Andrew cocked his head and looked over his shoulder and went back to the floorboards.

"That's right, Andy," Ken said. "Fuck the Etch-A-Sketch. You find the gun, and I'll take it from there."

Raymond kicked him into the door again.

Ken lowered his head and worked his way through a series of wet coughs. After they subsided, he said, "When we get to Wilkesboro, we're going to talk to that guy, Vernon Masters, and see exactly what's what."

Andrew remained crouched on the floorboards. He held up a red plastic flashlight and flicked it on, letting the beam play across the roof of the car.

"Good idea, the flashlight, Andy," Ken said. "Now the gun. Let your friend Ken put that combo to work."

Over the lip of the ditch, the sky was a pulsing wet whirl, the flurries gaining weight and speed the closer they got to the ground.

Raymond turned his head and ran full-face into the beam of the flashlight.

He blinked and looked away, trying to clear his vision. He heard Ken scrabbling up the seat, the tear and wheeze of his breathing, but this time Raymond's kick was late, coming after the punch that drove his head against the window, Ken grabbing the flashlight from Andrew before falling back.

Ken snagged the steering wheel and wrapped his arm around its column. He leaned over, raising the flashlight and bringing it down hard on Raymond's mangled hand.

The pain was otherworldly.

"In pain and out of luck," Ken said. "More of the former to come and tough shit on the latter."

Raymond's arm alternately burned and went numb.

Ken aimed the flashlight at the floor. "Over there, Andy," he prompted. "The barrel's showing, see? Right under that white bag."

Andrew grimaced and twitched. He looked at the flashlight in Ken's hand and rocked slowly.

"Not me," Ken said. "Don't look at me. Look where I'm pointing the light. Right over there."

Andrew stiffened and faltered in his rocking, its rhythm broken and uneven like an engine that had begun to seize up.

When Raymond tried to shift position, pain squeezed every synapse. He got off one kick, which Ken easily deflected.

Andrew picked up the Charter Arms Pathfinder.

Ken looked over at Raymond and smiled. He turned to Andrew and held out his hand.

Andrew lifted the pistol and shot him in the face.

It was over before Raymond could fully register what happened.

Ken lay against the driver's door, his head thrown

back and his mouth open, a small dark hole, no bigger than the blunt end of an unsharpened pencil, in the middle of his forehead and the surrounding patchwork of cuts and abrasions.

Andrew turned and pointed the Pathfinder at Raymond who reflexively held up the cuffed hand. Nothing in his son's face suggested that he understood he'd just killed someone.

And nothing in his son's face suggested that he wouldn't hesitate to pull the trigger again.

"Andrew, please," Raymond said.

"Everything is, and everybody rides," Andrew said. He nodded twice and slowly lowered the pistol and reached over to retrieve the flashlight. He replaced the Pathfinder under the white bag.

Raymond looked at the keys dangling from the Nova's ignition and spotted the small silver one that unlocked the handcuffs.

He thought about the farmhouse he'd seen before the car landed in the ditch.

Andrew lifted the flashlight and again held it on Raymond's face.

Raymond closed his eyes and carefully spaced his words. "It's time to go, Andrew. I'll bet you're ready. We need to go home. It's time. You and me, Champ. Your mother's waiting for us, and she misses us. She's at home, and that's where we'll go, but first, Andrew must listen some more. I will say the words, and Andrew will do them."

Andrew kept the flashlight trained on Raymond's face. Raymond forced himself to remain still, not wanting to do anything that might distract his son.

"I need you to be my hands, Andrew," he said.

He kept his eyes closed. The beam of the flashlight shimmered and wavered on the back of his lids. His left arm was on its way to going numb.

"Can you do that?" he asked. "Be your father's hands? Because that is what I'm going to ask you to be. Andrew is listening now to his father, and this is what Andrew will do. He will move down to the steering wheel and get the keys. Andrew knows keys. They unlock things, and they're shiny. Your father needs those keys so that we can go home where Andrew lives and see his mother, and that is just what Andrew and his father will do as soon as Andrew gives his father the keys. Andrew can take the flashlight with him when they go home."

The light remained on Raymond's face. He told himself to remain patient and started in again, repeating what he'd said and telling himself in the process that Andrew was his son and surely that had to count for something. He was a father, goddamnit. Some vestige of that connection had to be there, stubbornly suspended like a trace element in his son's psyche despite everything else the autism had swallowed.

All Andrew had to do was get him the keys. Raymond would wedge the key between his thumb and pinkie finger and work on unlocking the cuffs. There was still enough feeling in his arm to make it work. Then Andrew and he would climb out of the car and walk to the farmhouse.

Raymond gradually became aware of another sound snaking through his words and thoughts. He stopped and sat with his eyes closed and listened to Andrew repeat everything he'd said, exactly reproducing his words but emptying them of their content, his son's voice flat and inflectionless, filling the interior of the car like a damaged delayed-action echo.

A few seconds later, the light disappeared.

Raymond opened his eyes. His field of vision swarmed with after-images, and he was unable to raise either hand to rub his eyes. He tried to blink his way past small mobile pockets and explosions of light.

Andrew was in the middle of the front seat. He held the Etch-A-Sketch and ran his hand over its splintered face and looked around for the missing knob.

"Andrew, listen to me, please. Get me the keys. Okay? Reach over and get me the keys. Your father needs them. There's a pretty house down the road, and the people inside are very nice. They'll take us home, Andrew. But first, the keys. They're right next to you. Pull the keys out and give them to me, and then everything will be all right, I promise, but first you have to give your father the keys."

Andrew nodded at everything Raymond said.

He looked back and forth between the Etch-A-Sketch and Raymond's face.

Then he reached over and touched the knob on the radio, turning it.

For a while, there was nothing but the hiss and crackle of static, and then the station's signal centered. The front seat was suddenly filled with the sound of a ringing telephone.

Before Raymond understood what was happening, Andrew had climbed over the front seat and out the rear passenger window.

Raymond called out, pleading with him to come back, but Andrew scrambled up the side of the ditch and over its lip and walked away. Raymond kept calling his son's name. The snow and wind turned the night sky inside out.

The phone continued ringing, followed by another, then another, the rings building and overlapping and gradually diminishing, only to be replaced by the soft mellow tones of Tony Shephard who reminded listeners that this was a special follow-up to the New Year's Eve edition of *We're Only Human*. Tony Shephard wanted listeners to call in and let him know how their resolutions were holding up after a week. Were they *Steady? Shaky? Gone?*

Raymond tried to ignore the wind and the cold and the snow that funneled through the rear passenger window. The world had shrunken to one fact - he was alive - and Raymond was determined to fit himself to its dimensions and squeeze himself inside no matter how tight the fit and then stay there.

Tony Shephard took calls from Michael, Denise, Bill, Nicole, Wayne, Sheri, and Richard who maintained in the following year they had resolved to quit gambling on college sports, cut out caffeine, avoid speeding tickets, think globally, buy American, get into a size five, and use condoms. Their responses were a thicket of *Steady, Shaky,* and *Gones.*

Raymond looked at the keys dangling from the ignition.

A few feet, he told himself, that's all, and tried once again to lift his left arm.

He couldn't.

It was okay to be afraid, he told himself. Perfectly normal and expected under the circumstances.

Except the circumstances were no more normal or expected than the ones which had swallowed the lives of his parents and one hundred and eighty five others when the DC-8 crashed and burned, Raymond the sole survivor, the infant son of two people who up until that point had comprised his entire world and who in an instant no longer existed, their identities in the end only verifiable by something as paltry and insignificant as the record of the visits they'd made to a dentist.

The sense of abandonment eventually disappeared. The fear never quite did.

The trick was to find some way around the fear. It was a trick, he realized, he'd been trying to master his entire life. Raymond had always believed that what he carried up his sleeve would be enough to take him where he needed to go.

He leaned back against the seat. The sound of the wind mixed with the voices from the radio. Snow blew into and settled inside the car.

Diane, Phillip, Emma, Greg, and Louise had promised to give only constructive criticism, eat less red meat, cut up two credit cards, avoid any more DUI's, and learn to be a friend to herself, and they were *Shaky, Steady, Gone, Gone, and Shaky.*

Raymond shut his eyes when Tony Shephard segued with a string of toll-free numbers that would put listeners in touch with programs and support groups designed to help them follow up with their resolutions.

More voices then. Too many. Frank, Mary, Robert, Deborah, Larry, Susan, Todd. Voices squeezed from the air. Circling. Pressing in. As hard as he tried, Raymond could not shut them out.

He was not part of Tony Shephard's flock, he told them. No way. They could keep their designer sins and one-size-fits-all desires. They had nothing to do with him or what he was facing. He did not want his life excused, fixed, or enriched. He just wanted to know he'd had one. He was facing the prospect of dying, goddamnit, and wanted to be able to look at himself and know that his mistakes and misjudgments and wrongdoings and fuck-ups had been large and complicated enough to mean something. It was his life, and he couldn't afford to flinch, edit, or evade. He knew what he needed, and he knew he wouldn't find it on the radio with Greg and Joan and Tom and Louise.

He wanted two things.

To be worthy of his sins and forgiven for his love.

Tony Shephard broke in. *Cut the bullshit, Raymond. You watched your son shoot a man in the face over a flashlight and then walk away and abandon you handcuffed in a ditch. You can't move your left arm. You've started talking to the radio. You might be facing the prospect of dying, Raymond, but you're still trying to fool yourself. We've worked together, remember? I helped you launder Ken Brackett over there in the corner and a dozen or more of your other clients. We know how things work, but now all of a sudden you want to go Larger-Than-Life on me and play to the old Moment of Truth. That's PR talking, Raymond. Like everyone else in the country, you've taken the small change of your days and inflated its worth. Then you convince yourself it's hard cash and run out and buy some State-of-the-Art, Top-of-the-Line convictions. You're telling me you want to be worthy of your sins and forgiven for your love? You check the price tags on those lately? Out of your league, friend. Like it or not, you're part of my flock. Hell, I'm part of my flock. That's just the way things are now. We're all on the air. So let's get real, Raymond.*

Raymond blocked out Tony Shephard and tried to calculate how long Andrew had been gone, but he kept running into wall after wall after wall. Time had become something that didn't fit a calendar, watch, or pulse anymore.

A postscript here, Raymond.

No more. Leave me alone.

What? You're not going to freeze out your old friend, Frank Atwell, are you?

Frank? That you?

One and only.

You're dead though.

Of course I am. No need to remind me.

Does that mean I'm dead too?

You're the only one who can answer that.

I think I'm in trouble, Frank.

That's news? How you going to get out of it?

I don't know.

You should. I already explained how.

What do you mean?

Stories, friend. They're the only thing that can save us. I told you about stories, remember? You have to find yours and inhabit it and then let it inhabit you.

That's harder than it sounds.

Of course it is. We're talking about a life, Raymond.

Raymond shifted his weight to the door and rested his head against the passenger window. For a moment, all he heard was the sound of his own breathing.

On the exhale he opened his eyes and watched his breath condense on the cold glass. He waited for its reappearance and then watched some more.

He saw it then. A small boy carrying a flashlight and moving down a deserted road that divided an immense field, the flashlight bobbing with the boy's steps toward the farmhouse on the near horizon. All the lights in the house were out except for one, the house a stubborn presence in the dense swirl and fall of snow, its silhouette wavering like something on the bed of a fast-moving stream.

Raymond exhaled. He could see it then.

The farmhouse and the elderly couple upstairs in the bed they'd shared for the forty-odd years of their marriage. The headboard had a plain burnished maple finish. The nightstand, bureau, and dresser were matching pieces from the same set. Raymond was sure there was a framed reproduction of a stock landscape painting - something wide-vistaed and heavily wooded and cut by a meandering stream, everything done in muddied greens and browns - hanging on the wall opposite the bed.

As was his custom, the man had fallen asleep immediately, already slipping into the jagged snore that he inevitably denied whenever the woman brought it up during waking hours. The same held true for his occasional tendency to talk in his sleep.

Tonight, as on many other nights, the woman had a touch of insomnia, and she lay quietly next to her husband and looked at the ceiling, waiting for sleep to claim her.

Raymond exhaled. He could see it then.

Andrew standing in front of the darkened farmhouse and lifting the flashlight and playing its beam over the face of the house while the woman lay next to her snoring husband and sensed that something other than insomnia was keeping her awake tonight.

The feeling was not entirely uncomfortable or unpleasant. It held the same sort of quiet anticipation she'd experienced just before the phone rang and she knew before she lifted the receiver that one of her children was on the other end of the line. She welcomed the calls even though, with the exception of holidays and birthdays, her children, grown now and out in the world, only phoned when they had a problem. She'd then go on and listen with a curious inexplicable sadness welling up inside her that left her feeling happier than she'd ever imagined possible as her children went on to recount their struggles with the large and small lessons of love and work that she and her husband had tried but finally had not been able to prepare them for. She took the problems seriously, but they were never as important to her as her children's need to still see their parents as a refuge from and simultaneously the source of all their problems. Her children's appeals and accusations were a necessary lie and one she entered into willingly.

She could say the same thing about the man sleeping next to her. Forty-seven years of marriage, and there were times when the memories of her life before meeting him seemed to belong to someone else. They'd chosen each other in a way that her children, two of whose marriages stuttered, faltered, and dissolved, didn't understand. Their forty-seven years had not been easy or fun or glamorous, but at the heart of all those years there'd been the presence of that original choice, the sense of having chosen and been chosen, and she could still say she loved the oftentimes intractably stubborn, foolishly proud, maddeningly private, compulsively hardworking man lying next to her because the lies they'd lived by had always been necessary ones.

Those lies, however necessary, were still not enough to erase the occasional bouts of insomnia, those periods in the dead of night when longing reared and called to her from the darkened corners of the room or insistently tapped on the window like a tree branch in the wind. But in the face of her longing, the pull of missed chances and misplaced dreams, the slide show of other lives she might have lived, the lies held. In the end, they were more than enough. Much more than enough. The years had schooled her in a private arithmetic. She'd learned long ago that a marriage was always both more and less than the sum of its vows, and tonight, seven days after the birthing of a new year, she was blessed with just enough regrets to be happy and grateful for the chance to start over yet one more time and try to get it right.

Raymond waited with her. Sooner or later she would notice the pale beam of Andrew's flashlight wavering through the fall of snow and playing at the edges of the window or hear his soft knock on the front door, and the woman would smile, as if she'd been expecting it all along. Then she'd wake the sleeping man next to her, and together they'd get up and claim the lost boy outside.

Raymond could see it then. The three of them standing inside the doorway, Andrew slowly lifting his head and looking from one to the other. Every detail in the scene was *there*, perfectly clear, except for one that continued to elude him. Raymond could see the couple leaning toward the child, but he did not know their names. He waited, searching their faces, sure they would come to him at any moment.

END

About the Author

Lynn Kostoff is a Professor of English and the Nellie Cooke Sparrow Writer-in-Residence at Francis Marion University in Florence, SC. His other highly praised crime novels include *A Choice of Nightmares* (available from New Pulp Press), *The Long Fall,* and *Late Rain.* He has also taught at the University of Alabama, Indiana State University, and Bowling Green State University in Ohio where he received his MFA in fiction. His website is at www.lynnkostoff.com

Thank you for reading.
Please write a review of this book.
Reviews help others find www.newpulppress.com
and inspire us to keep bringing you the best in noir.

Newpulppress.com